I0535996

Iron Arm

Kimberly Loper

Copyright © 2019 Kimberly Loper

All rights reserved. No part of this publication may be reproduced, distributed, or transmitted in any form or by any means, including photocopying, recording, or other electronic or mechanical methods, without the prior written permission of the publisher, except in the case of brief quotations embodied in critical reviews and certain other noncommercial uses permitted by copyright law. For permission requests, write to the publisher, addressed "Attention: Permissions Coordinator," at the address below.

This book is a work of fiction. Any references to historical events, real people, or real places are used fictitiously. Other names, character, places and events are products of the author's imagination, and any resemblance to actual events, places or persons, living or dead, is entirely coincidental.

ISBN: 13:978-1-951908-00-3 (Paperback)

Library of Congress Control Number: 2019919779

Front cover image by Oliviaprodesign.

First printing edition 2020
Spanish Fork, UT

www.kimberlyloper.com

To Stephen for believing in me and this project even when I had my doubts. Thank you for all of the kind words and for sharing your excitement.

quivered and clung to her, all of them dressed in little more than rags. No man was visible, able or willing to defend them. Thus far, in his few previous raids, William had miraculously avoided coming into direct contact with any occupants, often wondering what his response would be when this day came. Now, it was here and still he had no clear idea of what to do. He knew what was expected; however, that was out of the question. He would not defile these innocents.

William approached and knelt near the terrified children who attempted to back away only to hit the wall. "I mean you no harm," he said to the young ones. Looking at the mother, he continued. "I offer you my protection. This will soon be over, and we will leave your village."

The quaking woman looked at him in confusion. "*Cosa vuoi? Non capisco. Per favore non farci del male!*" Her voice shook and rose in pitch and volume as words tumbled out.

William shook his head at his stupidity. He had not considered that they were now in Italy and these people would not speak his native French.

"Of course, Italian. Let me see." Grateful for what little Italian his uncle had insisted on teaching him before he left home, William stumbled, "*Non ti farò,* uh, *male. Sei,* er, *sicuro.*" He was unsure if his meaning was getting through to the woman. Continuing in French, he added, "I know my words make no sense to you, but I urge you to consider the safety of your young ones and allow me to stay."

After a few moments of consideration, she nodded in assent. William stood up, careful to not hit any of the hanging assemblage of pots and herbs that littered the ceiling. Going to assess the situation outside, he stopped beside a small square window next to the door. A few slats of wood were set to block the elements. William lifted the top board slightly to peer out.

"*Perché?*" the woman asked a few moments later, drawing William's attention back to her.

Recognizing her question of *why*, he took a few moments to consider. Again, he did not know enough Italian to answer fully, so he continued in his native French, knowing full well she would not understand. "I suppose because of my family. I cannot bear the thought of women being treated the way your friends and neighbors are now. I would hope that if my mother and sister were to find themselves in a similar situation, someone might step forward to protect them, as I am doing for you." With that he turned back to his vigil.

The shrieks of women and children struck a chord in William's chest. Should he leave this family to go aid another? That would leave this house open for the same treatment as whoever he rescued. Trading one woman for another had no overall benefit and would create a greater challenge. The men he travelled with respected him, but that would quickly change if he were to get in the way of their baser instincts.

He needed the men to respect him, for he hoped to lead them one day. He did not respect any of the others enough to follow them, so he had to lead. Currently, he shared the load of responsibility with several other knights, regardless of his inexperience, one of the benefits of his lineage. The remainder hailed from other respected households in France.

There had to be a way to inspire the men to be better than this. He would have to find it. Until then, he needed to find a balance between what the men wanted, and what his conscience would allow.

A man from his company charged the door where William stood. He carried an axe in one hand, and as William watched, swung it up to grasp it with both hands in preparation to break down the door. The barbarous look of the hardened warrior did not frighten William, yet he could not allow this man to see that he did not participate in the pillaging.

Thinking quickly, he rushed to the woman, saying, *"Fidati di me."* *Trust me.* Hearing the door crash open, he crushed his mouth down on the frightened woman's. Her lips were tense and matched his with loathing for this action. He imagined the discomfort she must be experiencing; her soft, supple body crushed against the cold metal of his armor. He would not carry the farce any further, but for her safety, she must suffer this insult.

The raider laughed callously, muttering something that was swallowed up in the sound of the children's cries, then retreated from the hut. William released the woman, who immediately shrank back amidst her brood. William knew he had terrified her, but could not retract his actions now.

"Perdonami," William apologized. Little though it was, it was the best he could do. He watched in agony as tears coursed down the woman's cheeks, mixing with the dirt and grime often found on working peasants. Knowing he was largely to blame for her distress, and having no way to correct the wrongs done, tore at his heart. The thought of what he had done shrouded him with shame, and he turned his eyes away from her, studying the scene out the window once more.

For all the damage done, the assault ended quickly, and he felt confident that he could leave this family in relative safety. Kicking through the remains of the door, William saw the last of his raiders riding out of town. He turned back to the frightened family.

They stared at him, wide-eyed, from the corner they had occupied through the entirety of the raid.

Struggling to think of the right words, he stumbled through instructions for the woman to stay inside. "*Rimani, ah, dentro.*"

"*Grazie, signore. Grazie!*" The woman hugged her children and spoke to them in soothing tones.

Passing through the shattered doorway, William found his horse where he had left him. Swinging back into the saddle he rode out to rejoin the rest of the men.

Losing track of time, one stretch of the journey seemed much like every other. They skirted around the larger cities in Italy, hoping to draw as little attention to themselves as possible. To alert the local nobility of their presence was to invite conflict. Thus far they had not been pursued, but they were still far from safe. They swept around Turin at the base of the Alps, then Genoa near the sea, following the vast expanse of ocean until they reached the outskirts of Rome.

Meeting a fellow traveler outside of Rome, they learned that they were a mere four days from Aversa—four days from possible employment with Count Drengot, a fellow Norman. The company swelled with a new sense of excitement.

Now, three days later, William sent Gregory and another young squire ahead to scout for possible danger. They had made scouting their surroundings a priority throughout their multi-country trek, and that would not change now that they were so close to their destination. William did not want to take any risks. The company had been on the move for about an hour when the scouts unexpectedly returned.

"There is a group of men moving this direction," Gregory informed them. "They are well armed."

"How large a group?" William's heart sped up in anticipation—for what reason, he did not know.

"Nearly thirty mounted, twice that on foot," Gregory responded.

Half our size, William thought. There wasn't any convenient place to leave the road and hide; it appeared they were destined to meet this other company. Knowing these men would not hide, or back down from a confrontation, William prayed the men with him would remain calm and no scuffle would ensue.

"We ought to continue on our way and hope these men are not looking for a fight," William said.

"But if they are, they are sure to find it!" shouted Drogo, William's older brother. The men cheered their agreement. He always knew what to say to rile the men.

Soon they saw the approaching company.

Hugh, a friend of William's who shared responsibility for their company, looked to William and said, "Hauteville, go and see if there will be any trouble."

"Me?" William asked. "You want me to speak for all of you?"

Hugh rolled his eyes at William's surprise. "You speak some Italian. We do not. Of course you will need to speak for us."

Drogo jumped in. "Just find out what they want and come tell us."

The other knights murmured their assent.

"Very well," William acquiesced. He spurred Valeur and rode away, leaving his party as they came to a stop. A man in the other group also separated himself from his company and met William in the middle of the two. William decided to speak first so as not to appear on the defensive.

"Buongiorno. Dov'è Aversa?" From his broken speech it was painfully obvious that William was not Italian as he asked directions to Aversa.

"Ah! Normans!" the man responded in French, smiling. "What takes you to Aversa? Are you off to join Drengot?"

"Yes, do you know the count?"

Ignoring William's question, he continued, "And what will you do once you are there?"

"We hear Count Drengot offers work for any Norman who wants it." William shifted in his saddle. He was happy to meet other Frenchmen, but he was also anxious to be on his way. The end of this journey could not come soon enough.

"My name is Sir Aimery. I am a knight of Duke Pandulf of Capua. Do you know of him?"

"We have just arrived in this area," William admitted. "I must confess we are unfamiliar with anyone here."

"Duke Pandulf is always looking for strong men. It's a great opportunity to work for someone who holds a great deal of power. What would you think about changing your course? A duke could certainly offer better opportunities than a count. He has more holdings and is in need of strong men to protect them." The man's gaze was steady, and he appeared to be at ease, which encouraged trust. William relaxed into his saddle.

Sir Aimery talked on about the benefits of working with the duke. William listened intently. They had planned on arriving in Aversa first and hoped for ready work. This man was offering them work before they had even settled in the area, and with their fellow countrymen. This could prove to be a great opportunity.

"My company and I worked with Drengot before he received his title. He worked for Duke Pandulf before that time as well. Is not that recommendation enough?" Sir Aimery certainly seemed to believe what he said. William found him rather convincing.

"Possibly. Although, I wonder why we should throw in our lot with the duke before we discuss it with Drengot?"

"Are you expected?" Sir Aimery inquired.

William did not respond. He did not wish to admit they were not expected by the count, as well as uncertain of any following livelihood opportunities. They had travelled from Normandy on the rumor of positions only.

Sir Aimery seemed to suspect as much. "I know it is common for men like you to arrive unannounced, merely hoping for employment. Duke Pandulf pays better than any other lord in the surrounding counties. He also lets us raid the surrounding lands with impunity, only asking for a small percentage of our gains."

"Hmm, this is an interesting offer. I will need to talk it over with the rest of the knights I'm traveling with. Just to satisfy my curiosity, what brings you and your men out this way?"

Sir Aimery smiled again. "Oh, just taking care of some peasant unrest." He winked as he smiled. William read his meaning perfectly—the peasants could take care of matters themselves, but Sir Aimery and his men benefitted from seeing to it.

"Take the time you need. We can wait." Sir Aimery turned his mount and returned to his own men.

Drogo came out to meet William, and they rode back to the rest of the knights together. William spoke with the company leaders, including Hugh and Drogo, explaining the offer he had received.

"This sounds perfect!" Drogo crowed.

"But we know nothing of this Duke Pandulf." William countered.

"What if we get there only to find out he isn't honorable?" another knight joined in, bringing a laugh from the others.

"Does it matter if he's honorable? We may have more success working for someone a little less upstanding," Hugh pointed out.

"Should we at least get to Aversa to see what other options there are?" one young pup asked.

"And who says there will be other options? A sure thing is always better than taking a chance."

"If you believe that then why are you here?" Hugh questioned. "Leaving your home and all your friends seems like taking a big chance."

William listened to the back and forth for several minutes, not participating much in the discussion. He didn't care where they worked. All he really cared about was what Drogo thought, as they had sworn to stay together. They weren't responsible for the others. None of them owed their loyalty to anyone as they were all there for similar purposes. The glory of battle in a war-ridden land provided opportunities for wealth. William knew that to reach his aim of ruling, he needed to begin at the bottom, learning all he could about the local nobility and working his way into their ranks. This would be as good a place as any to begin.

"Enough!" The men were maundering, and William needed to rein in the conversation. "Drogo, what are your thoughts?"

Drogo's eyes were calculating as he said, "It seems the wisest course is to continue on to Aversa where we know we are welcome. But, being welcome does not mean that we will be allowed to stay and work. Besides, where is the fun in being wise?" He laughed along with several others.

"William, what do you think?" Hugh turned to him, waiting for him to share his thoughts. The others all waited for his response.

"I cannot speak for all of you," he began. "Work is work. I will not say no to an opportunity that is falling into my lap. I am willing to take the chance and go see for myself what type of man this Duke Pandulf is. There will always be time to change our allegiance in the future if he proves to be no good."

"I'm inclined to agree with you, William." Drogo nodded. "This entire adventure is based on uncertainty. Why not see where it leads us? Although, I would like to know how far this new place is. I am definitely ready for time off my horse." The men all laughed again.

The group seemed disinclined to separate, and after some more deliberation, decided to take the offer. William mounted his horse once more, and as he approached, Sir Aimery rode out to meet him.

William spoke first. "We accept."

Chapter 2

Salerno – December 1035

A re you certain? You heard this from whom?" Guida asked Brunhild. The ever present chill in Guida's bedchamber was overwhelmed by the sudden heat of anger at hearing this news from a servant rather than her parents.

The nurse turned lady's maid nodded emphatically, continuing to brush her mistress's raven locks. "I overheard your mother speaking with the prince himself."

Guida yanked her hair out of Brunhild's grasp as she stood, nearly knocking over the wooden stool she had been perched on. Pushing past her maid, she stalked swiftly out the door and down the corridor, passing Maria's chamber and reaching her parent's rooms. Without knocking, she pushed the weighted wooden door out of her way and entered. Her mother, Lady Raingarda, sat in front of her looking glass.

Her mother's maid stood behind the noblewoman assisting in her morning ministrations.

Without preamble Guida demanded, "Are we leaving for Sorrento?"

Lady Raingarda turned her attention to her daughter as she waved her maid away. "Prince Guaimar is conferring the dukedom of Sorrento onto your father. You are now the daughter of a duke. Your father and I will travel to Sorrento and work on establishing the peace now that the conquest is over. You and Maria will remain here under your Aunt's supervision."

"What?" Guida cried out, her outrage heightened. "You cannot mean that. Aunt Gemma hates me! You would leave me at her mercy?"

"Hush!" Lady Raingarda ordered, glancing behind Guida to the still open door. Addressing the maids, she ordered, "Leave us. And secure the door on your way out." Turning back to her daughter, she continued. "You are much too old to have a fit of temper over this. And to speak so in front of the servants! You must contain yourself. You will stay, and you will be grateful to Princess Gemma for allowing it. Watch her. Learn from her. Prince Guaimar is a good man. As your uncle, he will look after you. You have a lot to learn before you will be a lady worthy of your father's new title. When the time comes for you to marry, which will come sooner than you think..."

Guida balked at the thought and interrupted, "I am too young to marry!" She began to pace around the room, which was much larger than her own, too agitated to sit still. Her heavy skirts swished with each movement, catching between her legs and threatening to trip her with each step.

"Nonsense. You are nearly grown and no longer a child." Lady Raingarda said. Then, softening her tone, she added, "All will be well, Guida. We must be strong."

"Why leave us behind? We are a family. We should stay together."

Lady Raingarda rose and walked calmly to her daughter, her own skirts rustling with her movement. Reaching out, she enfolded Guida in a tight embrace, comforting her as only a mother could.

"My dear child, I wish we could take you and your sister with us, but Sorrento is not stable. Your uncle has only recently taken control of the city. There is still so much unrest among the people, and I worry for your safety were you to accompany us."

Guida's heart constricted, and her strophium threatened to suffocate her, resulting in quick shallow breaths.

Lady Raingarda pulled Guida to the chair near the mirror and sat her down. Keeping a hand on Guida's arm, she repeated, "All will be well. You will not be alone. You will yet have Maria, your Uncle Guaimar, and your cousins for company."

"You know how Aunt Gemma treats me! With you and Father gone, she will have no reason to temper her tongue. I will be miserable here."

"She is not the kindest woman, I grant you, but you must not let one person influence your well being. This is a large castle. It need not be difficult to learn what you can from her, and stay out of her way the rest of the time. Besides, I need you to watch over Maria. She is only nine, and must be protected. I dare not take her with us. Sorrento is far too dangerous a place for a child. I am relying on you."

Guida considered her mother's words. The thought of being separated from her parents tore at her heart. She stood at a crossroads. She too had been a child before entering this room. Now, she was given new responsibilities: the care of her sister, the task of learning from her vile aunt. She would have no mother or father to fall back on. At only fifteen, she could kick and scream along the journey, but there was no turning back from this path. Propelled into this new role, Guida determined not to be a disappointment to her parents. Looking back at her mother, shoulders slumping, she responded simply, "Yes, Mother."

Lady Raingarda sighed her relief. "You are a good daughter, Guida. I knew I could count on you. And the distance between us is not insurmountable. We are sure to see each other again soon. I look forward to that time when we shall be reunited." She placed a soft kiss on her daughter's cheek, her usual rose scent tickling Guida's nose.

Looking up, the fight having gone out of her, Guida repeated, "Yes, Mother."

Shivering in the cold, Guida watched her parents climb into the carriage that would convey them to Sorrento. She stood with the rest of the royal family, slightly separate from her aunt and uncle. The courtyard bustled with mounted knights who would accompany the duke and duchess to their new keep. Servants shuffled around packing last minute bundles into bags strapped to the horses and into the carriages.

Holding her sister Maria's hand, they were nearly lost in the middle of all the activity. Maria was crying softly, but Guida refused to give in to her emotions.

The procession began its departure, taking with it Guida's parents, and her sense of security. Standing a little straighter, she reminded herself that she must be strong. The noise from the travelers slowly died as they passed through the castle gate, leaving behind piles of horse manure, and quiet.

"Two little girls, little more than orphans," her aunt, Princess Gemma, spoke from behind Guida. Prince Guaimar must have already left the courtyard. "Your own parents will not even take you with them. It simply breaks my heart to see it. Whatever shall we do with you?"

Guida knew the falsehood of the pretended care in these words. Gemma had never shown evidence that she had a heart, let alone one that could be broken. Guida also knew better than to answer such a question. Turning to her sister, she said, "Come along, Maria. We must get you out of the cold air." She stepped to walk around her aunt, but Gemma moved to block Guida's passage. Given that Gemma was but a few years Guida's senior, the two ought to have been close friends, however the bitterness that seemed ingrained in Gemma prevented Guida from wanting to be near her. Gemma was really only ever kind to her precious Gisulf, the fussiest babe Guida had ever seen.

Gemma's golden gown seemed out of place amid the dirt and grime of the courtyard, just as her softly spoken words were out of rhythm with her meaning. "This is a dangerous place for children. I do hope nothing happens to either of you." Gemma's words dripped with menace as her countenance screwed up in mock concern. She turned haughtily around and left the girls.

"Try not to let Gemma bother you," Gaitelgrima said. Gemma's step-daughter, who fell between the sisters in age, had also lingered. She moved to take Gemma's place in front of the sisters. "She is bitter and jealous. Besides, I am certain that she hates John and me more than she hates you two." It was true that Princess Gemma did not care for her stepchildren. She made no attempt to hide that fact from any, save her husband. "I sometimes wonder what has made her so disagreeable. I hope that she will one day let go of her grievances. But, we shall see."

"She has a tack in her undergarment," Maria replied, as if it were common knowledge.

"Maria!" Guida chided, swallowing her own laughter. "You must not say such things."

"But Brunihild says it!" Maria retorted. "I have heard her repeatedly say that is the reason for Aunt Gemma's cruelty. Aunt Gemma is in constant pain, and attempts to make those around her share her misery."

Gaitelgrima and Guida shared a knowing look, then Guida leaned down to look her sister in the eye. "You must not repeat things that you hear the servants say. I love Brunhild as I know you do, yet we would all be punished if we were to be overheard saying such things."

Giuda pulled a reluctant Maria along with her, making their way back to the castle. It was far too cool to keep Maria out of doors for much longer. Maria kept turning to look out the gate, seeming to expect to see her parents' return. Once inside, Guida found an empty room and pulled Maria inside it. Closing the door, she turned to her sister.

"Maria, you must listen to me. Aunt Gemma is not to be trusted. We must be careful when she is around. And we must watch our tongues always. Word could get back to her about anything we say. Do you understand?"

Wiping her tear-stained cheeks, Maria answered, "Of course I understand. I do not like her any more than you do. Do not worry, Guida. I know how not to be seen." It was true. Maria had an ability to go unnoticed that was nearly mystical, which somewhat eased Guida's mind. She would still need to watch out for her sister, but knowing her sister was on guard calmed her fears substantially.

Chapter 3

W illiam and Drogo's heavy boots thumped along the stone battlement as they made their way to the tower stairs. The jingling of their hauberks added to the mild cacophony, and William itched to be free of the heavy armor. Duke Pandulf insisted his guards be fully dressed for battle anytime they were on duty, and with good reason. Over the eight months since his arrival in Capua, William had learned just how many enemies the duke had.

Drogo sped his steps in his rush to get to the great hall. Having just finished their watch, they were now free to go to supper, and Drogo made no secret of his desire to arrive quickly.

William laughed at his brother. "Slow down. The food will still be there, even if we do not fly to the tables."

Drogo slowed, but grumbled, "Perhaps not, if Hugh arrives before us."

"You simply wish to see Lady Isolde's maid, Margaretha." William laughed.

"Can you blame me? She is better company than you, and if I do not get there first, several other men would gladly have a go with her." Drogo laughed as well, but his crass comment took the fun out of the conversation for William. There was no point trying to alter Drogo's way of thinking toward women. It was an old argument between the brothers.

The din from the great hall could be heard well before they reached it. Pandulf employed quite a number of knights, and meals were always a loud, festive time.

"Sounds like they started without you, brother," William said, as he slapped Drogo on the back.

"I better get to it, then." Drogo left William standing in the doorway as he went off to seek his prey.

William spotted Aimery and moved to join him. They had become friends and often ate together. Aimery had been born but two territories east of Hauteville in Normandy. It was close enough for the two men to feel some comradery, but not close enough to share any of the same acquaintances.

"Ah, William. You see Lady Isolde tonight? She gets lovelier every day," Aimery drew William's attention to the head of the room.

Lady Isolde was a lovely young lady, no more than eighteen, with dark brown hair and dark eyes. She carried herself with an air of innocence, but her eyes gave her away, seeming to dare those around to challenge her. She had arrived with her parents, the former duke and duchess of Sorrento, in Capua just after William and his friends. The prince of Salerno had conquered the castle in Sorrento, but the family had been allowed to leave peacefully, on the prince's orders. William

23

was unaware of the reason. It seemed a foolish decision without having more information.

"You set your sights too high, my friend. What of the new kitchen maid? What's her name again? Gweneth?" William could not help glancing at Lady Isolde regardless of what he said.

"Gweneth is, perhaps, a bit too eager. I like a bit of a chase." Aimery's eyebrows lowered as he scanned the room again.

Quite a few people were sitting at the front table: Duke Pandulf with his wife and unmarried children, the duke and duchess of Sorrento with Lady Isolde, and several men who served as Pandulf's advisors. Lady Isolde really was lovely, although her eyes seemed a bit too close together, and she pouted a lot. William watched as Pandulf fawned over her. It was enough to make a grown man sick watching the married man simper over another woman.

"Why does the duchess tolerate Pandulf?" William asked, while looking over at Pandulf's wife. It was not the type of question that he would want overheard.

"I doubt she has a choice," Aimery responded. "She does not appear too happy to me, though." Aimery turned his attention back to the food in front of him.

William thought of his father's house. Tancred of Hauteville would never dream of disgracing his wife in such a way. A hard man to be sure, one bent on being respected and feared, yet he loved his wife and anyone who saw them together would have no doubt of their shared affection.

William was under no illusion of thinking that most marriages were happy ones. Many marriages were arranged, at least within the nobles of the kingdom. It was not uncommon for the couple never to meet before the day of the ceremony. That type of beginning often led to unhappiness and men were prone to search for solace with someone other than their wives.

He made a mental promise that he would never behave in such a manner. When he married, his wife would never have cause to doubt his affection. He could not know for certain there was a relationship between the duke and Lady Isolde, but it would not surprise him if there was. That would certainly account for the duchess's countenance this evening.

"If you ask me," William said, "everyone is too focused on women at the moment. We need a distraction. Care to have a go of it in the training field tomorrow?"

"A few of us are leaving at first light to ride towards Benevento." A glint came into Aimery's eyes. "Duke Pandulf wants us to stir up a slight ruckus, but not too close to here. He does not want the peasants coming to complain to him about us again. His coffers are getting lower than he likes, and he needs us to replenish them."

Pandulf was a strong supporter of his men raiding the surrounding countryside, and few of William's fellow Normans had any problem obliging the duke.

William happened to be one of the few who refused to support himself through such means. He had ambitions as large as most men, but he refused to flat out steal from anyone. He did not agree with it, but he also would not speak out against it to anyone, save Drogo. His brother often chose to participate with the other men.

"Another time," William answered. Aimery had long since stopped trying to convince William to join them. The men had enough respect for William, due to his fighting ability and his good-natured character, that they allowed his peculiarity in this respect.

Chapter 4

T he wind blew Guida's hair away from her face as she made her way to the secret passage that would lead her out of the castle grounds. It was not a passage through a building as one would think. This was merely part of the wall that was easy for children to scale over. It required climbing a tree and shimmying over the wall from a branch that lay over the top. Once on top of the wall, Guida gathered up the length of rope she stored there. She always left it tied to the branch that traversed the wall. This rope had knots tied periodically throughout its length making it ideal for descending the wall, and later climbing it again.

The fullness of the tree hid any occupants from the view of the guards as well as passersby. Guida sat on the wall while she waited for John to appear. John was Guaimar's first born son and heir. He was a few years younger than Guida, but they had similar temperaments. Both felt trapped in the castle, and yearned for freedom. Last year they had discovered this secret way out of the castle grounds. The fear of being caught was nothing to the joys of being out.

This developed into a bit of a ritual. They never ventured to this spot together, thinking that would attract too much attention. Guida's maid, Brunhild, being older and able to roam where she chose, had the assignment of leaving through the gate with three horses. She would make her way around the castle and meet Guida and John. The three of them would then ride out for an adventure.

At times Guida felt guilty at not sharing this secret with Maria and Gaitelgrima, John's older sister. John had convinced her that the more people who knew of their secret activities, the greater their chance of discovery. Neither of them wanted that.

Guida and John relished their freedom. Brunhild rarely interfered with their plans the way a guard was sure to do. Guaimar especially could never find out. He would be furious to find that his heir had left the safety of the castle without proper supervision. Guida, herself, could see no harm in it. She was still young, and unaware of the dangers they could encounter.

John arrived, and Guida watched as he easily made the climb up the tree.

"Where should we go today?" he asked her.

"Wherever the wind takes us," she answered. She just wanted out of the castle. The actual location mattered little to her.

"How about a race, then?" John asked enthusiastically. It was his typical request. The boy loved a good horse race.

"Very well. What shall we have the prize be?"

A mischievous look entered John's eyes as he answered, "The loser must get the winner a cup of wine."

Guida had begun her descent, but at this challenge halted and looked back up. "You know your mother would have my head if I allowed that."

"Stepmother," he corrected. "And if you are afraid of her, then I suggest you try not to lose," he laughed.

Chapter 5

A s William finished his guard shift he was met by Aimery coming to relieve him. He had just returned from raiding and was not happy about having a night shift.

"I am one of the senior knights here. I have been with Duke Pandulf for years and have never given anyone reason to question my loyalty. Should not that get me out of working through the night? William, stay and keep me company for awhile. I will regale you with what you missed. Or do you have business elsewhere?"

William responded, "No. I'll stay for a bit, but I really am quite hungry." He did not particularly care for hearing what Aimery had to say, but it seemed politic for him to keep up on the local goings on.

They ended up talking for much longer than William had intended, but the two were friends, and William did not mind the distraction. By the time he left Aimery, supper was well over. There would be no food for him until morning, and he was less than happy about that. He grumbled to himself as he made his way through the castle.

Passing through a corridor that contained several bed chambers often used for guests, he heard a high-pitched scream from one of the rooms. He ran and pushed the door of the chamber open.

There was a flurry of fabric and human limbs on the bed. A woman screamed again from underneath a large man. She was giving her attacker a full fight. William pulled the man off the bed and threw him to the floor. Shocked, he looked down to find a very drunk Duke Pandulf. Starting to rise, the duke yelled incomprehensibly at William. He came toward William and took a sloppy swing. William answered with a much more effective blow that sent the duke back to the ground, this time rendered unconscious.

Soft crying brought William's attention back to the bed. Lady Isolde knelt there in a torn night dress.

"Are you well, my lady? Did he hurt you?" William spoke softly, attempting to soothe the woman. Gratefully, his Italian had improved dramatically since his arrival in Aversa. Hearing, and attempting to speak the language constantly, allowed William ample opportunity to learn.

She sniffled as she slowly crawled to the edge of the bed, but she did not say a word. William took a step toward her, and she shrank back. Noting her reaction, he stopped his forward progress. He held up his hands in a calming gesture. Speaking in what he hoped was a soothing tone he said, "I am not here to hurt you, my lady. I heard your scream and came to help." He took another tentative step forward. "Are you hurt?" He repeated his earlier question.

Lady Isolde slumped down to the ground. She pulled her legs up close to her chest and wrapped her arms around them. Burying her head in her knees, she cried. Her shoulders shook with uncontrolled sobs. Kneeling next to her, he wondered, *How can a grown woman appear so small?* He did not try to make her talk anymore.

Her tears finally slowed, and she wiped her face with the hem of her skirt. "I apologize, Sir. Please, believe that this is not my normal state of mind. What you must think of me!"

William stood up and reached a hand down to help her. She looked at him for a moment before taking it and allowing him to help her up. Her legs wobbled under her and William grasped her around the shoulders as he guided her to a chair, only letting go of her hand once she was seated.

"Perfectly understandable, my Lady. Where is your lady's maid? She should not leave you alone like this." As if hearing she was needed, Margaretha rushed through the still-open door and ran right to Lady Isolde's side.

"Oh dear! What has happened?" Margaretha looked thoroughly concerned, but William couldn't help but notice her disheveled appearance. Her hair was a bit mussed, and her cheeks were thoroughly flushed. Of course. She must have been with Drogo, the cad.

Before Lady Isolde could answer, William spoke. "Margaretha, go fetch Lady Isolde's parents."

Margaretha did not hesitate. In no time at all the duke and duchess of Sorrento entered, the duchess rushing to her daughter's side.

"What is going on here?" the duke demanded, as he shut the door behind them.

"Your Grace," William bowed his head. He then recounted the events leading to them all being here. It was not difficult to believe, seeing as Pandulf was still sprawled out on the floor. Lady Isolde quickly corroborated the tale.

"I believe it is time for you to leave Capua, Isolde," the duke said.

"But where can she go?" the duchess fretted. "We have lost our home already. We have nowhere else to go."

The duke thought about it for a moment. "What of your sister? Would she be willing to take Isolde?"

The duchess looked at her husband as if he had lost his senses. "Gemma? How can you think that? Her husband is the one who took our home from us! He would never allow it."

"His quarrel is with me. I do not agree with him on many things, and heaven knows I do not care for him, but, Prince Guaimar is a fair man. I do not believe he would turn away an innocent."

"He may accept Isolde into his household, but he would never allow us. Are you intending to send her alone?" Her incredulity was evident in every word.

William stayed off to the side, watching this exchange. It was not his place to give his opinion, nor his responsibility to decide a course of action. He was entirely surprised when the duke turned to him.

"Sir?" the duke asked.

"William, your grace," William supplied.

"Sir William. As you can see, we are in an impossible position. I need a man I can trust. My own men were forced to remain in Sorrento. You have saved our daughter tonight, which has placed us in your debt. I must, however, ask yet more of you. I pray my trust in you is not misplaced. Would you take my daughter, tonight, to her uncle's castle in Salerno?"

"Do not be absurd!" the duchess said. "Riding out at night with a complete stranger could possibly be worse than having Isolde remain here! Her reputation would be every bit as damaged."

The duke ignored his wife, not shifting his eyes from William. Shocked by this request, William considered his options. His actions tonight would hardly ingratiate him to Duke Pandulf. It would be best for William to leave, and the sooner, the better. The duke might be drunk enough to not remember this night. However, was that a risk William was willing to take?

"I will need some time to prepare for the journey," William responded. "Have the lady packed and down to the stables in one hour. We will take Margaretha, as well as my brother. We will have our squires. Your daughter and I will not be alone. Her reputation should weather this."

The duke offered William his arm, a gesture above William's station. "Keep her safe, Sir William, and I will be forever in your debt."

William bowed low, then turned, and quickly left the room. He wondered, *How will I explain this to Drogo?*

William and Drogo kept a steady pace to make it easier for the women. It was dark and William did not want to risk losing them. He did not want anyone calling out to be found. Even at night, one never knew who could be listening. William had learned over the past six months that Pandulf had informants everywhere. If they were found it could very well mean his death, as well as Drogo's.

William looked back again to assure that the women were still with them. Once they conveyed these ladies and the duke's request to the prince of Salerno, it would lose Duke Pandulf his greatest ally. William had never met the prince, but he knew of few men who would allow the attempted rape of a relative to go unanswered.

It was not terribly far from Capua to Salerno, only about an eight hour ride. At the speed they were going, they could be there just after dawn. When they were safely within the walls of the castle they would feel some peace, assuming they were welcome.

William had no idea how they would be received. The prince had a reputation of being a fair and honorable ruler. Would those same qualities be evident within his familial relationships? Would the prince be as outraged as William would be if their roles were reversed?

William had killed before, but always at the whims of his liege lords. Never had he taken a life out of the need for revenge. That would change if a man were to treat William's sister in such a manner. He felt the heat of hatred rising in his throat just from the thought. It was best not to think on it. He attempted to keep his mind on the road.

The area between the two strongholds was heavily wooded and, thankfully, provided ample places to hide if the need arose. The road itself was frequently travelled, and the full moon allowed enough light to make it easy to follow. They first glimpsed the castle just before dawn. It was located on a hill overlooking the city of Salerno opposite the road from Capua.

William was beginning to relax, but then Drogo started talking and William tensed again.

"How do you think the prince will react when we arrive? And what do you plan to do once this is done? There is no chance that Pandulf will take us back now, and Prince Guaimar is not known for hiring Normans."

"I know. I did not force you to come. You chose to join me on your own."

"That is because I was half asleep! I would have agreed to go anywhere just to get you to be quiet. And that is not an answer to my questions."

"Honestly, I'm hoping that the prince will be grateful for our assistance to Lady Isolde and will allow us to work for him. If not, we could inquire with Count Drengot in Aversa; just go back to our original plan from last year. For now, we should pray that God will guide us where he wants us to be." William always fell back on his faith in God during times of uncertainty. It never failed to give him comfort.

"You know I don't pray," Drogo said.

"Now may be the time to start," William replied, with a long look at his   brother.

Chapter 6

Salerno – August 1036

Guida sat entirely ensconced within a crenel on top of the back wall of her uncle's castle. These breaks in the top of the battlements were some of her favorite places. She was small enough to fit completely inside with her back against one edge and her legs bent up to her chest. In this position she could not be seen from either corner of the wall, although no real lady would sit in such a way. Gratefully, Guida still had some time before she would be expected to always behave like a lady.

Brunhild hated that Guida would sit here. She would go on and on about how dangerous it was. She was always saying, "What if you were to fall? It would be a shame to have your life cut so short."

Guida would grant her that it was a terribly long way to drop, but that never stopped her. In fact, it made it that much more exciting. She just loved the feeling of being so high and looking over the surrounding area.

Today was different, though. Today, she came for the escape it provided, not the adventure. She had awoken early from a bad dream. Making her way here, she hoped the cool air of morning would clear her mind. It was not working, though.

The leaves of the trees fluttered in the breeze, as if afraid of remaining still. Guida watched as a falcon circled over a particular section of forest.

"What are you searching for?" Guida asked the bird. She watched as the beautiful creature swooped down toward the tops of the trees and frightened a clutch of smaller birds out of their hiding places. The falcon gave chase to one, quickly snatching his prey with his talons. Guida gasped at having witnessed something so deadly happen so fast. As she continued watching, the falcon swooped down within the trees and was lost from view.

Shuddering, Guida's gloom nestled on her shoulders as sure as her winter fur. She told herself it was just the nature of beasts, yet it felt somehow meant just for her. A sign of the future? An omen like the servants often spoke of? How she wished to speak with her mother. Perhaps Guida would mention this in her next letter to her parents.

It had been months since Guida's parents had left Salerno. Guida had settled into a daily routine of monotony since then. She and Maria joined with Gaitelgrima in lessons each day. Once she completed her lessons, she was allowed to venture basically anywhere that her legs could carry her, provided she not go alone. Uncle Guaimar would be upset to know she was alone now. He was proving nearly as overprotective as a parent.

"Guida!" the voice of her maid reached her from the tower.

Knowing that the longer it took Brunhild to find her the angrier she would be, Guida leaned her head out and called, "Here!"

Brunhild rushed over to her, and Guida knew what she was about to say, so she said it first. "I know. I know. I should not be up here, especially sitting on the wall like that. I know it is dangerous, but I just love the view! Please do not be angry."

"Oh, child," the older woman sighed with exasperation. "I just worry so! Could you not just look through the crenel? Do you have to actually sit up there? And what if Maria were to see you and attempt it herself? You must think of the example you set for that child."

Not wishing to think on her failings as a guardian, she chose to change the subject. "Brunhild, when do you think my parents will come back?" She turned to look back out the crenel. "I dreamt last night of them travelling here. They were set upon by bandits on the way and both were killed. Then, just now, I saw a falcon kill a bird in the air. Are these evil omens? Is something terrible about to happen?"

Brunhild's wrinkled face scrunched up in a comforting smile. "There, there, child. What would your mother say to such ramblings?"

"I am asking you, Brunhild, not my mother. I know you have different beliefs than my family. I truly wish to know."

Brunhild's eyes shifted and she wrung her hands. Guida knew she had made the woman uncomfortable and regretted pushing her.

"I apologize, Brunhild. I know omens are not real. Father says they are the explanations of the uneducated to explain circumstances. Bad things may happen, but we must place our faith in God and let Him guide our hearts."

The older woman's face relaxed and, taking Guida's arm, she guided her towards the tower stairs. Feeling slightly mollified, Guida followed her maid's lead.

Guida notice a bit of fabric flapping from within the final crenel in the wall. Recognizing it as part of Maria's dress she grabbed her skirts in her fists and ran the remaining distance. She quickly transferred her grip from her skirts to her younger sister's nearest arm and yanked with all her might. With a mighty scream the two girls crashed onto the rough stone floor.

"Have you gone mad?" Maria indignantly yelled as she clambered off Guida.

Panting from her quick sprint combined with having the wind knocked from her, Guida sat upright. "What were you thinking climbing up there? A fall from up here would kill you!"

"You climb up there all the time!" Maria pushed against Brunhild, who was attempting to brush off the gravel from the little girl's hair and clothing.

Guida had to stop and consider her next words. Maria was right; Guida did often do the exact thing she was now chiding Maria over. What could she say? "I am nearly grown! You are still a child. Do not do this again or I shall be forced to speak of it with Uncle Guaimar."

"Being nearly grown does not make it any safer for you than for me."

"Of course it does! Men go to war, not boys. Women know better than little girls. Now, cease arguing. Return to your chamber and stay there until supper."

Maria continued to grumble, but obediently walked away.

"You see the damage you have caused with your own reckless behavior?" Brunhild said.

"I see my failing quite clearly, Brunhild. There is no need for you to chastise me."

"Perhaps. In many ways you are still a child yourself, my dear. I am merely trying to help."

"I know. I feel unequal to this task of caring for Maria. She needs her mother." Her sister was only nine, six years younger than Guida. The heavy weight that had settled over Guida's shoulders earlier threatened to make her knees buckle. A lone tear slid down her face, and her lower lip trembled.

Brunhild looked at Guida, then pulled her into an embrace. "I know it is hard now, but it really is for the best that you are here. There is much that you can learn from Princess Gemma about being a lady, Maria, too. You will have better opportunities to meet marriageable men. And you still have family here. Your uncle dotes on you as if you were his own daughter. And you have Gaitelgrima. This is the only home you have ever known. You do not understand what it would be like to say goodbye and leave. You must trust me. Trust your parents. This is where you ought to be. For now." She stroked Guida's back as she spoke the soothing words in her ear.

"What I can learn from Gemma is how to be a vindictive old hag. She knows nothing of kindness or charity. I do not understand why I must learn anything from her."

Brunhild looked stricken, and she glanced around to make sure they had not been overheard. "You must not say such things!" she hissed. "If the princess were to know you spoke against her, she would not hesitate to have you punished. I shudder to think what that woman is capable of."

Frightened by Brunhild's countenance, Guida returned to her previous concerns. "I do not feel like an adequate guardian for Maria. You are right; she is learning all of my bad habits. How can I do this?"

Guida didn't often share her insecurities, but today she felt despondent. Instead of keeping it bottled inside, she desperately wanted to talk about it. She was often uncertain when she thought of the future, but she worked hard to hide that from those around her. After all, she was the daughter of a duke, a lady in her own right, and the niece of the prince. She was always being told that she needed to be strong, and she strived to appear so, even if it was all just an act. However, this was a moment of rare vulnerability. Perhaps it was the scene with the falcon that she had witnessed making her feel more like a child than she should.

"Dear child, we cannot live in the world of 'what ifs.' That only serves to make us anxious and miserable. We must focus on what is in front of us. Look out there." She gestured out behind the castle. "What do you see?"

It was Guida's turn to sigh. She did not want to get into a philosophical discussion. She just wanted to share her feelings, but she played along with the older woman.

"The sky, trees in the distance, birds flying, the road, and," she squinted to try to see further, "some men making their way to the castle. Who could it be? Quick Brunhild, I wish to see." This might be the distraction she needed to shed her feelings of insecurity.

With that she took off like a bolt of lightning, running toward the stairs. The company she had seen were still far enough away that Guida would be able to reach the castle gate before the newcomers. In the back of her mind, she knew her despondent thoughts would return, but for now a distraction was welcome.

She was short of breath when she made it outside and reached the gate, but that didn't abate her excitement in the least. She ran straight for the gate so as to greet the company immediately on their arrival, stopping just short of running into the guards. Her chest rose and fell in rapid succession as she waited. Brunhild was still making her way out, having taken a more careful approach than Guida had. If Brunhild did not make haste, she would miss the arrival. Guida was fairly bouncing, overcome with excitement.

Thinking better of her position, Guida sidled next to the wall, attempting to be inconspicuous. As much as she wished to see these strangers, she was less eager for them to see her.

Upon their approach, Guida was struck by the oddness of the company. The two women looked like native Italian women. It was evident that one was a noblewoman as her dress was of the latest style. The other was dressed in much coarser material, and Guida guessed her to be a lady's maid. They both had dark brown hair and olive-toned skin, similar to Guida's. The men, on the other hand, looked entirely foreign. Instead of the brown hair and olive skin common to Italians, they were all fair skinned and relatively clean shaven, which was uncommon in this area. Guida did not recognize a single person.

One of what looked like the men's squires displayed a coat of arms that was unfamiliar to Guida. It had a blue background with a slanted line of red and white checkered squares. It was quite plain when compared to Guaimar's coat of arms that was displayed in many places throughout the castle boundaries. Guaimar's was a complicated design filled with white and red stripes going first one direction and then another, mixed with blue crosses filled with yellow crescent moons tipped on their side.

The man in front, who looked to be the leader of the company, was strikingly handsome. His hair was cropped short which left his eyes in full view. Being clad in full armor, it was impossible to get an accurate sense of what was underneath, but it spoke to his size and strength that he could wear it. She had the impression that no one would dare go against such a formidable-looking warrior.

As if sensing her gaze, the man turned and looked directly at her. Their eyes met, and briefly held. Guida experienced a brief moment of wishing she were five years older. This man was easily ten years older than she, yet she felt drawn to him.

Brunhild finally caught up to her and tried to guide Guida back to the castle. Guida remained rooted where she was, unable to tear her eyes from those of the stranger. After a few more moments, the man turned his attention back to the guards. Only then did Guida allow herself to move again. She turned and ran back into the castle, Brunhild's agitated voice calling after her. She did not seem to see anything as she ran to her chamber and threw herself onto her bed. She could not stop the vision of the stranger from replaying in her mind, nor did she wish to.

Chapter 7

Salerno – August 1036

W illiam, and the others with him, reached the gates. The guards stepped out in front of the men.

"State your name and your business," drawled a guard. He gave off an aura of boredom, as if actual security was not his priority.

"Sir William and Sir Drogo, lately of Capua. We are here escorting Lady Isolde, Princess Gemma's niece. It is urgent that we speak with the prince."

The two guards spoke quietly to each other. While he was waiting, William noticed a little slip of a girl, not quite a woman and not quite a child, a few paces away. She was gazing up at him with the most peculiar expression. She looked a bit windswept, like she had just been running. Her cheeks were rosy from exertion, and her eyes were wide. Something about those eyes drew him, and he could not look away.

The girl's beauty rivaled Lady Isolde's. Her olive complexion was framed perfectly by raven hair. Several tendrils escaped her pins and curled alluringly around her heart-shaped face.

His reason for being here briefly left his mind. All he could think about was what would make such a girl look so serious. *Why is she staring?* Perhaps because he was a foreigner. It was obvious he was not Italian. His light hair and complexion could not be hidden. His obvious time in the sun could not make him match the shade of those Italians he had met since coming to this country. His blue eyes were also evidence that he did not quite belong here.

Feeling uneasy under her continued scrutiny, William forced his mind back to reality and the guard still speaking to him.

"You may take your mounts to the stables. Then return here and I will escort you into the main hall. The midday meal should be beginning soon. I will let the prince know that you are here to speak with him."

"*Je vous remercie*," William dipped his head to the guard while he thanked him. They turned their horses toward the stables. Turning back to look at the girl, he found that she was gone.

Since the great hall was being set up for the meal, the two men were escorted to a separate chamber attached to it. There they were met by the prince and a few of his guards. "Now," the prince addressed William and Drogo, "what has happened to my niece?"

Lady Isolde had been escorted away, presumably to her room. She had not spoken much to her uncle, leaving the unenviable burden of retelling the events of last night to William. As William prepared to speak, he quickly tried to assess Prince Guaimar. He appeared to be in his early thirties, although it was difficult to tell with the full beard that the man wore. He had a reputation of being levelheaded and honorable. William hoped the reports of his character were accurate.

He felt Drogo's eyes on him, expecting him to take the lead. William did so, considering it had been him who had witnessed the attack.

"Your Highness, my name is Sir William of Hauteville, and this is my brother, Drogo. We left my father's home in Normandy last year and have been working for Duke Pandulf of Capua since arriving in Italy. Over this past year I have been able to assess Duke Pandulf's character as one of the vilest of men. I do not wish to go into detail, as I am sure you have neither the time nor the inclination for such an accounting."

"I care only for what pertains to my niece." The prince waved his hand impatiently.

"Lady Isolde arrived in Duke Pandulf's household a few months back. Duke Pandulf immediately flooded her with his attentions. It appeared, to those of us close to Pandulf, that he was laying the groundwork to build a relationship with her. That would have been inappropriate, considering he is already married. Unfortunately, Duke Pandulf is anything but honorable."

The prince nodded his agreement. William quickly retold the events of the previous night. The prince's face contorted with anger, but he remained silent.

"I stopped the attack, and sent her maid to fetch her parents. The duke then asked me to bring her to you. We set off immediately. I assure you that she kept her personal maid with her at all times on our journey, my Lord."

"I thank you, both of you, for bringing Lady Isolde to me," the Prince responded. After a short pause, he added, "I wonder what it is you expect to gain from this? I assume you have not helped her out of the goodness of your hearts. I'm sure you realize that Pandulf surely will not take you back after this."

"I have been quite discontent working for such a man as Duke Pandulf. I am well aware of your reputation, however. My brother and I would like to offer you our allegiance and hope for a place in your household."

William felt Drogo's eyes on him again, and hoped that he was making the right move for his brother as well as for himself.

"I see," the prince mused as he crossed his arms over his chest, affecting a thoughtful pose. "I have heard tales of you men of Normandy. Tales of raiding, stripping villages of anything of value, taking advantage of the women that you run across, ransacking and defiling churches. I have no patience for that sort of behavior and have never had Normans in my employ. Tell me honestly, would the two of you abide by the rules that I would lay forth, if I do decide to let you stay?"

The account of Norman behavior was not without truth, however horribly it painted William's people. Knowing that Drogo was not opposed to such enterprises, William was surprised to hear his brother speak.

"My Lord, my brother William has never once initiated any raiding parties, nor has he taken pleasure in such. I, myself, have, on occasion. I would never do so on my own. As you said, you have never employed Normans, so a raiding party of one is all there could be. I am not such a fool to think that I could take on a village on my own. You would need not fear about our activities while here."

"That is rather persuasive. However, I do not make rash decisions. I will take time to consider your request. I am only considering it because of the service that you have rendered to my family. You are welcome to stay with my other knights, as long as you are good to your word, and I will send for you when I have made my determination."

"As you wish, my lord." William bowed and left the room with Drogo at his heels.

Guaimar summoned Guida to the solar that afternoon. This room, where the family often took their leisure, was not a place that Guida enjoyed. It was lovely, with enormous tapestries draping the walls, and padded chairs around the fireplace. There were shelves lining the walls with carvings and figurines, treasures from places that Guida had never been, along with a few precious books and scrolls. Guaimar occasionally allowed Guida to read from those, and Guida loved the new information that flooded her mind. Yet, this room was often occupied by Princess Gemma, who never hid her displeasure of having Guida nearby.

Prince Guaimar normally summoned Guida after the evening meal, on those nights when he had time to visit with her. He was insistent that he finish his work for the day before he made time for her. It was still a solid hour until the evening meal, which was why this summons felt different. She assumed that someone had disclosed her activities to her uncle, and he was calling to chastise her for being up on the wall. He did not approve of anything that could compromise her safety.

Guida was surprised to see Princess Gemma with her uncle. Gemma wasn't often present when Guaimar summoned Guida. In another corner of the room Gaitelgrima and John spoke with a young woman whom Guida had never met. Guida recognized her as being one of the travelers who had arrived earlier that day.

"Uncle Guaimar?" Guida's voice sounded timid, even to her. "You wished to see me?"

"Yes, my dear. Come in." He waved her to a chair near his own. "I did not see you at the midday meal, and I wondered if you were having a difficult day. I thought perhaps you would wish to talk about it." He spoke gently to her, just as he always did. She felt reassured, yet still uneasy about this break in routine. Gemma sighed as if already put out by Guida's presence.

Not wishing to confess the thoughts that had been racing through her mind, she decided to not be entirely honest. "I was just feeling a bit homesick. Do not worry, it shall pass."

"Very well. Now, Brunhild informed me that you have been up on the wall again. Guida, that must stop. You are far too intelligent to place yourself in such unnecessary danger."

"Yes, Uncle." Guida's anger flared at Brunhild for this betrayal. Her lack of freedom to do as she wished rankled her.

"Such a foolish child," Gemma growled, as if she were more than a few years older herself. "That kind of behavior will not be tolerated. This is your only warning."

Her uncle tried to lessen the rebuke. "I know it is not easy being away from your family, but remember that we are your family, too. I want you to feel at home here. I do not know how long you will stay, but I want you to enjoy it while you can. Let this be your home." He took one of her hands in both of his, and he squeezed it comfortingly.

"I have a surprise for you," he continued with a smile. "I will give it to you tomorrow. Meet me outside the great hall doors after the morning meal, and I will take you to it."

Aunt Gemma was aghast. "You are going to reward her?"

Uncle Guaimar looked at his wife sharply. "This is unrelated, and I will do as I wish!" He turned back to Guida. "Now, I would like to introduce you to Gemma's niece, Lady Isolde. She has just arrived, and may be staying with us for some time. I would like you and Gaitelgrima to help her get settled. I hope you three will become great friends."

Guida's feelings were all a jumble. She was excited to finally have another young lady close to her age to speak with, but nervous at the same time. *What if she doesn't like me? What if I don't like her?* she thought.

She was a bit embarrassed to be rebuked by her aunt and uncle, and to have this new girl witness it. Hopefully, Lady Isolde had been too engrossed in her conversation with Guida's cousins to have overheard. Guida stood up and curtsied as she had been taught. "It is a pleasure to meet you, Lady Isolde."

Chapter 8

Salerno – August 1036

The dining hall was only half full the next morning when Guida arrived to break her fast. It had taken Brunhild longer than normal to help Guida dress. Full of excitement and curiosity about her uncle's surprise, Guida had found it difficult to remain still during Brunhild's ministrations.

Guida barely tasted her food as she forced it down. She always had trouble eating when she was excited. Gaitelgrima arrived just after Guida, and sat next to her.

Leaning in conspiratorially, Gaitelgrima asked, "What do you think of Isolde?"

Looking at her cousin, Guida answered honestly. "I do not know what to think, yet. She spent most of last evening speaking with you and

John. I did not have much time to interact with her. What are your impressions?"

"She is nicer than Gemma, but that is not difficult. She spent most of the time speaking of herself. You ought to ask her why she is here. Her tale is intriguing."

Asking the question she was dying to have answered, Guida said, "Do you know who she arrived with? I saw her ride in with some strange men."

Gaitelgrima's eyes widened with excitement. "They are Normans. Actual Normans from France. Isolde's father sent her with them because she was no longer safe with Duke Pandulf. I must find a way to speak with them. I have so many questions about their part of the world."

"I thought Normans were men to be feared." Guida's confusion was evident. "Do you not know what they do? They pillage and plunder, and ruin lives. Why would you wish to speak with such men?"

Gaitelgrima scoffed. "These men have been trusted by Isolde's parents enough for her to travel with them. My father has allowed them into the keep, and is considering allowing them to stay. You know he would not do that if he did not believe them to be honorable. I shall be safe enough to have a simple conversation with them."

"Yes," Guida conceded. "I suppose that is true."

Excusing herself from her cousin, Guida worked her way through tables that had yet to be cleared. She was almost to the doors when she tripped on the hem of her gown. She would have landed flat on her face if it had not been for two large hands grabbing her arms and keeping her upright. She looked up to find the foreign knight she had just been speaking of.

He gazed down at her and said kindly, "Careful, now. Steady." He was much larger than her, even larger than Guaimar, making her feel more like a child. "Good morning. My name is Sir William." He bowed to her.

Still not knowing if this Norman could be trusted, she stepped back, suddenly wishing for more distance between them. Yet, he spoke kindly and his soft blue eyes told her that she need not be afraid.

"Guida." She curtsied, and then cursed herself for her breach in etiquette. A noble lady ought never to show deference to a man so far beneath her station. Aunt Gemma would surely mock her if she knew.

"I saw you yesterday. You were near the gate as I rode in." He smiled, and Guida's legs quivered. The world around her disappeared and all that was left was that smile, directed at her.

She shook herself, and looked away from his eyes that were the blue of a lake at midday. She needed to gather her thoughts and extract herself from this moment that had become awkward with her lack of response.

"Yes, Sir." *Wonderfully engaging,* she thought sarcastically.

"I am happy to meet you, Lady Guida. It is always a pleasure to see a friendly face." He winked at her, so quickly she thought she must have imagined it.

"Yes, Sir." Guida said a bit breathlessly as she felt blood rushing to her cheeks. She could not seem to utter another rational sentence. She felt even more like a small child, one who did not understand appropriate social rules.

"I won't delay you any longer, my lady." He bowed to her with a twinkle in his eye, then turned and walked away.

Guida was left standing there, staring after the foreign knight. She had a tightness in her chest and her mind was a mass of confusion. She had never felt anything like this before and did not know what to make of it. She thought about asking Brunhild what these new feelings meant.

Brunhild would likely say they were caused by the moon being in a certain position in the heavens, or the way the wind was blowing, which was why she decided she would not tell Brunhild about it. This seemed like something best kept to herself. Brunhild always tried to explain everything away, but Guida felt some things had no explanations.

Taking a moment to remember where she had been going, she turned back to the door. She found Guaimar standing just outside the great hall. He took her hand and laced it through his arm as they walked toward the stables. One of the servants stood just outside the stable next to the prettiest young horse Guida had ever seen. She gasped and looked up at her uncle. He smiled down at her and simply said, "Go."

She did not waste any time. She sprinted the rest of the way and came to a stop a few paces from the filly. Guida examined the horse from head to hoof. She was mostly black, with just a few white spots on her head and a small patch of white in her mane. Her hair was so silky smooth that Guida longed to reach out and run her fingers through it, but she knew that she needed to gain the horse's trust first so that she would not get spooked.

Guida slowly walked the rest of the distance between herself and the horse. She held her hand out as she approached. The animal snorted at the proffered hand, but did not retreat. Guida reached up her other hand and began stroking the filly's neck.

Guaimar came up behind her. "This filly is only a few years old and still being trained, but she is yours. You will continue your usual riding lessons on my horses and only ride this one when I am able to be with you. We must ensure she does not hurt you. I want you to come to the stables often to visit with her so that she gets to know and trust you."

Guida finally tore her gaze from the filly. She threw her arms around Guaimar's neck.

"Thank you!" she breathed.

"He really attacked you?" Guida's shock was evident.

She had taken an immediate liking to Lady Isolde, who was only a year older than herself. Along with Gaitelgrima, the three had spent a good deal of time together. Their personalities were all so different, but still they enjoyed each other's company.

Where Guida was a bit shy and unsure of herself, Lady Isolde's mere presence exuded confidence and pride. Gaitelgrima was confident, yet fairly quiet. She often said there was no reason to announce her intelligence to the world. Lady Isolde said exactly what was on her mind at nearly the moment it popped into her head. Guida preferred to let her thoughts simmer in the back of her brain for a while before sharing them with anyone.

Lady Isolde was sharing why she had come to Salerno so unexpectedly. "Shocking, isn't it? I was there to try to find a suitable husband, and that awful man would not leave me alone for a moment. He was often drunk, and would slobber over his food while he talked. It was horrendous! And then there were the glares from his wife. As if I had deliberately encouraged his behavior!"

"How did you get away?" Guida was hanging on every word, and Isolde appeared to love having such an avid audience.

"One of the guards rushed in and knocked Pandulf unconscious! He was even kind enough to escort me here safely." Isolde's face showed her satisfaction at being the center of such a tale, making Guida wonder if she was truly unaffected by such an experience.

"I may have met him the other day," Gaitelgrima contributed. "I know there were two who arrived with you, and one was helping my brother, John, with his riding."

Guida did not feel the need to share her interaction with Sir William. Let Lady Isolde think Guida had a bit more finesse than tripping over her own skirt. She was curious about Pandulf's court, though. Having lived her entire life in Salerno, Guida was often curious about other places. She wished she could ask Isolde, but she felt too unsure of herself.

"Now, what of the men here?" Isolde asked. "I know my father will be more at ease once I find someone suitable to marry. I would rather not marry right away, but I do enjoy looking."

Guida wrapped her arms around herself as if with a sudden chill. "Does it not bother you that we really have no say who we marry? I hate the idea of being married off to some decrepit old widower simply because of his rank. It makes me shudder!"

"Of course it bothers me, but it is our duty. To do anything else is unthinkable. So we will do it," Isolde said emphatically. "But, we are not married yet. There is no harm in just looking at the available men, is there?" She needed no answer. "And a bit of flirting never hurt anyone, either." Her eyes took on a sly look. "I am excited to see what sort of men there are here in Salerno. Have you noticed anyone?"

Guida blushed and lowered her gaze. Isolde squealed and laughed. "You must tell me all about him! I simply must know everything."

There was no way that Guida was going to tell Isolde about Sir William. They had only just met, and she was still unsure about Isolde's fundamental character. It would be disastrous for Guida if Aunt Gemma found out about her growing interest in a Norman.

"I, for one, am in no rush to find a man," Gaitelgrima offered. "Happiness in marriage is not common enough to entice me."

Chapter 9

Salerno – October 1036

T raining with Guaimar's men was taxing. The prince insisted on his knights being well trained. It had taken all William had to withstand the many blows of the day. Since the prince had allowed them to stay, they had been training each day with the other knights, who mostly treated them as equals. The men were severe, yet relatively good natured. Although, there were a few who seemed to dislike the brothers simply because of their nationality.

They all pitched in to replace the weapons used throughout the day. Then they removed their armor, leaving it for servants who would mend and polish and return it to them in the morning.

They had been added to the guard rotations of the castle and were starting to feel a little more settled. The other knights held the prince in high esteem, which made William grateful for his change of location.

These knights drastically differed from Pandulf's men, who were mostly savage and greedy with little honor. William knew that was typical of his countrymen, who made up the majority of Pandulf's forces, but it still did not sit well with him. There were a few, Aimery among them, whom William respected regardless of some of their actions.

Drogo and William followed the others back to the castle for supper. Glancing up, William looked once again for the woman he had seen up on the wall on his arrival. Since seeing her, he had taken to glancing up, thinking he might see her again. He had been surprised by her presence there. Having guarded his share of castles, he knew the wall was not often visited by those not needing to be there. He also knew the dangers of playing there. Stories were frequent of those who had plummeted to their deaths from such a height. He found it foolish and irresponsible for anyone who did not need to be there to spend their time in such a way. Telling himself his irritation was irrational, as he had no connection with this woman, did nothing to relieve his tension. He had looked for her again and again, and realized he had been waiting to hear the screams and shouts that would signal her fall.

Upon entering the dining hall, his eyes went straight to the dais where the prince and his family sat. Through conversations with the other men, William could now name the majority of the royal family. Princess Gemma was a severe woman with rather common features. Her eyes often pinched together giving her a calculating air which William distrusted. Lady Isolde flitted her eyelashes at any man who crossed her path, eager for attention. John, Prince Guaimar's first born son and heir, laughed frequently as he sat near Lady Guida and across from his sister, Gaitelgrima.

William could just see her face now through a gap in the people seated across from her. His eyes traveled from her raven hair pulled behind her with only a few random strands curling down in front, to her face, and his heart skipped a beat. She was also laughing, and her joy radiated through him as sure as any flame.

Continuing his examination, he noticed she wore a dark blue over dress with light blue sleeves. The dress had gold embroidery stitched throughout. Recognition flooded him as he realized it had been her he had seen at the top of the wall.

William's irritation at her foolishness threatened to spoil his appetite. A foolish woman with little regard for her own safety held little interest for him. Just as he came to this realization, Drogo noticed his inattention.

"Stop staring, man! People will start to speculate," Drogo whispered as he pulled on his arm to guide him to a table.

Barely having sat down, they were approached by a servant who bowed before stating, "Sir William, the prince insists that you join him on the dais this evening." The servant bowed again and turned to return to his duties. William's plans for avoidance evaporated.

William and Drogo looked at each other dumbfounded. William asked the question they both had, "Why would the prince want me up there?"

"Maybe he has more questions about Pandulf?" Drogo suggested.

"If that was the case, would he not choose a more private meeting place? There are too many listening ears here." William was on edge, not knowing what had prompted this breach of etiquette. William's social standing was nowhere near high enough to warrant being seated with the ruling family.

"Well, don't make him wait. Come find me later. I want to hear all about this." Drogo guided William where he needed to go with a slight push forward.

William walked up to the head of the room and bowed low.

"Ah, Sir William! It is good to see you again. Please join us. There is an empty chair next to Lady Guida."

"Thank you, my lord."

As he walked around the table to the seat indicated, Guida looked up from her conversation with John.

"Good evening, Sir William." Guida greeted him softly while avoiding direct eye contact with him.

He bowed low to her. "*Bonsoir*, my lady. I hope I am not interrupting your evening with Master John." He gave John a slight bow as well.

"No, nothing too serious. John was just telling me of a prank he played on his tutor today. I should not have laughed, but I really could not help it." She laughed a little just thinking about it. It was a lovely sound.

"Please, do not stop on my account."

Isolde and Gaitelgrima sat opposite them. "How are you faring this evening, Lady Isolde?" William asked her.

"Much better than when last we met, Sir William. And you?"

"I am quite well, my lady."

Where is Maria? Guida wondered once more, debating if she ought to get up and find her. Yet that would draw attention to herself as well as to her absent sister.

Pursing her lips in thought, Guida noticed Isolde lean slightly forward and purse her lips at the handsome knight. Would William be taken by Isolde's beauty and her obvious tactics to be noticed?

Not wishing to find out, Guida interrupted. "Sir William, have you met my cousin, Gaitelgrima? She has been anxious to meet you."

"Lady Gaitelgrima," William inclined his head in greeting.

"We have heard of your heroics, Sir William," Gaitelgrima began, blushing from the attention. Guida wondered if there was a woman within the keep who was not taken with this handsome man. "I hope to hear more exciting tales of your adventures some time."

"Perhaps," he hedged. "Although, many may not be appropriate for innocent ears."

Guida spoke again, "What will you do now, Sir William? Given you have brought Lady Isolde to us safely, will you be returning to Capua?"

"My brother and I have the good fortune to be staying in Salerno."

Guida grinned, unable to hide her pleasure. "I am happy for you, that you do not have to return to Capua. I hope you will enjoy your time here." Her smile faded. "I have been to Capua, many years ago. I did not care for it. Uncle Pandulf is an odious man."

William choked on his ale. He coughed a few times, then repeated, "Uncle Pandulf?"

"Well, he is actually my great uncle. He is my father's and Guaimar's uncle. Do not worry about any family loyalty, however. Uncle Pandulf has done many things over the past few years that have my father and Uncle Guaimar concerned. His treatment of dear Isolde unfortunately is not uncommon." She chanced a glance at Isolde, who had turned back to conversing with Gaitelgrima, and was not following Guida's conversation.

She suddenly felt like a child caught pilfering the kitchens. Glancing at Guaimar, who was speaking with the captain of the guards, she began taking back what she had said. "Oh, dear. I really should not be talking about this. Please do not tell Uncle Guaimar what I have said. I will be in so much trouble." She felt her cheeks heat and felt she was no better than Gaitelgrima.

"I will not say a word, my lady." He smiled briefly and winked at her. "I am simply surprised at the connection, given his actions toward Lady Isolde."

"Unfortunately, one cannot choose their relations. Pandulf is an awful man; even more so when he has had too much to drink. I do not think any woman is safe from him when that is the case, regardless of her relation to him."

As she was speaking, Guida's eyes lit upon Maria, who was attempting to sneak up to the table unnoticed.

"Maria!" Guida hissed. "Where have you been? And why are you so filthy?"

Maria sat in the empty chair next to Sir William, forcing the sisters to speak around him to each other.

"I found a new chamber upstairs that is being used for storage." Maria answered. "I lost track of the time while exploring it."

Glancing back to assure that Gemma had not seen the filthy child approach, Guida turned back to Maria.

"Eat quickly, then have Brunhild draw you a bath. You must not allow Gemma to see you like this. Honestly, Maria, you have cobwebs in your hair!"

Guida was mortified that Sir William was witness to this conversation. Attempting to distract him, she changed the subject back to the original topic. "Do you plan on staying here for long?"

"I am not certain," William laughed, then returned to his former serious state. "There is talk of the Roman battles in the south. My brother Drogo and I are thinking about joining up with the Roman army. They pay well, and it is something to do. It is not good for Drogo to sit around. When he is inactive he tends to act foolishly and get into trouble."

"Oh, would you be leaving soon?" She could not hide her surprise. "You only just arrived."

"We have no definite plans yet, so it is hard to say. It would not be immediately anyway." Relieved, she began to relax again.

"Can you explain to me about the conflict in the south? Why are there always reports of fighting, and no signs of peace in the region?"

"Do you really have an interest in politics, my lady?" William asked, surprised.

"I am beginning to. My uncle speaks of these matters with me on occasion. But I must confess, he raises more questions than he answers." She lowered her eyes, breaking their connection. "I know it is not considered the place of a woman, but I do find it fascinating."

William was impressed. He had spoken to Fressenda, his stepmother, a few times about different issues facing the regions near their home in Normandy, but that had been the only time such things had come up with a woman.

As he prepared for bed that night, he recalled his conversation with Lady Guida. She had known more of the southern conflict than he would have guessed, and she was not satisfied with the simple response that the Romans have control, and the Lombards wish to take it back. They had spoken of the Pope, the Romans, the Arabs, and the Lombards, as well as Charlemagne. Her grasp of politics intrigued him. It was refreshing to converse so freely about important topics with someone other than Drogo.

Besides enjoying the conversation, William had noted that Guida's large brown eyes rarely left his face once he began his political lesson. Rather than feeling scrutinized, as he would have from anyone else, William relished the feeling of openness that they shared.

She had continued to amaze him with the intelligence behind her questions. She was clever, and he found his good opinion of her growing. Witty, too. There had been several times she had made him laugh aloud as she attempted to lighten the mood from such a heavy subject.

It had truly been with regret that he turned his attention to Prince Guaimar. The prince had wanted William's account of crossing the Alps, and William realized that was the reason for him eating at the high table. He looked forward to his next opportunity to speak with Lady Guida, and hoped it would be soon.

Chapter 10

G uida was entranced with Sir William and constantly on the lookout for him. She had been surprised with how he spoke with her at dinner. Taking time to explain important political matters, he had not just brushed aside her questions. And he had been patient with her as she strove to understand.

She was not used to being treated in such a way by any other than her tutors and family. The rest of her uncle's men had no interest in speaking with her at all. A few of them had begun leering at her and making lewd comments as she passed by. These attentions had been increasing over the past year, as her body took on more womanly curves. Unlike Isolde, who seemed to relish such attentions, Guida was unsettled by them.

Sir William was different. He treated her differently, and she liked it immensely. His smiles felt genuine, and he would speak to her, not about her from a distance.

She was currently watching him train from up on the castle wall. It was too far away to see any facial expressions. She knew he was unlikely to see her, but she was able to see how he bested nearly every opponent. It often looked like he was teaching the other men.

He was so large, and Guida couldn't imagine how terrifying it would be to have such a man charging toward her in battle. But even as the thought terrified her, it also thrilled her. She imagined all sorts of scenarios where she was a damsel in distress, and he was her knight come to rescue her. The imagination of a young lady knows no bounds.

Interrupting her daydreams, John said, "I should have known you would pick the most dangerous place around to sit in. It is just where I would have chosen."

Guida had been so preoccupied with watching the training field that she had failed to hear her cousin approach. Thankfully, she knew John would never betray her to Aunt Gemma. John was a loyal son, to Guaimar. For Gemma, he was more than an annoyance; he was an obstacle to her ambitions. She had been openly hostile to him since the birth of her son, Gisulf.

"John?" Guida quickly climbed out of the crenel and looked at her cousin. "What are you doing up here? You ought to be studying."

"Master Geoffrey was feeling ill so he gave me the day off. I came looking for you."

"You know me too well. Perhaps I should find a different place to pass the time," she teased.

"Perhaps I should start coming up here more often," he teased back. He moved to take her place in the crenel.

"I think we had better not. It is one thing for me to be reckless. It is quite another for the heir of Salerno."

John looked disappointed. "Then what should I do with my day off? Do you want to go for a ride?"

"I would love that! Let me go change into my riding habit and find Brunhild. I will meet you at the tree." The chance to get out and get some air was too tempting to pass up. She would not be able to ride her new horse yet, but one of Guaimar's other horses would work well for now.

She changed quickly and hurried to meet John. As she left the castle, she glanced at the training field to see if William was still fighting. Not seeing him anywhere, she began walking faster. She did not want John to have to wait long.

Just as she was turning her attention back to the path in front of her, she rammed into something solid. She tumbled down onto her backside. She looked up to see William holding back laughter. She had run right into him! Why did she have to be so clumsy? Mortified, she felt the heat rising in her cheeks.

"My lady, I am beginning to suspect that you *like* being on the ground." Despite his teasing tone he reached out his hand to assist her up.

She decided to tease him back. "It is a good way to assess how gentlemanly a knight is. Frankly, I am surprised that more women don't avail themselves of such a strategy." She had tried to keep a straight face while she spoke, but knew that she had failed miserably. She gave up and started to laugh at herself. William joined in.

"Now, where were you off to in such a hurry?" He turned to move in her same direction, and began walking.

Thinking quickly to ensure she did not give the secret away, she answered as truthfully as she could. "I am to meet John. We are going for a ride."

"What luck. I was just about to go for a ride myself. Would you mind if I joined the two of you? I am sure your uncle would feel better about you two venturing out if you took a guard with you."

Guida's heart raced with excitement and her breathing sped up just a touch. But how to manage this without getting herself or John into trouble? "My uncle is quite insistent that we do just that. He never permits John to leave the castle grounds without a guard. I am also required to have Brunhild nearby, unless I am with a member of the family and there is a guard present. Brunhild is on her way to the stables to ready our horses. I need to fetch John. We will meet you soon."

With that, she turned and fled, leaving a bewildered William behind. She needed to reach John and fill him in on the change in their plans.

They had stopped on the banks of a small stream in order to let the horses drink. John wanted to climb some of the nearby trees. He enjoyed feeling like a wild animal when roaming the forest. Guida was left alone with William, and they had quickly taken up the conversation that they had to cut short before.

"So what do the Romans wish to do with that area?" Guida asked. "What makes it so important?"

"Land will always be important," William answered. "Without land, men are always dependent on other men. Land is sustenance. Land is power. Yet, it is more than that. What is it the pope works toward? The conversion of the world. The entire world's population to come unto

God. What are the Arabs? Infidels. Non-Christians. The pope cannot sit idly by and allow people to believe in false gods, now can he?"

"But, how can he do that?" Guida wondered. "How can you convert an entire country, let alone the whole world?"

"The pope gains land," answered William, "then builds monasteries and chapels, sending priests and other church leaders to these new centers of religion. Over time he hopes to spread his influence throughout the whole world."

"So the Romans wish to prevent the pope from gaining control?"

"I do not think it is a problem with the pope specifically. The Romans simply wish to control the land, and if the pope controls it, then the Romans do not."

"What of Emperor Conrad? Is he opposed to the pope as well?"

"The emperor wants to take the land back from the Romans. The more land that is in his empire, the more taxes can be collected. Then more men can be enlisted into His Majesty's army. I believe he is on the side of himself, much like the Roman emperor is."

She was amazed how patient he was with all of her questions. "It sounds like it would be mutually beneficial for the pope and the emperor to share the land. Why are they at odds on this point? It just does not make sense to me."

She knew that Isolde often acted dumber than she was in order to encourage men to talk to her, explaining things that she already knew and understood. Gaitelgrima rarely asked questions, preferring to glean what information she could through quiet observation. This was a subject that Guida was truly interested in, and she really did not understand. She kept expecting William to grow impatient with her impertinence. It was not common for a woman to be so inquisitive when it came to political matters.

"It would be good for both of them. The problem comes when you try to decide who has the most power. They are both strong leaders, but which one is the strongest? Which one has more men at their disposal, and which one really has control?"

"Oh, I see," Guida said, pausing. She then ventured to offer her opinion. "It is difficult to compare men of such different positions. I would not wish to be the one to decide between them. I would hope that more men would follow the pope, since he is the mouthpiece of God."

"Well, let us pray that we never need to choose," William answered. Offering her a sidelong look, he changed the subject, "What do you do if you cannot find an available guard to go with you and John?"

Looking away to hide the guilt she was sure shone on her face, she answered, "There are more ways out of the castle than the front gate."

"What?" William's shock was evident. "Do not tell me you sneak out of the castle unprotected." His brows pulled low over his eyes and anger radiated off him.

Unprepared for his reaction, Guida grew defensive. "Why not? I am not a child."

"You may not be a child, yet you are far from being able to handle the dangers in the world. John is a child, besides being Prince Guaimar's heir. Do you not think he deserves to be protected? You know too little of the world if you think there are not men who would take advantage of finding the two of you alone." He turned his back on her and took a few steps away.

Why is he so angry? Guida asked herself. She decided that she did not wish to talk about it. "Perhaps we should collect John and return home."

Chapter 11

The service on Sunday was incredibly difficult for Guida to sit through. She sat on the end of the pew next to Isolde, who would not stop whispering. Guida had been taught to be silent during the bishop's sermon, but apparently Isolde had not. Luckily, Isolde needed very little response, and Guida let her mind wander since she could not hear most of the sermon.

She sat in the second pew, near the front of the chapel, a privilege of being part of the royal family. Her aunt and uncle occupied the first row, along with their children. Gemma had relegated Gaitelgrima and John to the second pew, with their cousins.

She did not look back to see who else was attending, but she somehow knew that William was there. He had attended mass every week since his arrival in Salerno. He must come from a religious family and have faith of his own to attend so faithfully. Few people outside of the prince's family attended every week. Most would come once every month or two, or on special occasions such as when they had a visiting dignitary, which did not happen often.

She wondered how God felt about the poor attendance of His people. Was He pleased to see that she was here? Did His heart break for those who forgot to think on Him as they should? She tried to picture Him in the clouds of heaven looking down on her. *Holy Father,* she prayed, *Please watch over my sister, Maria, and my parents. Keep thine arms of safety securely around them, and thwart the plans of any enemies. I pray for the wounds of Isolde, those that are not shown, that they will mend.*

Her mind strayed to her recent conversations with Sir William. She knew that she wanted to pray for the victims of the recent battles in the south, but she was not quite sure which side to pray for. She, of course, wanted to be loyal to the empire, but she also wanted to be loyal to the Pope. How could she support two opposing factions? *Father God, turn thine all seeing eyes on the innocents in this conflict. Watch over and protect those deserving of thy care.*

She glanced up at Isolde who had stopped whispering at some point and found her watching the Bishop. Guida was grateful to be able to hear the rest of the sermon.

"What were you thinking about?" Isolde inquired after the sermon ended. "I cannot for the life of me pay any attention to what that old man talks about. I wish Uncle Guaimar didn't insist that we all attend every week."

Guida walked with the family back to the solar after mass. "I cannot always pay attention, either. When I get lost with the sermon I use that time to pray. There always seems to be plenty of people to pray for."

"What makes you so pious?" Isolde asked with disdain. "Do you really think that God watches over any of us? If He was, why would He let such awful things happen? Do you think God was watching over me when Pandulf attacked me? Are you really so inexperienced?"

Guida stopped walking. Why on earth would Isolde get so worked up so fast? Was she possibly blaming God for her recent experiences? "Of course God watches over us! How else do you explain Sir William showing up just in time to save you, and then bringing you here to safety?"

"Coincidence! Honestly, Guida, you cannot be so naive. There is no way that God could watch over every single person in the world all the time. And if He cannot do that, why would He take the time to help me?"

"Because He loves you. He blesses those who are faithful and who follow His teachings, which includes you."

"Guida, you have been too sheltered. Just wait until something bad happens to you. Then you will see that God does *not* care for all of us."

Was Isolde right? Was it merely a coincidence? Did God not really watch over and protect His people? Guida's mind reeled as she considered this new possibility. She needed to be alone. Turning around, she walked back to the chapel.

She walked directly up to the altar and knelt down. Looking up at the windows beyond she saw the colored glass depicting Jesus Christ who willingly gave His life for the salvation of man. Her father had taught her to put her faith in God. She had learned that all people were His children, and that He loved all of His children. What else, other than love, could induce anyone to willingly sacrifice themselves? He did not back down from the prospect. He showed us how to be perfectly brave and noble.

These teachings had always felt right. But if He loved all of His children, why did He allow bad things to happen? Guida had overheard stories of the horrors of war: raiding parties ransacking villages, women ravished by conquerors, and children trodden under the thunderous legs of war horses.

But if these teachings were false, then did that mean that God was false? Or was it truly possible that there was no God watching over the people? That would mean that there was no one watching over Guida herself, save her uncle. Guida suddenly felt more alone than she had ever been in her life. This made her frightened. She had always trusted in the peace that came from her belief in God.

Bowing her head, she prayed. *Oh God, I am lost. Please send thy peace to comfort my soul.* She knelt quietly for a few moments.

"You seem so deep in thought," Sir William's voice echoed through the chapel. Guida gasped with the unexpectedness of it. "I wonder what could be so important as to draw you back here after mass has ended."

"I thought I was alone. I am sorry if I am interrupting your prayers." *How could I have missed him there?* He was leaning against a pillar a few yards off to the side of the altar.

"It is no matter, my lady. I was merely praying for my family back in Normandy."

"I often pray for my family, too. I have not seen my parents for so long. Do you miss your family?"

"I do. My family is often in my thoughts."

They spoke of their families. William's mother had passed away and his father had remarried. He had one sister, four full brothers, and five half brothers. Guida's shock was evident on her face. "So many! I have no brothers and one sister only. How wonderful that must have been growing up with so many to love you." Guida was not well acquainted with loneliness, having been surrounded by family most of her life.

"Well, I do not know many of them. I was sent to train as a knight when I was six. Luckily, Drogo and I were both sent to the same household to train, so we are close. I have not even met one of my half brothers, since he was born after I came here."

"But you pray for them?"

"Of course."

"Well, I will leave you to it. I must return to the solar. Uncle Guaimar will be wondering where I have gone."

Sir William bowed to her as she turned to leave. As she walked, she realized that peace had returned to her while she had been with him. Halfway down the corridor she met her uncle coming to fetch her.

"Guida, what were you doing? I thought you would have stayed with us."

"Yes, Uncle. I was just coming."

"Since I have you alone, there is a matter that I have been meaning to discuss with you." Guida was suddenly on her guard due to the gravity of his voice.

"You are a member of the nobility. As such you will be expected to marry primarily for political reasons. Your father has tasked me with finding someone suitable. He would like you provided for and protected."

Guaimar was quiet for a moment before continuing. "Gemma comes from a powerful family. She has a brother, who you may have met at our wedding, Giovan. Your father is intending for the two of you to marry."

"What?" Guida scoffed. "Giovan is a scoundrel. I could never be happy with him. Uncle, you must change father's mind on this matter."

"I will attempt to find someone that will better suit your temperament, but there are no guarantees. You are getting older, and will soon be of an age where marriage will be expected, and I do not wish you to be unprepared."

She paused as something new occurred to her. "How likely is it to be happy in marriage when someone other than myself is to choose who I will live with for the rest of my life?"

"Unfortunately, it is not about happiness, Guida. It is about alliances and keeping the lords appeased. Do you think that I am happy in my marriage? Do you imagine that Gemma is happy? Your own parents did not know each other when they were wed. There are few who are able to find happiness, but that is rare. I pray that you will have such a match, but that is not the overall goal. I am not trying to be harsh; I am merely trying to prepare you for the inevitable."

She paused and turned to Guaimar. "I know, and I appreciate it."

"Luckily for you, Giovan is currently traveling out of the country. He will not be back for some time. Until such time, you are still free to live your life here."

"Thank you, Uncle. You are always so good to me." She rose on her toes and kissed his cheek, then resumed walking.

"Of course. You deserve all the happiness we can manage for you, my dear." Reaching the solar they joined the rest of the family.

Chapter 12

Salerno – June 1037

Guida was nearly out of her mind with ennui. Her uncle had sent William with a few other knights to investigate some reports of unrest to the south. With him had gone her favorite pastime: watching his every move. It was unknown how long they would be gone. It could be a matter of days, or even weeks. It all depended on how quickly they could straighten everything out.

She could not understand why she always looked for him. He was handsome, she supposed. Could that be her reason for wanting to see him? Was he simply nicer to look at than most of the other men? Somehow she thought there was more to it than that.

Perhaps because he was a foreigner? She tried thinking of any obvious customs that he observed that were different than her own. She really did not know him well enough to come up with any. He was not socially awkward, like some of the fighting men she had contact with.

He was pleasant and social, but he was not overly attentive. She figured he only paid attention to her because of his allegiance to her uncle.

For now, she needed something different to do. Over the last few days she had wandered the castle too many times to count. She had gone exploring in the nearby forest with Brunhild several times as well. She enjoyed her time with Brunhild. Isolde and Gaitelgrima did not enjoy exploring. They would rather spend time in the castle, but Guida sought any opportunity to be out in the wild forest.

She decided to go to the stable to check on her horse. It had taken months for her to settle on a name for the beautiful creature. She had finally chosen Adrina, meaning happiness, for that was what Guida felt anytime she saw her.

This horse had become a symbol of freedom, of independence. She embodied the idea that Guida had a way to escape the pressures of life at court. Riding her meant shrugging off the heaviness of her responsibility to watch over Maria, and the overwhelming feeling of being completely alone in a castle bursting with people. One day, Guida dreamed of riding off with Adrina never to return to this place of self doubt she currently occupied.

Walking into the stable, Guida went directly to Adrina's stall. The scent of fresh straw, combined with the less savory aspects of a stable, assaulted her nostrils. Stepping carefully to avoid obstacles, Guida grabbed some oats from a bucket near the wall. The young horse snorted her pleasure and stuck her head over the wall of the stall so that Guida could feed her.

Riding lessons had been a vital part of Guida's education, but she was only allowed to ride Adrina with supervision. Guaimar tried to be there with her most of the time, but occasionally he would allow her to ride with one of his trusted knights watching over her.

Well, Guaimar was not around. He had ridden into Salerno to check on some matter of business. Guida looked around to see if there was anyone who could saddle Adrina for her. Her eyes found a young man who had been training with the stable master. She could not remember his name, so she decided to simply walk up to him and start talking.

"I would like you to saddle my horse." She used her most authoritative voice and attempted to seem more self-possessed than she was. She had been learning from Isolde that a woman could often get what she wanted if she demanded it with confidence.

"Yes, miss." He jumped up and began the work. He must not have known of her uncle's restrictions. Good.

Soon he had her horse ready, and led the horse out of the stable. Guida followed as they made their way to the paddock where she always practiced her riding. Once they were all through the gate and it was closed, he stepped over and assisted her into the saddle.

"Thank you. You may go," Guida ordered as she settled herself into the saddle.

There was something pulling William home. He could not explain it. The feeling was subtle, yet persistent. Drogo rode beside him, trying to engage him in conversation. They had spent only two days with those peasants working through their concerns. The townspeople had been sure that the Arabs were encroaching on the prince's land. It had not taken long to assess the validity of their statements. In the end, it appeared that the Arabs were correct in their assessment of the boundary, but convincing stubborn men of that had taken several hours.

All William had been able to think about was how much he wanted to be back to Salerno. Now that he was on his return journey William was anything but calm. They were moving at a snail's pace, and he had no power to speed up the procession. It was maddening! If only there were some reason for him to ride ahead. He glanced around and saw that Drogo was staring at him.

"Pardon?" he asked.

"You have not heard what I have been saying, have you? What could you possibly be thinking about so intently? Please, share it with me. I am in need of some diversion. Anything to take my mind off how bored I am with this journey!" Drogo had never travelled well. He was not one who enjoyed silence, and he struggled with the monotony of simply riding forth, mile after mile.

"I was not thinking about anything in particular. I just was wishing that we could move faster. I would like to be home."

"Why? You are not normally so anxious to be done riding. Is anything amiss?"

"I cannot explain it. I simply feel the need for haste."

Sir Enzo, the leader of Guaimar's guards who had led this journey, overheard their exchange. Now, he joined in, "I had been thinking about sending a messenger ahead to make sure everything is readied for our arrival. Perhaps this would be the perfect mission for you, William." Sir Enzo smiled at him.

"Thank you," William said with relief. He quickly spurred his horse and left the procession behind.

William rode hard the rest of the way to the castle. As he approached, he slowed Valeur to a more reasonable pace. He still could not figure out what had him so uneasy.

"Ho, Amatus. Sergius." He greeted the two guards at the gate and halted his horse.

"William! Where are the rest of the men?" Sergius looked behind William trying to see the company.

"I came ahead. How have things fared since we left? Any news?"

"Nothing of interest. You really have not missed much." Sergius attempted to stifle a yawn.

Amatus, one of the youngest knights at the castle, joined in. "I bested Josef with spears for the first time!" The lad was fairly shaking in his boots with his excitement.

"Perhaps you should challenge me, Amatus; then I can see just how improved you have become. Shall we plan on the morrow?"

Amatus suddenly looked pale as a ghost, like he was going to be ill. William was arguably the best fighter here and everyone knew it. It was not surprising the young man felt apprehensive about going up against him. William and Sergius laughed at Amatus's discomfort.

Questioning his own intuition, he wondered why he was so unsettled. He had felt pulled here, yet there appeared to be no reason for it.

Continuing into the open courtyard, he turned Valeur toward the stables. Guida was in the paddock riding her filly, which William knew was not permitted without close supervision. He also knew the reasoning behind that restriction. The stable master had not finished with the animal's training and there was still a bit of unpredictability with the animal.

Surprised that she would so blatantly defy the prince, he reminded himself that he did not know her well. A handful of conversations were not enough to know the full measure of a person. She was quiet and a little reserved, but William saw glimpses of an intelligent, fun-loving, slightly mischievous woman beneath her outwardly cautious persona.

Watching her now, he could not help but grin. She was so graceful and made it look like she had spent her entire life riding. Her body moved in tandem with the horse's movements. The grace of the two was entrancing. He felt a stirring inside that he had not experienced before, and he was not sure what to make of it.

He reminded himself that she could also be foolish. He often saw her on top of the castle wall, and it irked him each time. Her easy conversation and wit could not replace common sense, which she seemed to lack. And now she was riding a horse which could become out of control at any moment.

His irritation grew the longer he watched her. And yet, he could not tear his eyes away from her, nor did he wish to. He knew that there could be nothing between him and the lady. She was a member of the prince's own family, and he a mere knight. But even those thoughts could not distract him from the sight before him.

As he watched, he saw a stray dog run into the paddock and begin barking and snarling at the horse. The filly reared up on her hind legs. Guida, miraculously keeping hold of the reins, screamed as the horse shot off toward the far end of the enclosure.

William spurred his horse after them and deftly jumped the fence. Keeping his eyes on Guida, he watched as her horse came to an abrupt stop just before running into the fence on the other end. Guida, however, did not stop. Her small body flew over the fence, and she rolled to a stop on the ground beyond.

William reached her as fast as possible. He dismounted Valeur at a run and threw himself down next to Guida's still form. Rolling her onto her back, he checked for breathing. Her eyelids fluttered, and he felt relief roll through him in giant waves.

He quickly assessed her for injuries. Brushing his hands quickly down her arms and then down her legs, he tried not to think how improper it was. He longed to do so more slowly and tenderly. For now, he checked for broken bones. There did not seem to be any. Still, he would take her to the healer to be checked more thoroughly.

"Guida, wake up. Look at me," he softly commanded as he cupped her cheek and rubbed it with his thumb. Her eyelids fluttered again, but still she did not open them. He could tell she was not unconscious, but for some reason she did not open her eyes.

"Guida, I need to know that you are well. Can you please open your eyes? Come on, *cherie*." She slowly opened her eyes and stared directly into his. He had never been more excited to have someone looking at him. The relief he felt was palpable.

"*Bien, ma cherie*." He grinned down at her. "That was quite a tumble. Are you hurt anywhere?" She blinked a few times, and he saw pain in her eyes. "I am going to take you to see the healer now. May I pick you up?" His stepmother, Fressenda, had taught him never to touch a woman without her consent. He had already done that, but now that she had her eyes open he would ask permission. He did not wish to upset Guida after she had already suffered through an ordeal. She nodded and William quickly and gently scooped her into his arms. He was amazed at how light she was. Tired as he was from his journey, he still could have carried her for hours and not complained.

She rested one hand on his chest in a rather hesitant fashion. "Thank you, William," she whispered, and William barely heard. She snuggled into his chest as he walked. Her face was tense, scrunched up in pain. It nearly broke his heart to see her like this. If only he could ease the lines on her forehead and to kiss away her hurts. He forced his feet to move faster.

Arriving at the healer's rooms, he set Guida in a chair near the fire. Addressing the healer, Berta, he explained, "She was thrown from her horse. I do not think anything is broken, but thought it best to have you examine her."

"Of course I should examine her!" Berta was not known for beating around the bush or dealing with the niceties that other people often did. She believed in getting right to the heart of any problem. This made her a great healer, if not a great conversationalist. She did not sit around when she knew she could be helping someone who was sick or injured. Berta began poking and rubbing at Guida's body to assess for injuries. In a softer tone she addressed Guida. "Where does it hurt, child?"

Guida's lip quivered and her eyes grew watery. "Everywhere!" Then she shifted her position so that she was sitting up straight in the chair. She sniffed, and rubbed the tears from her eyes.

William bent down next to her. "You just went through a painful experience. You are allowed to cry, my lady." He took one of her hands in his. Her hand was so small and cold. He rubbed it in an attempt to transfer some of his heat to her. He looked in her eyes and was amazed at the strength of spirit he saw in this beautiful maiden.

"I am not a child, and I refuse to cry like one," Guida said matter-of-factly. It was unclear whether she was trying to convince him or herself.

"I am astounded at your strength, my lady. If only I could be as brave." He winked at her as he brushed a loose strand of hair behind her ear, and then stood, before he found himself doing something even more inappropriate. "Berta, I will leave her in your capable hands." With that he left the room.

"Sir William," Guaimar began. "I find myself in your debt once again. This is the second time you have come to the aid of one of my family." William had been summoned to speak with the prince soon after leaving Guida with the healer. "I confess I am intrigued by you. You ask no reward for your actions. If you had sought one, then one might begin to think that you had some sort of hand in devising such dreadful circumstances. Since you do not ask for anything, I am inclined to think better of you." He paused, but William did not know how to respond, so he stayed quiet.

"You do not fit the description of the Normans that I have heard. You are not brutal or selfish. You do not search for trouble, or for an excuse to fight, yet you are excellent in combat. I have witnessed this in the training field. You are well liked and seem to have no enemies. This shows a possibility of leadership potential. That, combined with the services that you continue to render me, makes me inclined to keep you close. I am considering allowing you a more prominent role in my household. Now, what do you think that I should do with you?"

William was shocked to hear his character laid out so succinctly. "My lord, I am at your service. You may do with me what you will."

"Hmm. If I were to promote you to be one of my advisors, I would like to know that you would actually advise me. I have no need of an advisor who will not openly share what he assesses of any given situation."

"Advisor, my lord?" William could not have been more shocked if the prince had begun to levitate. He cleared his throat. "There would be advantages and disadvantages to having me as an advisor. I believe that I could be an asset to you. I do not like to make decisions without careful consideration. As you said, I have trained hard to make myself a strong warrior. But, I am a Norman, a foreigner. That could be a potential problem for some of your men who think that they would make a better advisor than me. It could also be beneficial for you in any future dealings with Count Drengot. It could go a long way in maintaining him as your ally."

The prince smiled as he stood up and took William's arm. "Yes, I am certain we can find a better place for you."

Chapter 13

Salerno – July 1037

The sun warmed Guida's back as she finished the picnic lunch. She had snuck John away from the castle for an outing before the weather turned too cold. Always happier outside than in, she needed to get out for some air, and this gave her the perfect opportunity. The clean air instantly lifted her spirits. Vermin scurried through the underbrush of the forest, rustling dead leaves. The songs of the birds filled her with excitement and set her imagination wild.

At times, she saw herself as the damsel in distress, destined to be rescued by her strong and handsome hero. This role had begun to be filled by William in her mind. Other times she was the heroine of her own story. She would fight off brigands who meant her harm, rescue children who were being beaten, and thwart the evil plots of assassins.

She thoroughly enjoyed coming up with her stories. They made her feel bold and powerful, so unlike her usual feelings.

Coming out of her thoughts, she found Brunhild packing up the lunch items. It was so peaceful that Guida did not wish for it to end, but they had been out here for some time. If they did not return soon they would surely be missed.

"There won't be many sunny days like this left before the rains come." Brunhild had been just as eager to get out today as Guida had.

"Yes, I am not looking forward to being caged up in that stuffy castle. Why does winter have to last so long? It seems by far the longest season." Guida relished sunshine and loved being out of doors. It always revived her spirit.

"Yes, it does seem long." Brunhild agreed. She often agreed with Guida, which made Guida wonder if she would have voiced an agreement to anything that had been said. Her father had often voiced discontent with men who would agree with him based solely on his position as nobility, and not because of actual likeness of mind. Perhaps Brunhild was turning into that type of servant.

"Where has John gone off to? He ought to have returned by now." Guida felt sudden concern that something might have happened to him, which she attempted to squash. He had run off earlier to explore nearer the brook. The water was not high, and John was a strong swimmer. Shaking off her feeling of unease, she told herself he should not be in danger.

"I will go find him," Brunhild said as she stood up and walked off in the direction of the brook.

Guida stood up and started to meander through the meadow, picking a few wildflowers to take back to the castle. They would brighten up her chamber for a few days before they became too wilted.

She loved the fragrance of the flowers and was surprised to find so many still in bloom. Isolde and Gaitelgrima might like some also, so Guida picked enough to share. Wandering back over to their picnic spot, she put the flowers in one of the now empty food baskets.

Turning back towards the brook, she was unsettled, not seeing Brunhild or John. *Where could they be?* "Brunhild!" she called. "John! We really must be getting back!" She waited, but there was no answer. Dread crept into her heart, spreading its sinuous tendrils throughout her chest. Trying to shake it off, she spoke aloud. "They are likely just enjoying some distraction. Perhaps they found a beaver dam." It must be something of that sort.

Fear began to take over as Guida's imagination ran wild. She pictured John getting washed away with the currents and Brunhild drowning trying to save him. And then she chided herself for her foolish imagination.

With each step taking her nearer the wall of trees blocking the brook from view, her heart sped up. She wiped her clammy palms down the side of her rough wool skirts and attempted to take slow, steadying breaths. Where could they be?

It was not like Brunhild to tease her by not answering her calls. John would absolutely do it, and have immense fun at her expense, but not Brunhild. Why did they not bring a guard with them? It suddenly seemed like the most foolish decision to leave the castle with no real protection.

Reaching the brook, she turned to look up and down the path of the water. The trees were quite thick here and it was difficult to see into the inky shadows of the forest. She paused, trying to hear anything that might tell her where they had gone. Searching behind trees and up into the depths of their branches, she hoped for some sign that would lead her in the right direction.

The intensity of the silence threatened to suffocate her. She did not expect the sounds of other people. Being this far from the castle, hearing any noise from it would be impossible. But even the symphony of the forest was hushed. She imagined that she could hear her heart beating an unsteady rhythm which increased her sense of foreboding. Hearing a twig snap somewhere behind her, she rounded to investigate. A man stepped out of the trees on the other side of the brook.

"You should not be walking alone, my lady." The man's grin was incongruent with his verbal warning. His clothes were old and stained, and even from this distance Guida saw the gaps left from missing teeth. "You never know who you might meet." He hopped easily across the water and came to stand just in front of her.

She quickly backed up a few steps. The scent emanating off of this stranger, a combination of body odor and ale, was overwhelming. She attempted to not show her distaste for him as she responded, "I-I am looking for my companions. H-have you seen anyone else n-nearby?" Her voice was shaky and gave away her fear.

The stranger did not respond. However, he continued to advance, and she continued to retreat, until her foot tripped on a rock and she fell backwards. Pain exploded in her hands as they were cut on sharp rocks and small twigs.

The man stood over her, laughing. "Oh, what a lovely reward for my service. Pandulf certainly would not object to me taking you as my prize." His lecherous eyes roamed over her body, and she suddenly felt filthy. She tried to roll over so that she could stand back up, but the man grabbed her by her hair and yanked her up. His arm circled around her waist. "You are not going to fight me, are you, *my lady?*" His voice dripped with sarcasm on this address, as his breath polluted her ear. Guida nearly lost the contents of her stomach.

Throwing her hands up to her head, she attempted to pry his fingers off her hair, but his grip was as sure as the portcullis at the castle entry.

"Let me go!" she cried, as she found her voice again. "What do you want?"

The man snorted, then spoke softly and menacingly into her ear, "You know what I want."

"No! Let me go!" She repeated her command, but instead of letting her go, he managed to tighten his grip. "Where is John? What have you done to him?" She had to think of something other than her pain. Perhaps she could distract him.

"John? Oh, would you like to see?" He dragged her over to the tree line. There, lying under one of the trees, was John's small, lifeless body. There was blood running in a line across his throat, pooling on the ground. His eyes stared blankly at the sky. Guida couldn't contain the scream that ripped from her chest.

"You can scream all you want. We are quite secluded here, and too far from the castle for you to be heard."

"What do you want?" She could barely choke out the words through her sobs.

"Well, I've completed my mission. Now it's time for a bit of fun." His hand around her waist shifted up, and he grabbed onto one of her breasts. Even through the fabric of her dress, it hurt. She tried to recoil, but he held her too tightly for her to get away. Pulling her to a nearby tree, he quickly twisted her around, pinning her back against the tree. She was now face-to-face with him.

Letting go of her hair, he used both hands to restrain her. His lips travelled roughly over her face and finally clamped over her mouth. Her stomach heaved at the taste of him. He stuck his tongue in her mouth, and she bit down, hard, drawing blood. Crying out, he backed off a step. Spitting his vile blood from her mouth, she told her legs to run.

She did not make it far before she was knocked to the ground with the beast again on top of her. He rolled her over until he was sitting on her stomach. "This may be the more satisfying because of your spirit, milady." His words sounded a little off, due to his wounded tongue.

Using every ounce of strength she had, she hit his chest, but it did not faze him. He used his legs to keep her where he wanted her. Pulling out a knife, he brandished it, stilling her struggles. Slowly, as if savoring the moment, he sliced through the front of her dress, from neck to waist. She trembled as terror threatened to overwhelm her. Tossing the blade, he resumed his two handed groping. Her screams resumed as she clawed and hit his arms and chest, anywhere she could reach. None of it slowed him down. He brought his face back down to kiss her again, but she turned her head just as he reached her. As she did, she found herself looking into the open eyes of Brunhild lying a few feet away. She had a matching line of blood on her neck like John's, and a look of terror in her lifeless eyes. Guida screamed again and turned her head away from the gruesome sight.

And then the weight on her was gone. Sitting up, she saw the man knocked onto his back on the ground. Sir William stood over him with his sword drawn and pointed at the stranger's neck. "Who are you?" he growled out.

"Don't kill me! I'll tell you anything you want to know, just don't kill me!" It was hard to believe how quickly this man went from terrifying and overpowering to a sniveling coward.

"Guida, I left my horse in the clearing. Run back to it and get my rope out of my saddle bag." William did not even glance at her. She had never seen him so angry. Fury fairly seethed out of him. Every muscle was taut and he was poised for battle. His very breath threatened to inflict injury. Keeping focus on her assailant, he repeated his instructions. His voice was gruff and his face contorted. Finding herself afraid of what he would do if the other man did not comply with William's every command, she sat as still as the corpses nearby.

The quaking of her spirit began manifesting throughout her body. Her limbs felt somehow separate from the rest of her. *Can I even stand?* she wondered. If she could, would she be capable of walking? All she could do was stare at Sir William, as if he were the emperor himself.

"Guida! Now!" Sir William's sharp words drew her back to reality. Finally processing his commands, she grabbed the tree next to her and pulled herself up. Holding the cut fabric of her dress close across her breast, grateful her shift was still intact, she made her way back to the clearing. Her legs seemed to regain strength with every step she took, and soon she was running. She found the rope in the saddle bag and turned to run back to Sir William.

Sir William deftly tied up the villain. Leaving him, William slowly approached Guida. "Are you hurt?" His voice was surprisingly gentle, considering its harshness just a few minutes before, and the rage that still filled his eyes.

Guida did not know how to answer. She was hurt, both physically and emotionally, but she did not want to admit any of it. Her eyes lowered as she looked down at herself. One hand still held the ripped fabric of her dress closed. She looked at her other hand and saw that a few of her fingers were bleeding where she must have scratched her attacker with enough force to rip her nails from their beds. It seemed like such a small complaint compared to what would have happened if Sir William had not arrived.

William approached her and wrapped his arms around her in a comforting embrace. "You are safe, *mia caro*. I'm here now. He will not hurt you anymore."

She finally found her voice as she whispered against the safety of his nearness. "John and Brunhild. He k-k-killed them! He killed them!" Her entire body began to quake again and blackness encroached on the outskirts of her vision. No! She could not faint. Not now. She had to be strong. Taking deep, calming breaths she willed herself not to cry.

William released her, and she was left with a sense of emptiness. She found herself longing for the return of the safety of his embrace.

"We need to get back to the castle," he stated. "We must take this *lichieres pautonnier*," his depth of feeling was evident by him slipping back into his native French, "back to the dungeon and get you to safety. Then I will return with some additional men to recover the bodies. Can you ride?"

"I believe so," she responded. Turning toward the horses, she only travelled a few steps before doubling over and retching. Spitting out what she could, her breaths became quick and shallow. She could feel hysteria rising within her. Her eyes darted back and forth. Thinking of how scared John must have been, her heart broke for him. Hot tears escaped her eyes, and she could not imagine them ever stopping. "No one should die like this, especially a child."

"You cannot help them now. You must think of yourself, and that means getting back to the safety of your uncle."

She knew he was right, but it broke her heart again to leave them there. She also knew that her brain was not working to full capacity. She had been through an ordeal, so she would leave the rational thought to William and do as he bid her.

Making their way back to the castle, thoughts assaulted Guida as surely as her attacker had. Trying to focus her mind on anything else, she began counting her horse's steps. This became difficult due to the nearness of the other horses. William rode his horse as he led John and Brunhild's steeds behind him. Guida's attacker had been flung over the back of Brunhild's horse with his hands and feet still bound. When this tactic of counting steps failed, Guida guided her horse up next to Sir William's.

"I do not believe that I properly thanked you for saving me," she began. "It seems inadequate, but thank you."

Sir William glanced over at her. "There is no need, my lady."

"How?" she asked.

"How what?"

"How did you find me? How did you even know I needed finding?"

William sighed. "John was missed. Prince Guaimar could not find him and he commanded every available knight to search for him. I remembered you saying there was more than one way out of the castle."

"Well, I am most grateful that you did. You seem to be making a habit of coming to my aid." She tried to laugh about it, but her emotions were still too raw for it to be believable. The tears were too near the surface. She knew that she had never been able to hide her emotions. They always showed on her face for everyone to see. She hated that about herself, but she had no notion of how to change it.

Sir William looked at her again, as if weighing what he would say. "Guida, how could you do this? I warned you that no good would come from sneaking out of the castle. The world is a dangerous place, and I cannot be around every time you choose to do something foolish." His words were like a slap in the face.

"Are you saying that I am to blame?" She could not believe it.

"Perhaps not entirely," he hedged, "but you must face the reality that you could have, and should have, had a guard with you. You ought to have known better. Having someone here to protect you may not have changed the final outcome, but we will never know now."

She did not understand. "So, my actions have led to the deaths of two of my closest companions? How could I have known that we needed protection? We come out here often and have never encountered any trouble."

"Until today."

Yes, until today, she silently agreed.

"My lady, you are in a position that puts you close to the prince of the region. You cannot simply do what you wish. You are not a child who is constantly watched over. This means you must use your head! You must realize that there are evil men, like Duke Pandulf, who would seek to use your position as a way to reach Prince Guaimar. You do not have direct influence over what your uncle does, yet his actions could very easily be manipulated by someone seeking to do you harm. You are not a fool. Do not behave like one. You sneak out of the castle unaccompanied, you risk your life at the top of the castle wall, and you foolishly ride horses unfit for you. This reckless behavior must stop! You must think about your actions and the possible consequences of them. I should not need to explain this to you, but it seems necessary."

She could not get any more words out. How she wanted to! How she would have loved to rant and rave and curse him for his insinuations. But she could not. Somewhere in the back of her mind was the thought, *What if he is right?* He was chastising her like a child, and she had never felt more deserving of that correction. She had acted foolishly, and John and Brunhild had paid with their lives.

"I am not saying that you set out to have this happen, my lady. But would it be too much to ask for you to think about what you are doing *before* you do it?" His face was turning red as his anger was stoked again. "Besides putting yourself in danger, you brought the heir of Salerno with you! I know you have been instructed to have a guard with you at all times when outside of the castle. Can you not follow simple instructions?" His voice had been rising in volume throughout his rant, but Guida had stopped listening. She felt his accusations like a knife to her heart.

Her words came out so soft that William had to lean toward her to catch them. "You are right. It is all my fault. I have been foolish and short-sighted, and John and Brunhild are dead because of it." She could not fight back her tears. He must think her childish and foolish. She hated adding the embarrassment of giving into her emotions to his long list of her faults.

Concentrating on her horse, she swayed with its movement and tried not to relive the past hour in her mind. The reality of what had occurred was bad enough, and her imagination was threatening to add details to fill in the gaps of her memories. She thought, too, on what she could possibly say to her uncle when she saw him upon her return. Neither she nor William spoke another word the entire trip.

The ride to the castle had been one of the most uncomfortable of William's vast experiences. He had not tempered his opinion as he ought to have with Lady Guida. Unable to control his anger, he had lashed out like a poisonous serpent. It was a character flaw that he was well aware of, and he had made many efforts to correct.

When Lady Guida was involved, however, all his progress disappeared. He could only assume it was this situation that was bringing out the worst in him. Why could he not master his emotions when faced with a woman in peril? He thought again of the women he had protected during raids. And now Guida. Why was it that women always seemed to need rescuing? The thought that the gentler sex could not defend themselves seemed too simplistic. Instead, he wondered why there were always men who would take advantage of their greater size and strength.

His rage bubbled up inside him once more as the image of Lady Guida flooded his mind, screaming and scratching at her assailant as he ravaged her. Glancing at her, he saw she held her horse's reins with one hand as her other was needed to hold her dress together. One hand was not sufficient to correct the damage done, and he could see more of her shift underneath than was proper. Tearing his gaze up to her face, he tried to ignore the fury that still burned within.

He expected to hear sobbing, but the lady was oddly silent. Her cheeks were wet, tears running in streaks through small smears of blood. He was unsure as to whose blood it was. The villain had been quite scratched up by the time William had separated the two. He was strangely proud of Lady Guida, despite his earlier words. She had used the only weapons at her disposal, when she could have easily given up in the face of such circumstances. He respected her fighting spirit.

As they neared the castle they could see a group of six men and women clustered together, laughing with one another. They were next to the wall, but off to the side of the gate so as not to block the way. They were all being rather free with their affections, to put it politely. It was a rather disturbing display given the harm that had befallen Lady

Guida today. William was certain the lady would not enjoy seeing such actions, yet he was powerless to prevent it.

As they drew nearer, one of the men rose and approached the gate so as to arrive at nearly the same moment as William and his charges. William groaned inwardly at the sight of his brother. Typically, William would have had much to say to Drogo about his choice of activities. Under these current circumstances, however, his priority was to get Lady Guida to the healer to be checked for injuries. Then would come the unenviable task of apprising Prince Guaimar of what had befallen his oldest child and beloved niece.

Drogo spoke first. "Ah now, what have you been up to?" His eyes skimmed over Guida, taking in her dishevelled appearance and ripped clothing. William wished he could spare Guida these looks, but knew that everyone who saw her entering the castle would look at her similarly.

"Not now, Drogo," William's tone warned against argument.

"Why not now? What is so pressing?" Drogo appeared to have genuine interest as he also took in the prisoner. "When you finish with the lady, you should come back and join us. It is a great way to end the day." Drogo looked back over at the people he had left.

William glanced over at Lady Guida. She had continued on and was almost to the gate, allowing him the privacy to speak openly with Drogo. "You know I do not participate in such disgraceful displays. I wish you would not, either. We were not raised this way, and our parents would be ashamed."

"And why is that? Why deny ourselves some fun when it is readily available? Where is the harm?"

William did not have time for this. He had more pressing matters to see to. "We shall speak of this later, Drogo. I must go." He left his brother standing in the road as he spurred Valeur to catch up with Lady Guida. He did not wish for her to have to explain everything that had happened to Prince Guaimar. He could not fix all the damage done today, but he could take that burden off of the lady.

Chapter 14

Salerno – July 1037

When Guida awoke, the long fingers of shadows were seeking to snuff out what little light had been peeking through the windows. One of the shadows moved along the edge of her vision, and she turned to find a servant lighting candles. As Guida rolled onto her back to stretch, her muscles screamed in protest. Memories of the previous day assaulted her mind.

She had been rushed to her chamber as soon as they had arrived back at the castle. Berta had been sent for, and Guida had been forced to tolerate her ministrations. Once the cuts and scrapes had been tended, Sir Enzo entered. As captain of the guard, it was his duty to extract the story from her. Refusing to let her emotions take over, she attempted to remain calm while recounting what had transpired. The mortification of others knowing how she had been sullied nearly undid her. How would she ever look this man in the eye again? Or any man?

The questions seemed endless, as Sir Enzo attempted to piece together the fabric of events. *Will I ever wake from this nightmare?* Guida asked herself.

When everyone had left, she was alone with her thoughts, which were almost worse than the interrogation had been. Laying on the bed, she stared at the wall. Each time she closed her eyes she saw those of John or Brunhild looking back at her: lifeless orbs robbed of the years that should have been theirs. In the silence, she heard the cries of their spirits calling for help that she could not give. Were they blaming her? Did they begrudge her for being saved? Were they even real? Was she going mad?

"Oh, *bene.* You are awake." Alys, a maid who had been assigned to take Brunhild's place, rushed over to the bed. "I have been so worried about you, my lady! How are you feeling?"

How am I feeling? Had this woman really just asked such a question? It was to be assumed that the entire castle knew of the tragedy. How was Guida to answer? She chose to respond as lightly as she could. "My head aches a bit, and I am still quite exhausted." Guida could not remember being as hungry as she was at that moment. Realizing she had not eaten anything since the previous afternoon, she added, "Would you be so kind as to bring me a tray of food? I am famished, yet I have no desire to break my fast with my family."

"Oh, it is much too late for that, my lady. You have fairly slept the day away. Of course, I will fetch you some supper. Your uncle would like to speak with you as soon as you are able. Shall I go fetch him?"

"Help me get dressed first. I do not wish to keep him waiting, but I also cannot receive him like this."

"Very well, my lady," Alys said as she rushed to her side. "Tsk. You really must have a bath. There is dirt and broken leaves in your hair. I will send for the water, my lady." Alys proved quite efficient, and soon Guida was undressing.

Alys gasped, and Guida looked at her naked body. She was covered in bruises; some of which were easily recognizable as finger marks. Scrapes etched across the landscape of her skin, as well as claw marks from her attacker's fingernails. Dirt smudges blended with the bruising, and she wondered how much of the foreign color would wash off. Guida thought her body matched the filthiness she felt within her.

The warm water began to soothe her physical aches. Once she was as clean as she could get with a bath, she dressed. Sending Alys for her uncle, Guida sat down at the small table she used for eating when she did not go to the great hall. Dread at how her uncle would respond to this tragedy snaked its way through Guida's gut. Would he still love her? Would he send her away?

Gratefully, it was not long before Alys was guiding Guaimar into the chamber. Overcome by emotion, Guida stood and rushed into his arms.

"Dear Uncle Guaimar, I am so sorry!" He held her with all the gentleness of a loving parent. She did not wish to add to her uncle's burden, but still the tears flowed. He guided her back to her chair and took the seat opposite her. Guida had rarely seen her uncle more careworn.

"Guida, sweetheart. There is nothing to forgive. I wanted to tell you what we learned from the man who attacked you. He was sent by Duke Pandulf."

That was not news to Guida, remembering Pandulf's name being mentioned in the forest.

"Pandulf has not been happy that I removed my support of him after the incident with Isolde," Guaimar continued. "He wants to hurt me in any way he can. Deciding I would be too difficult a target, he sent his man to watch the castle and attack when he saw an opening. I am so sorry, Guida." His face was full of anguish. "I ought to have seen this coming, been more vigilant. I will not make this mistake again." His face was grim and there were tears in his eyes, but they did not fall.

"No, Uncle," Guida insisted. "The fault is mine. I was foolish. I did not appreciate the danger. How could Pandulf do this? To his own family?" It was beyond Guida's understanding.

"You are little more than a child yourself, my dear," his words stung, although they were kindly meant. "It is for others to protect you. I do not blame you for this. I also thought you should know; I have sent for your father. I expect your parents will be here within a few days."

Guida's heart constricted as she said, "Did you give my father the details of what happened?"

Guaimar's face softened as he answered, "No, my dear. That is your story to tell, should you choose. For now he knows only of John."

Guida would have to think about how much to tell her family. For now, she wished to stop thinking about it all together.

The lovely fall morning held no enjoyment for Guida. The sun was high in the sky, and the air was still. The forest was alight with a riot of color. The changing leaves boasted all shades of reds, oranges, and browns; yet there were still a few trees hanging onto the greenery of summer, making the contrast brilliant.

Guida walked along the top of the castle wall with Alys. It had been a week since the incident. And she had not left her chambers for any reason except to visit the garderobe, and even then she insisted on having Alys wait just outside for her. This morning she decided that she was done sulking around in her chamber and that it was time to get out. She wanted to see the view of the city and forest from the top of the castle wall.

Watching as leaves slowly fell to the ground, Guida soaked in the feeling of calm. This was her favorite time of year, watching as God gave one last spectacular display of His power before the harshness of winter set in. A priest had once told her that this was proof of God's existence and His love for His children. Normally, Guida was inclined to agree, but now she was confused. Why had God allowed John and Brunhild to be killed? She had always thought of God as loving, but if He loved His people, would He not protect the innocents? Her past conversation with Isolde came to her mind. Perhaps Isolde had been correct, yet Guida still was not prepared to let go of her faith.

Guida was grateful for the chance to get some fresh air. She had felt so closed in since her attack. Self inflicted though it was, she had no other way to cope with her experience. The feeling of safety she had always known was gone, and she did not know if she could ever regain it.

Gaitelgrima came often to visit, yet rarely gave any insight as to what was happening around them. It was clear that Gaitelgrima held no fault with Guida over the loss of her brother. Ever the pragmatist, Gaitelgrima took this heartache for what it was: proof of the cruelty that exists in the world.

Isolde visited once or twice, but felt little affinity for Guida's grief. Guida began to wonder if Isolde had any depth of feelings. She held herself so aloof from others and seemed inordinately concerned with her own cares. Having shared a similar experience, Guida had supposed they would exhibit greater empathy for one another's sufferings. She was disappointed in such a hope.

Stopping at her usual crenel, her gaze drifted down to the training field. She could see Sir William as he went through practicing with his spear while on his horse. She knew this was an important skill in battle and had seen him practice it many times. Watching as he dominated his opponent, she was reminded of his aptitude in the field. He was clearly one of the most advanced knights at the castle. He was taller than most of the other men, with his body filled out in perfect proportion to his height. At times, he would remove his helmet and his blond hair would once again distinguish him as a Norman. She loved the difference.

She had not spoken to him since he had placed the blame at her feet. She could not imagine that her presence would be welcomed by him, given his low opinion of her. Why what this man thought of her should matter to her was a source of endless frustration. Wishing she could forget his opinion, she was determined to carry on with her day. She had more pressing concerns than what a single knight thought of her.

She did not need to see him, nor converse with him on a regular basis. Up until now, the majority of their interactions had been over various meals. Since she was not currently attending them in the great hall, she was confident that their acquaintance would remain a passing one. She no longer needed to think about him.

"Alys, I need a diversion, but I am afraid. What if something else happens?"

Alys sighed heavily, "I am certain it will get easier in time, my lady. You need to associate more with people. The more you do, the easier it will be. You will see, there is nothing here to be afraid of. Your uncle and his men will protect you." She gave Guida's hand a firm squeeze.

"You are right." Guida straightened up. "Enough wallowing. I believe that today is market day. Will you come with me into Salerno? We will not stay long, just long enough that I can tell my uncle I went out."

The two women had barely ventured out of the castle before a commotion in the courtyard arrested their attention. Several carriages rolled through the gate, circling around to the castle entry to allow the passengers to disembark.

"Oh, no." Guida's heart sank as she recognized the coat of arms being displayed. She knew her parents were expected to arrive, but had not known there would be other visitors.

"Who is it, my lady?" Alys asked beside her.

"Gemma's family," Guida ground out. "Besides Gemma herself, these are the most unpleasant people we are likely to ever meet."

"My lady! You must not speak so of the princess's family." Alys's shock was evident.

"No, Alys. You must never speak so of her family. I may say what I will," Guida insisted.

"You are too reckless, my lady. The princess will not have any qualms about seeing you punished for speaking against her. I wish you would be more careful."

Her maid's worried look was enough to chastise Guida. "Do not fret, Alys. I will say no more."

Chapter 15

Salerno – July 1037

Williiam watched for Lady Guida each evening when he entered the great hall. Days passed, and he never saw her. Desperately wanting to apologize, he was not entirely surprised by her absence. How foolish and shortsighted of him to blame her for her own attack!

He had been angry. Angry that someone had dared to harm members of the prince's household, that someone would harm innocents. Angry that he had not gotten to her sooner, and that he could not take away her pain. And angry with himself for taking it all out on her. He must learn to control his anger.

Now, he did not know what to do. Hardly in a position to speak with her anytime he wished to, he had watched for her, yet she had eluded him since they had returned to the castle. The entire family had been mostly absent as they dealt with their grief.

Tonight, however, as he entered the great hall, William was stopped by a young servant. The lad informed him that Prince Guaimar and the family would be present this evening, and they had once again requested that William join the family on the dais. Looking up to the front of the room, William saw the royal family were indeed all in attendance. Lady Guida was positioned across from the prince and princess. They were all surrounded by several people William did not know. One man, seated next to Prince Guaimar, shared similar features with the prince, and appeared to be slightly younger. William was curious who these strangers were, and why his presence would be requested. There were also several new faces interspersed around Lady Isolde, on the side of Princess Gemma.

Putting aside his curiosity, he was more concerned about this being his opportunity to address Guida. But what exactly was he to say? How to put what he felt into words? Especially in public.

Prince Guaimar greeted William as he approached. "Ah, Sir William. Allow me to make some introductions. This is Guida's father, and my brother, the Duke di Sorrento." He gestured to the man next to him. That explained the similarities between the two men. Then, turning to the duke, he gestured to William. "This is William di Hauteville. He is becoming quite invaluable to me. I believe he will suit our purposes quite well. William, please have a seat next to Guida."

Doing as he was bid, William wondered at what the prince had spoken. Guida did not look up at him as he sat down. "Good evening, my lady." She nodded her head a fraction, but made no comment.

William and Guaimar spoke occasionally over Guida, but nothing seemed to draw her out. She was focused entirely on her food, and nothing else penetrated her notice. *This is foolish.* He decided to begin speaking with her like nothing had happened between them.

"Who are those people around Lady Isolde? I have not seen them here before."

Guida still did not remove her eyes from her trencher, but she answered, "One is Princess Gemma's brother, Sir Giovan, and one is their sister, Grimelda." Her answer was informative, yet formal.

Getting caught up in conversation with the prince and his brother, William was not able to focus more on drawing the lady out.

When the meal was winding down, Guaimar turned once more to William. "I would like to change your responsibilities, Sir William. I no longer wish for you to rotate with the castle guards. Instead, I would like you to take over the charge of Lady Guida's protection." At this proclamation, Guida's eyes finally lifted and met those of her uncle, who ignored her attention. "She has not been easy since John's death, and her father and I would feel more at ease knowing she was fully watched over. You have assisted her a few times now, and I would feel better knowing that my niece is under your watchful eye. I believe she would feel better knowing that there was always someone watching out for her."

Guida looked thoroughly mortified. "Uncle Guaimar! You cannot be serious. I would never dream of taking one of your knights away from his duties simply to put my mind at rest. Besides, I have Alys. She would feel so slighted to be replaced like this. Please, Uncle, do not take any more pains for me."

Guida may have different reasons, but her displeasure with this proposal mirrored William's own. However, Guaimar ignored Guida's pleas and continued. "Besides protecting her, you are to make plans for her; activities to get her out of her chambers and help her begin to enjoy life again." Turning to Guida, he added, "I have placed Gaitelgrima under similar restrictions. I will have the women in my care protected."

"What? Uncle Guaimar, be reasonable! Only this afternoon I went into town. I am getting better on my own, and this is hardly work worthy of a knight. Please!" Her voice took on a shrill quality, and there was panic in her eyes. She took up a different tactic. "Father, can you not reason with your brother? Please, this is not necessary."

Duke Guy responded, "Guida, do not argue. Guaimar is doing this at my request. Alys has other duties, and I have quite made up my mind on the matter. I have decided Maria shall return with me to Sorrento, and I do not wish for you to be alone. Sir William, you will begin now."

As much as he would have also liked to protest, William knew his duty lay in whatever direction Guaimar pleased. So he stood up, bowed, and replied, "Yes, my lord." He waited for Lady Guida to rise, and the two of them left out the side door. Lady Guida walked slightly in front of him, and he saw the stiffness in her shoulders. How could he set her at ease? He did not know why, but that was suddenly important to him.

"My lady, I hope you can see that your father is merely attempting to protect you. Your uncle was thoroughly shaken with your," he paused, thinking of an appropriate term, "experience, and I believe he just wants to prevent anything else from happening to you. He has already lost one child, and I do not think he could bear it if something else were to occur. Besides, I am not that bad to be around." He knew it was a poor jest, yet hoped she would find a little humor in it.

She stopped in the middle of the corridor and turned to look at him full on. It was the first real look she had taken of him all evening, and he was shocked at the difference in her countenance. Gone was the laughter in her eyes, replaced with something new. Grief, certainly. And something more. Fear, perhaps? And, suddenly, anger.

"How dare you act concerned for my feelings? You have made it quite clear what you think of me. I do not appreciate you attempting to appease me now."

Having prepared himself for her outrage, he replied, "It was wrong of me to speak to you so, my lady. I apologize for my earlier behavior, and ask for your forgiveness." He bowed as he said the words, hoping her anger would subside, and she would forgive him.

After a pause that felt like an eternity, she took a deep breath and began, "My reluctance at being guarded has nothing to do with you. I am merely frustrated with my current situation. I am grateful for the assistance that you have shown me since we met, and I would like to consider us friends." She sighed heavily and leaned her back against the rough stone wall. "I find that I truly do not know what to do with myself these days. I believe that you will find only dissatisfaction with your new assignment."

"Why do we not give this assignment a chance, my lady? You never know. I may be able to draw you out of your melancholy." He suddenly wished to.

A sardonic laugh escaped her. "And how would you go about doing that?"

He smiled conspiratorially, "You will just have to wait and see, my lady."

"That, my dear knight, is something I would *love* to see."

Chapter 16

Why would you agree to such a ridiculous assignment?"
Drogo's face scrunched up in disgust. "He has turned you
into a nursemaid."

"It is my duty." William scowled with displeasure and rolled over on
his pallet. He had related the prince's directives to Drogo and was now
wishing he had been a bit more discreet.

"Are you angry with me? Or your situation?" Drogo did not even
attempt to hide his amusement.

William sprang to his feet, drawing stares from some of the other
men in the east corner tower where the knights were housed. Feeling
out of sorts, he began pacing the floor. "What am I to do with her? I do
not know what to do with a lady. I am a warrior! I have trained my
entire life to fight, ride, and fight some more. I can affect a certain

amount of gentility, but to maintain it for any prolonged amount of time? God, help me."

"God help us all, if indeed He cares." Drogo's smile continued to grow.

"You are enjoying this!" William gave him his most withering glare, to no effect.

"Oh, immensely!" Drogo laughed. "This has got to be the best news I have heard since coming to this country. I have never seen you like this. Unsure of yourself. Wondering how to proceed."

"I hope you never see it again, brother. Now, unless you can help me with this dilemma, leave me. I must give this matter some thought."

The next day dawned sooner than William wished. He had spent the majority of the night thinking up activities and outings that he was going to use in an attempt to brighten Guida's mood. He knew it was not a physical ache that time alone could mend. She was suffering from something much more difficult to treat. Having seen his share of the depravity of men, he was well aware of the ramifications of such actions. Men often had similar struggles after battle. Haunted dreams and anguished thoughts often accompanied changes in behavior. He did not know just how deep the lady's wounds were, but he knew they were there and he was determined to help. If he could keep her occupied enough, perhaps she could begin to forget. Then she could work to move past it.

Making his way to Lady Guida's chamber door, he relieved the guard that had been stationed there through the night.

Convincing Lady Guida to go for a ride with him was not so easy. She was obstinate, but he had persisted until she agreed.

As they rode, William took the opportunity to watch her. She wore a pink dress, with intricate white stitching. Her hair was braided down her back, with black tendrils already working loose and framing her flawless face. He found himself wondering how it would feel to twirl those tresses through his fingers. *No!* He stopped the thought and tightened his hold on his reins, looking away. He needed to focus on the task at hand, not on what he would like to do with her hair.

She was ill at ease, and her head constantly moved back and forth as she scanned the surrounding area. When she turned in his direction, he saw how tight the muscles of her face were. No lady should be so weighed down. He hoped that his plan today would help.

When her eyes met his, her cheeks reddened. Breaking their eye contact, she turned slightly in the other direction. "Exactly where is it that we are going?"

"There is a nice clearing in the forest up ahead. I thought we could stop there today."

She looked over at him with a small grin. "Oh, I know the place. It is not large. It should not take long to explore it."

"That is just as well. I have something else planned that will take up more time."

She tensed, and her face turned fearful. He realized his mistake immediately. Of course she would not feel safe going to a secluded area with a man that she did not know well. Not after her recent trauma. It was his turn for embarrassment.

"No, no! I realize how that sounded. Please, do not worry. You will be perfectly safe, my lady."

She softened a little, but did not fully relax. He would have to work hard to earn her trust.

The rest of the ride was silent and uncomfortable. Neither one of them knew what to say. Luckily the clearing was not far and they came to it quickly. The summer wildflowers were all gone, and the grasses were already turning brown. They dismounted, and he tied the reins to a tree.

"Well, here we are." The awkwardness of the situation was nearly palpable, with neither one of them at ease.

"My lady, I must say something before we continue," he said, taking a fortifying breath. "I want to apologize again for my thoughtless words the other day. I truly do not hold you accountable for what happened. It was wrong of me to suggest it was in any way your fault. Please forgive me."

She sighed. "Do not make yourself uneasy, Sir William. I am fully aware of my role in what happened. Your words could not add to the guilt that I already feel about the situation. However, I thank you for your apology."

"Well then, shall we begin?"

"Begin? With what?"

"Your first lesson." With that, he took out a bundle from one of his saddle bags and held it in one hand. With the other hand, he reached to guide her to the center of the clearing. She skittered back from his touch.

"I am so sorry!" She immediately apologized. "I am struggling a bit with being touched. I do much better if I am given a little warning. Please do not be offended by it."

William gave her an appraising look. "My lady, I know things appear bleak now, but I would like to help. You do not have to recover from everything on your own."

"Why?" she asked skeptically.

"I have a sister in Normandy. I would hate for her to be in your position and to feel the way that you seem to. I know that there may be few ways that I can truly help you, but I wish to do what I can. Starting now. I would like to take your arm, to help guide you to where we are going." He held out his arm and waited for her to accept it.

It was her turn to appraise him. "Very well." She gingerly placed her hand on his arm and let him guide her about ten paces from the edge of the woods.

"Now, my lady, lesson one. How to throw a knife."

"What? You brought me out here to play with knives?" The skeptical look was still on her face.

"This is no time for questions, but yes. I believe that you would feel more at ease if you were better able to defend yourself. I happen to be proficient with this skill and have decided that this is a good place to begin."

He proceeded to unroll his bundle which contained several knives of different sizes. They were all fairly plain with few embellishments, but that was better for throwing, in case any were to be lost.

"How hard can it be to throw a knife?"

"I believe you will be surprised." He was curious to see how this would progress. Would she be terrible and refuse to practice? Or would she take up the challenge and work to prove herself?

"You are smiling," she said when she caught him looking at her.

"Yes. This is one of my favorite pastimes. I find it immensely satisfying, and it relieves a lot of tension. A very worthwhile activity."

"Wait, you said this was lesson one. Does that mean there are more lessons you have planned?"

"All in good time, my lady." He picked up one of the knives. "Now, you will grip it by the tip of the blade between your thumb and first finger, like this. Then raise your arm back as I am doing and aim for that tree." He let the blade fly, landing with a satisfying *thunk* in the trunk of the tree. "Now it is your turn. Select a knife."

"Right. How hard can this be?" she asked. Having no notion which knife would be best, she picked a mid-size knife from the bundle.

Following his instructions she threw with all her might. It flew down to the ground and landed just a few feet in front of her. She burst out laughing, and it was one of the most beautiful sounds William had ever heard. He realized he liked her a little bit more for being able to laugh about her limitations.

"Oh, that was awful!" she gasped with mirth. "This may take more than one day of practice."

"That depends on your ultimate goal, my lady."

"Would that not be to throw a knife accurately?" Her eyebrows drew together showing her confusion.

"That is one goal, certainly, but not the goal I set out to accomplish today."

"And what was that?"

He leaned in conspiratorially. "You are smiling."

Chapter 17

Salerno – August 1037

Y ou are teaching her to throw a knife? Why?" The prince's moods were getting easier for William to understand. He was often short with words, yet every decision was made only after careful consideration. William knew how much he cared for his family. It stood to reason that the prince would wonder at William's chosen course as it pertained to Lady Guida.

"Your Highness, I am a warrior. I have been trained for battle, with many different kinds of weapons. It is what I know. You have given me a task which is not something that I am familiar with, and I am doing the best I know." William was not even convinced there was any wisdom in what he was doing, so how could he convince the prince?

"Are you dissatisfied with what I have asked of you?" Prince Guaimar looked discerningly at William.

"I am merely in unfamiliar waters, my lord." It did not seem wise to answer honestly.

"Hm." Prince Guaimar looked unconvinced, yet continued. "What else do you have planned for her?"

"I was considering archery. These are merely ways to get her mind off of what has happened."

"Distraction can be good, but is it enough? Why not try some exercises to help her work through her fear of people? She never used to be afraid to associate with anyone, but now she has a difficult time even being around the family."

It was as if a heavy weight had been placed on William's shoulders. *How am I supposed to accomplish that?* "My lord, are you certain that I am the right person for this? I am happy to serve you, but I am not…"

"Do not question me on this," the prince interrupted. "I have my reasons for choosing you." Guaimar glowered at William, who fought back the urge to shudder.

"Of course, my liege." William bowed his head, "My apologies." Hating that he had no right to question further, he kept his peace.

"Keep at it, Sir William. This may be just the right tactic for getting through to her. I would like you to continue your lessons, at least for now. We will see how she responds."

William bowed again, then walked backwards out of the room, careful to not turn his back on his lord. He would find Drogo and drown his frustrations in as much ale as he could find.

Several hours later, after the evening meal, Guida was summoned by Guaimar to join him in the solar.

Tentatively knocking on the partially open door, she heard a deep voice bid her enter. That voice, which was typically full of tenderness and love when he spoke to her, had lately sounded deep and serious. Her relationship with her uncle was changing, and she did not know what the final outcome would be. She wished that everything could just go back to normal.

Guaimar was standing at the window and turned toward her as she entered. Upon seeing her, his face softened in what she took for pity. He held out his arms to her as he had often done in the past. This familiar practice held no comfort for her, however. She did not want pity, especially from one who had lost so much more than she had. Instead of going to him like she would have done in the past, her body stiffened and she stayed where she was.

"Oh, my dear." He lowered his arms in disappointment. "I heard about your outing today. I am very pleased with Sir William and quite certain we will all be happy with the results. I believe that he will be a good influence on you."

"Yes, I think you may be right," she agreed, skirting the edge of the room in an attempt to avoid eye contact. "I am so sorry for my earlier reluctance, Uncle."

"Guida, you know that I love you like a daughter. Your happiness is very important to me. I would not do this if I did not believe that you would benefit from it."

"Of course." Guida realized she had been waiting for Guaimar to blame her for the loss of his son. She was relieved that he had not done so, yet she still felt it was inevitable.

Her uncle paused for a moment before saying, "Guida, do you wish to remain here? If it is too much, you could return with your father to

Sorrento. You have been through so much since coming here. I will understand if you wish to leave."

"No, Uncle." Guida cringed inwardly at how flat her voice sounded in her ears. "I love it here. This is the only home I have ever known. Just give me a little more time. I am sure that this will pass." Her heart beat faster, and she recognized the persistent feeling of panic that was becoming a frequent visitor. The idea of leaving the castle filled her with apprehension. She knew that outlaws frequented the roads between the two keeps, and she did not feel equal to the task of facing that danger, even accompanied as she would surely be. Her breath became shallow as she waited for her uncle to reply.

"Very well, if you are sure. This will be your home for as long as you require it."

"Yes, Uncle." Taking deep breaths, her heartbeat began to slow back to normal.

"Guida." Prince Guaimar paused. "Why have you not shared the fullness of what happened with your father? He has noticed how different you are now, and he worries about you."

Guida answered in a whisper, "I do not wish for them to think less of me. Not even Maria knows the full tale. Perhaps one day I will be able to tell them, but not yet." Wanting an end of this conversation, Guida decided to change the subject. "How about a game of chess? It has been awhile since we played. I would like to check my skills to see if I can best you yet." She tried for a smile and a light tone of voice.

"Not tonight," he answered, still looking troubled. "I must finish some letters. I am writing to our Emperor Conrad and Emperor Michael of the Romans, trying to persuade them to take action against Pandulf. Besides what he has done to us, he is targeting monasteries in the area. He loots them for the artifacts. It is time to do something, but I cannot openly move against him without the emperor's sanction. But tomorrow, after you have broken your fast, I want you to meet me in the chapel. There is something more I wish to discuss."

Guida awoke, sweating and chilled. Looking beside her, she assured herself that Maria was still asleep. Rising from her bed as silently as she could, she found the washbasin near the window. How she wished simply splashing her face with water would wash away the wrongs that she relived in her sleep each night. How long could a person survive without a decent night's rest? She might just find out. Each time she managed to sleep, the visions and emotions swooped in and wrested away what little peace she had pieced together during the day.

"You are going to rub your entire face off." Maria had been awake after all.

"What a spectacle I will be." Guida crept toward her sister with her fingers out in front of her like claws. "I will frighten all the little girls, and the boys will all test their courage by challenging me to battle." Guida pounced on her sister and commenced a quick tickle fight.

Maria's laughter rang through the room, lightening Guida's foul mood.

"Now, go to sleep, my little angel. You have a long day before you tomorrow." Guida sobered as she remembered that her father and sister were leaving for Sorrento in the morning. Sleep eluded her, yet she did not rise again for fear of waking Maria.

After what seemed like days, Alys entered and assisted them into their dresses. Together, the sisters made their way to the great hall, where Guida ate as much as she could. It was not enough to keep a sparrow alive, but it was all she could manage. While chewing what tasted like tree bark, but was in actuality a piece of bread, she was greeted by Gemma's younger brother Giovan. He sat next to her and began to fill his trencher from the platters in the middle of the table.

"Lovely morning, is it not, Lady Guida?" He certainly was adept at sounding pleasant, but there was always something lurking in his eyes that set her hair on end. Scrutinizing him now, she noted that he was rather handsome, tall and dark, with seeming perfect symmetry in his face. His eyes were unreadable, however, and gave off no hint of warmth.

"Yes, I suppose it is." She was in no mood to entertain this morning. Maria had quickly finished eating and left to assist Alys with last minute packing. She attempted to focus on her food so as not to invite more conversation, but the ruse did not work as she had hoped.

"I shall be going into Salerno today," Giovan said. "I would love some company. Would you consider joining me?"

Guida looked up at him. Her palms grew sweaty, and her heart sped up. Attempting to calm herself, she thought that perhaps she should join him. It would surely do her good to get out of the castle like she used to.

Just as she had made up her mind to agree to the outing, Giovan moved his hand in an obvious attempt to brush hers. She jerked her hand away and quickly stood up, knocking her chair to the ground behind her.

"I-I am sorry, but I am quite busy today. Perhaps another time." Her heart raced as she looked away, searching for the quickest escape from the massive hall. She needed to escape. *Where is William?* Was it not his duty to protect her? Did that not include keeping her from the unwanted advances of men she hardly knew?

After performing the quickest curtsy of her life, she was soon working her way through the tables and the servants, moving through the great hall, searching for some safety. She was nearly to the door when she met Sir William moving toward her.

"Good morning," she said, slightly breathless. "I, uh," she hazarded a glance behind to assure herself that Giovan was not pursuing her. "I had been wondering where you were."

"Is everything all right, my lady?" His concern was evident.

Glancing once more over her shoulder, she then turned to really look at William. "Where were you?" She tried for an unaffected tone but was still a little breathless, and she was certain she had not fooled him. Now that her immediate threat was at an end, anger took over, and her eyes flashed with fury. "Are you not tasked with my protection? How do you intend to fulfill your duty if you are nowhere to be found when danger presents itself?"

William's eyes flashed, and he spoke between clenched teeth. "What has happened?"

Shocked with his reaction, not knowing if he was angry at her again or upset that he missed something of importance, she took a deep breath to help gather her thoughts.

Attempting to focus on anything else, Guida scrutinized the man before her. She could not fail to notice the fine features of his face, and she often felt out of breath when he first came into her view. He had such broad shoulders, and was so tall that her eyes came to the middle of his chest. From this proximity, she could see how blue his eyes were, with little flecks of green. His short blond hair did not distract from the ruggedness of his face.

Noticing how much calmer she felt, she chose to ignore her previous scare. "Nothing has happened, really. I merely had not seen you yet this morning."

His face relaxed and he smiled at her. Realizing she had been staring she turned to leave, wishing to outrun her embarrassment.

"Where are you off to?" William asked as he moved in step with her.

"I am to meet Uncle Guaimar in the chapel." She shifted her focus to look down the corridor.

"Would you permit me to walk with you?" he asked, even though he already was.

"That is your job, so I suppose that you must." Tilting her head slightly she let out a sigh, even as her lips curved upward. She hoped making light of this would ease the awkwardness that her earlier outburst had caused.

Ignoring her obvious jest, he continued, "I thought we would take up archery this afternoon. Are you available?"

"I, uh, I believe so. I will know more after speaking with Uncle Guaimar. I do not know if he has anything else planned for me. He seems to want to take control of my every move these days." Guida was pleased to note that she said the last part with no bitterness in her voice. She really could not blame her uncle for wanting to protect her in any way that he could. If she were honest with herself, it was a relief to be told what to do.

Guida found her uncle kneeling in the chapel. Moving next to him, she knelt down leaving just enough space between them that they were not touching. She did not wish to disturb him, yet she wanted him to know she was there.

His face was drawn, and he had deeper wrinkles than Guida had noticed before. He seemed to have aged ten years in the past fortnight, looking far older than his thirty years. How desperately she wished she could remove his grief. What she would not give to be able to relive that terrible day and do things differently.

"Guida, do you believe in God?" Her uncle did not turn toward her, or even open his eyes. He merely asked the question.

She ought to have anticipated this type of question, given their location, but it still somehow took her by surprise. "Yes, I do."

"As do I. And if I believe in God, then I must believe in the teachings of the priests. We are taught that men are saved so long as they are baptized. John was baptized soon after his birth, so I know that he has been saved from perdition. Now, you say that you believe in God, so you must also believe that John is saved. This is something I want you to remember."

Turning to her now, he stared into her eyes to emphasize his words. "You need to know I do not blame you, and I need you to forgive yourself. I know you do not wish to speak to me about this, and I assume you have your reasons, but this is important to me." He reached out to grasp her shoulder. "I love you, Guida, and I know that you would never have knowingly let anything happen to John. But, it has happened, and now you need to move on, as we all must."

Guida wrapped her arms around Guaimar. How she longed to speak with him about all that was in her heart, but she could not. Not wishing to add to his burden in that way, she would be strong, if only for his sake. She owed him that much.

Chapter 18

Salerno – September 1037

It was time for Gemma's family to leave, at least Guida thought so. Maria and Sir Guy had left a few days past, leaving Guida nearly friendless. Isolde rarely spoke to her now. Gemma had likely been filling the girl's head with lists of Guida's undesirable qualities. Gaitelgrima also seemed to be more withdrawn, likely due to her own emotions regarding the death of her brother. And Guaimar seemed busier than ever with business conducted behind closed doors.

So, Guida was left alone to combat Gemma's family and all their unpleasantness. One could often hear the shrill voice of her sister Grimelda throughout the grounds, screaming about some slight offense or another, and her husband was only slightly better controlled.

Giovan was a different sort of creature all together. Alys had informed Guida that he was often caught stalking any number of the servant women, and had managed to take advantage of several. They all feared being caught alone with him. He was not known for his gentleness. Guida shuddered listening to Alys's accounts, memories of her own recent experience still fresh in her mind. She brought his behavior up with Guaimar, who assured her that it would be taken care of.

Giovan's attentions did not stop, however. Nor did they remain trained on the servants. Guida was aware of the way his eyes lingered on her whenever she saw him and the way that his hand *accidentally* brushed hers during their meals.

He was getting bolder, too. Now and again, Guida felt his hand on her back while they walked through the castle. At times, his hand would slip down just a little further than was appropriate. It was like a game to him. He was trying to see how far he could push her. She always made her excuses promptly and attempted to leave his presence, but it seemed to be getting more difficult to avoid him.

William was not always able to be next to Guida, even with Guaimar's overprotective directive. He had to continue his own training so as not to grow complacent and weak. Guaimar also required his presence at times, pulling him away from her side. Occasionally, she would have another guard, but they would not intervene against a man of nobility like Giovan. He knew how to go about his designs undetected by watching eyes. Guida also suspected that he bribed the guards to look the other way.

Then, Guida heard the news that they were leaving. Only after watching the company mount up and leave the castle grounds did she realize that Giovan was not with his sister. Fear crept back into her mind, and she went in search of Alys. She would surely have heard by now why Giovan was to stay. Rounding a corner near the tower, Guida nearly collided with Giovan.

"Oh! Giovan, I thought you were leaving with your family," she said. Hopefully this would open him up to explain why he remained.

"I have decided to stay." His eyes pierced her, and she moved to go past him. He blocked her way, putting his hand against the wall. Turning to go the other way, she was stopped again as he quickly put up his other arm on the other side of her, pinning her between himself and the wall. Leaning his face close to hers he murmured, "The company here is much more pleasant than at home."

His breath was hot and filled Guida with memories of another man's breath as she struggled against him. Her panic rising, she pushed against him, but he was solid and immovable. Her breathing quickened.

"Giovan," she began, "please let me go." Hating that she had to plead, she realized just how much she still had to learn from William about protecting herself. *Where is he?* He never seemed to be around when he was needed.

"No, I do not think I will, *my lady*," he said with disdain. "You talked to Guaimar about me. There are consequences for that." His face grew hard, and anger radiated off him. This was the first time she had seen him angry, and she felt she was seeing his true character at last.

Without another thought, Guida stomped on Giovan's foot. Using his surprise against him, she brought her knee up with as much force as she could muster. Her knee connected with him squarely between his legs, and he doubled over.

Just as this happened, William came around the corner. Quickly taking in the scene before him, he took Guida's hand and led her away from Giovan.

"I have been looking for you, my lady. It is time for our lesson," he said calmly, belying the anger that flashed in his eyes.

Yanking her hand out of his grasp, she sputtered, "D-did you not see what just happened? Where were you?"

William turned and looked intently at her, as if he were trying to work out a problem. After a moment, he again grabbed her by the arm and pulled her into a chamber set a little off from the stairs of the tower. It was an armory. There were several of them located throughout the castle and the grounds, so that in case of an invasion there would always be weapons and armor nearby for those men who could use them.

Once they crossed the threshold, she wrested her arm out of his grasp, still not at ease with being touched, even by him. She knew that it had nothing to do with William himself, since she had the same reaction with any number of people.

"What happened? Tell me everything." He leaned against the wall next to the door, blocking her escape.

"Ah, yes. As I am your assignment, of course you would be concerned." She did not even attempt to stem the sarcasm from her voice.

William took a deep breath, and then said, "I do not wish to know because you are an assignment, Guida."

At the sound of her name, her emotions threatened to overpower her. *I will not cry. Not here,* she told herself. Then she related what Giovan had done. What he had said.

"I felt so powerless! What else could I have done?" she asked.

"What you ought to have done was not be in that position to begin with!" His eyes again flashed with fury as he took to pacing the room. "Do you not know what kind of man Giovan is? You are a beautiful woman; of course Giovan would take notice." Almost to himself, he added, "Why can you not stay out of trouble?"

Shocked as she was by his outburst, she clung to one thought that left her breathless. "You think I am beautiful?" she whispered. She wiped her suddenly clammy hands down her skirt.

He seemed as shocked as she was, as though he just realized what he had said. Not acknowledging it, he countered, "That is not the issue at hand. You simply must be more careful."

Irritated by his demeaning manner, she fought back. "Where was my guard? You are tasked with my protection, are you not? And yet when the need arose, you were not there, again! Finding myself in that situation was every bit as much your fault as it was mine!"

"I do have other duties, my lady. However difficult it may be to believe, you are not the center of the world." As his anger increased, his frustration with his current role in her life became apparent.

She gasped. *Is that what he thinks of me?* "I am not so much a child as to believe that. I know that I am a mere woman, small and insignificant. But I refuse to sit by and allow every man I meet to do with me what he will! Regardless of your personal feelings for me, I do not believe that I deserve to be treated like a plaything, or bend to the will of those around me!"

William stepped closer to where she stood. "What I know," his voice was calmer, and quieter, "is that you are a passionate young maiden who is still discovering what she is capable of. I think we shall both see in due time what that entails." He seemed to have been comforted by her outburst, if that were possible.

They stayed where they were. Guida could not drag her eyes away from his. He had come at her with the fury of a lion, yet she had stood her ground. Now, his face had softened, and the lines of anger had fled.

What would it feel like to kiss that face? That mouth? Embarrassment coursed through her as she realized the pathway of her thoughts. She took a step back, breaking the spell that had encompassed them.

"I-I would like to go to my chamber," she stammered.

"Very well, my lady."

Neither of them spoke as they walked, side by side, back to her room. He looked straight ahead. She watched his hand swinging at his side. What would it feel like to take his hand? To have her small one encompassed by his?

He turned to her just outside her chamber door.

"You are not insignificant, Guida," he said calmly. "In spite of my initial reaction, I am proud of how you handled Giovan. And yes, you are quite beautiful," he said as he brushed a stray strand of hair behind her ear. It happened so quickly, and he was gone before Guida could formulate a response.

Why had he spoken to her that way? It was his charge to protect her, not to work on the fundamentals of her character. And where had that fire in her come from? He had to admit that he did not know her that well. He merely knew the surface of her personality, which he knew had changed due to recent events.

He had seen glimpses of an intelligent, clever woman before anything had happened to her, and he longed to see that woman again. He was achingly aware that she was building a fortress around her heart. He worried that nobody would be able to reach her if she were allowed to finish.

Would he be able to weaken her defenses while at the same time making her a stronger, more capable woman? Did he want to? Yes. He very much wanted to see her without the facade of strength and anger that she was developing. He did not wish for her to end up a bitter, confrontational person. He would need to be more careful with his tongue in the future. The last thing that he needed was to get her ire up each time they were together.

His relief was palpable knowing that she had defended herself against Giovan. If that vile man touched Guida again, William might not be able to stop himself from taking immediate action. The thought of running that blaggard through was tempting. As her protector, he might be justified. Although, as Giovan was the brother of the princess, there would be trouble.

"That odious man!" Guida spat. "There is nothing good or kind in him. He thinks only of himself and of his own pleasure." Unleashing her frustrations upon her helpless maid did little to diffuse her remaining anger over her encounter with Giovan. The argument with William was confusing, and she did not wish to think on it. It was easier to be angry, and she was certainly furious with Giovan.

"Hush now. You must put Lord Giovan from your mind. You need your rest, and you will not be calm as long as he haunts your thoughts." Alys ushered Guida over to her bed, having finished preparing her mistress for the night.

Guida followed Alys's bidding and crawled into bed. Once the door closed and Alys was gone, she crawled right back out. What was the point of trying to sleep? This was quickly becoming her least favorite time of day, even when she was not riled up as she was tonight. She had too many memories, too many ghosts in her mind for her to find rest.

Walking to the window, she curled up on the bench. She looked out into the vast darkness beyond the castle and wondered what William was doing. Was he thinking of her? Did he wonder how it would feel if they could be together? It was foolish of her to consider such things. Recalling his anger from this afternoon, she thought briefly what William would have done if he had rounded the corner a minute sooner. Would he have rushed to her rescue? There was a moment when she had been proud of how she had taken charge of her own protection. She felt powerful, and strong. Did William see that? Or did he really just see a woman who could not keep herself out of trouble?

His eyes crept into her mind. They watched her, waiting, for something. She did not know what. Was he waiting for her to fail? Or was he hoping for something that only she could do?

Shaking herself, she looked back to her bed. The place where Maria had slept before leaving with their father now lay empty and cold. She imagined Maria now, in Sorrento, sleeping peacefully. Guida envied her. It was the sleep of the innocent, something Guida would never be again. Leaning her head back against the window, memories of her sister swirled through her head.

"You know we are not allowed to venture this far from Sorrento," Maria *fretted. "Papa will be quite vexed when he learns of it." Her nervousness shone through her words.*

"No one is forcing you to come, Maria." Guida countered. "Although, it would be a shame for you to miss out on the refreshing, clear water, and the soothing music of the waterfall. But then, you never were one for enjoying nature." She knew just the right things to say to get Maria to go along with any scheme. This time was no different.

Maria smiled, and looked askance at her older sister. She spurred her horse faster and called out, "I will beat you there!"

Guida's body tensed with exhilaration as she raced to overtake Maria, but Maria was no longer in front of her. Guida slowed and looked from side to side. Where had she gone? "Maria? Maria, where are you?"

Fear gripped Guida as she quickly dismounted. Walking away from her horse, she stumbled through the trees. She pushed through and scratched her arms as the bushes stretched out their long bony fingers, clawing at her. She continued to cry out for Maria as a feeling of being pursued overtook her. She began running, but from what, she did not know. She knew, without a doubt, that if she stopped running all would be lost. What exactly that meant, she had no notion.

A gentle roaring could be heard over the pounding of her heart and her feet racing over the forest floor. The waterfall! That must be where Maria went. Guida changed her course slightly to head in the direction of the sound. Just before reaching the edge of the trees, she stopped. Her feeling of dread had not dispersed, and her heart pounded louder than ever. She was sweating, but whether from her exertion or her fear she could not say. The pounding of her heart continued to rise in volume and intensity. Thump, thump, thump! Thump, thump, thump!

Startled awake, Guida realized the pounding was actually someone knocking on her bedchamber door, and not her heart after all. She sat up from her slouched position on the bench and attempted to calm her breathing. The knocking continued so she rose and went to open the door.

"Sir William?" She was surprised to see him so late.

"You were calling out, my lady. Is everything well?" He tried to look past her, into the chamber.

"Yes, all is well. Just a bad dream. Forgive me for causing a disturbance." Her cheeks burned with embarrassment. She had not realized that she had fallen asleep and was not happy to know that she had called out in her fear.

"Are you quite certain? Should I check your rooms?" His light blue eyes were filled with concern. *Have they always been that blue?* Looking into them now filled her with a peace that she had not felt for months. She was comforted by William's mere presence, but felt it inappropriate to say so. The idea of him in her bedchamber filled her with a desire she had never felt before, and she longed for it. She knew she must decline his offer, but the thoughts were not so easily set aside.

After a moment's pause she pulled herself together enough to respond with a quick, "I am certain. Good night." She then closed the door and collapsed against it as she tried to catch her breath for the second time in the last few minutes.

The next afternoon Guida worked hard through another long practice session with William. She was beginning to manage with a few of his knives and had been able to actually hit a tree with the majority of her throws. It was a great improvement, and it filled her with pride.

"Not bad, my lady." William's look confirmed his approval.

"Why, thank you, my good sir," she responded in a falsely superior tone. "A lady is nothing if she cannot wield a knife to rival her fiercest adversary."

"Quite so," he played along. "Although, I do believe the trees could use a respite from your constant assaults." His smile was infectious, and Guida wished she could stay in this moment.

They packed up their supplies, mounted their horses and began their return to the castle.

"Sir William, why are you here?" she asked as they rode side by side. She had so many questions about this man. They were spending so much time together, yet she realized how little she knew of him.

Looking at her dubiously, he responded, "I am here to protect you, my lady." The words were polite, yet his eyes made her feel like a simpleton.

Eager to redeem herself in his eyes, she clarified, "I do not mean why are you riding with me. I mean why are you in Italy?"

His face relaxed as he responded, "My father has a small amount of land in Normandy, but nowhere near enough to split between nine sons. So, my brother Drogo and I knew that we needed to leave home in order to secure any sort of future."

"Oh, my. Pardon my saying so, but that is an enormous family! Your mother must be a saint."

"She is. Fressenda is my father's second wife, and she has striven to instill each of us with the values most becoming of men. And it is no small feat to keep that many boys from killing each other." Guida could hear the smile in his voice.

"You love her. I can tell. It must be difficult being so far from home. I can see why you travel with your brother."

He turned to glance at her as he shifted the focus off himself. "What of your family?"

"It is just Maria and I. It sounds insignificant next to your large numbers. My mother had difficulties bearing children. Berta thought she was going to lose my mother when Maria came, and advised my parents that it would not be wise for my mother to have more children. I am close with my uncle, Guaimar, and my cousins, Gaitelgrima and, well…" Her shoulders drooped and she lowered her gaze as she thought of John. "I had been."

William was quick to redirect the conversation away from John. "What brings you here instead of residing with your parents?"

Guida's good humor was quick to return. "Did you not know? I am in want of a husband." She attempted a flippant tone to detract from the seriousness of her words. She knew she should not speak so openly, yet she wanted to see how he would react to her honesty.

William was quiet, which unnerved Guida somewhat. *Does he think me grasping? Hinting for him to do something?* She was suddenly mortified with what she had said.

"Forgive me. I ought not speak so openly. I did not intend to cause you discomfort."

"Do not think on it, my lady."

The rest of their ride was uncomfortable and quiet.

Chapter 19

Salerno – November 1037

G uida, a word." Guaimar appeared to have anticipated her return from the village. She had ventured out with Alys and a guard while William had been training.

"Yes, Uncle." Handing Adrina's reins to a stable hand, she followed Guaimar into the great hall. From there he led her to another chamber where he often conducted his business. She had rarely been allowed in this room. There was a large table surrounded by chairs where she supposed he met with his advisors. Parchments were scattered upon it, interspersed with inkwells and quills. Shelves lined the walls filled with scrolls and a few precious books.

Guida tensed as she wracked her brain to discover what offense she was guilty of that would warrant her being here.

"Please sit," Guaimar gestured to a few chairs set near the fireplace where a pleasant crackling helped warm the otherwise chilled space.

Sitting on the edge of the chair, she could not relax. Sitting opposite her, Guaimar appeared at ease, adding to her confusion.

"I wished to speak to you of Giovan," Guaimar began.

Guida released the breath she had not realized she had been holding. "What, exactly, would you like to address about that vile man?"

Guaimar's eyes narrowed. "I am well aware of your opinion of him, and I am sorry to see that it has not improved upon further acquaintance." Sighing, he leaned forward. "I have received a message from your father. He wishes to pursue Giovan as a possible husband for you."

"What?" Guida shot up out of her seat and squared off as if to battle her uncle. "He cannot be serious. I could never be happy with such a man. Uncle Guaimar, you must do something! Write to father, convince him of the folly of such a match." Her voice was rising and took on the beginnings of hysteria. She began marching through the room, balling her fists and digging her nails into the palms of her hands.

"Guida," her uncle soothed, "I will do all I can. I have no desire to see you with such a man, yet I may be unable to stop it. Look around you and tell me how many marriages you imagine are happy ones? You must find a way to be at peace with whatever decision your father makes for you."

Trying a different tactic, she argued, "I am not ready for marriage. Surely my father would not rush this, would he?"

"There is one thing that will work in your favor. Giovan is leaving in a few days time for an extended journey. He is to accompany his father to the Kingdom of Germany, and is not expected to return before a year is past."

Guida scoffed, "Ah, I am to have a slight reprieve before my world ends."

Guaimar's eyes flashed. "Stop. I know it appears bleak, but the future is not firmly decided. A lot may happen over the course of a year. Arguing about it and making caustic comments will not change what your father is setting in motion. If you wish to change this outcome, the best you can do is supplicate with the Almighty. At this point, He may be your only hope."

Feeling thoroughly chastised, Guida stopped her pacing and faced her uncle. "I apologize. I ought not to have spoken so freely." She returned to her seat, this time slumping in defeat.

Guaimar reached across the space and grasped her hand. "All hope is not lost, my dear. You never know; perhaps Giovan will be detained and not return when he is expected. Your father may yet hear of another man who would suit you better. No marriage contract has been drawn up or signed by either party. Circumstances may still change the outcome of your future."

Grasping the hope that he offered her, Guida squeezed his hand. "Yes, thank you."

Chapter 20

Salerno – January 1038

Illiam rubbed his neck, warming it as it was exposed to the chilly winter air. It had been a mild winter thus far, yet it was still quite cold. He wondered if Guida's heavy fur cloak could really protect her from the elements. William had dragged her out to the forest for this next lesson, as he did not wish to have them overheard.

"You must learn to disguise your feelings, my lady. You display your emotions for all to see. Anyone who looks at you knows exactly what you are feeling at any time of day." William's frustration was evident in the tone of his voice. Over the last few months he had taught Lady Guida knife throwing and archery, skills he believed were making her more confident. He knew her uncle would never approve of her learning any sword skill, and she was too slight to be able to throw a spear with any amount of efficacy. So now they were beginning to work on less tangible things.

"I know! I have always been dreadful at hiding anything. My face gives me away every time." She slumped in defeat. The sound of their voices marred the otherwise serene atmosphere. Gone were the sounds of the forest that were common during the summer months—insects and animals no longer adding their music to the leaves in the trees.

"What is it that gives you away, do you think?" He could easily tell her, but it might be more meaningful for her to figure it out on her own.

"My face," she answered quickly.

"Yes, that is obvious." His exasperation was beginning to show again. "But, what is it about your face?"

"I do not know! If I knew, do you not think that I would change it?"

"Do not become ill-tempered. I think the easiest way to work on this would be for you to learn how to lie. Once you can lie proficiently, we will work on teaching you how to conceal something. Once you master those two skills, you will be able to hide your emotions more effectively. After all, concealing your true emotions is essentially lying, would you not agree?"

Guida stood there, gaping at him. "You cannot be serious. To lie is to break one of the sacred commandments given to Moses! How on earth could you ask me to do such a thing?"

Is she really this naive? William wondered. He had faith in God, but he also knew the way the world worked did not always fit with what was taught about God. Lying was indeed named as a sin. But so was killing, stealing, and various forms of debauchery, which were all done frequently by men of the world. Whether he agreed with them or not was beside the point.

He took a deep breath to try and calm his frustrations. "You do not have to make a habit of lying, my lady. You do not have to do it at all, save here with me. When we are working on this skill, I will know that you are lying, so I do not think it can really be called a sin."

After a moment, she sighed and said, "So how do we go about this?"

"I thought to start by having you tell me a few things about yourself, telling mostly the truth, but throwing in a lie somewhere. If I can pick out the falsehood, then I can tell you how I knew. After you become proficient with that, then we will move on to you just throwing in a few lies at any time during our times together. If you fool me, you must tell me about it later, then we will know that you have mastered this."

"Very well. Let me see, you already know a bit about me, so I am assuming I should start with things that you do not know." She paused for a moment. "I have lived my whole life here in Salerno. My father is now the Duke of Sorrento. My two sisters are still…"

"Stop," he groaned, shaking his head. "You do not even need to finish the sentence for me to know that you are lying about your sisters. Can you tell me how I knew?" This was perchance the hardest task he had taken on, and it took all of his willpower not to rub his eyes and yell in frustration.

"No! I was simply talking. I did not change anything that I am aware of." She sat down heavily on a nearby rock, blowing into her hands to warm them. He was obviously not alone in his frustrations.

"You looked away from me and smiled just a little, but I could tell that you were fighting it. If you had been telling the truth there would be no reason for you not to smile when speaking of your family."

"Oh dear, this is going to be difficult. I did not realize that I did that." She looked at him in disbelief. Standing back up, she shook her shoulders and stretched her neck from side to side, as if getting ready for battle. "Again."

How could that simple phrase dispel his foul temper? He did not know, and yet it did. Perhaps it was the way she said it rather than the words themselves. Looking closer, instead of seeing a job to be done, he saw a beautiful, strong fighter. He had lost sight of the respect that he had for her as he had focused on all of her faults as a pupil. Gazing upon her now, he knew that he had never met another young woman whom he would rather teach.

Chapter 21

S itting on a stump near the sparring field, Guida watched as William and Drogo fought each other. They were nearly evenly matched and could both swing a baton, the wooden sword used in training, many times before growing weary. She was to ride with William this afternoon, but he had insisted on getting in some training before leaving.

Guida found that she enjoyed watching William every bit as much now as she had when he first arrived in Salerno. He was truly a sight to behold. The sheer strength that was needed to fight in full armor was incredible to her. She could barely lift her uncle's hauberk. William was a larger man, so his armor would be even heavier.

The two were fully armed with hauberk, helm, and shield. Once their helms were on, it was difficult to tell who was who. Her current vantage point allowed for her to recognize William as he was slightly taller than Drogo. The times she watched from the castle wall, she could only guess which fighter he was.

She imagined the clang of metal that would result had they been using actual steel swords, those used for battle. How would it feel to wield one herself? Of course, as a woman, she was not permitted to even attempt it. Swords were completely within men's domain.

Uncle Guaimar had spoken to her about his sword once, when she had been a young girl. Having found him in one of the armories cleaning his blade, he had explained to her the different parts of the weapon. There was a groove down the center of the blade, which she had thought was merely decorative. It was actually to make the blade lighter. He spoke to her of pommels, which were used as counterweights to also make the sword seem lighter and easier to wield. Showing her how the sword was designed to resemble the cross of Jesus, he taught her that the infidels would refuse to pick them up in battle and use their enemies' swords against them.

She turned her attention to Drogo. Roughly the same build as William with similar features, their familial relationship was obvious. Drogo was a little darker, and his eyes a bit wider apart. Having not had many interactions with the younger de Hauteville, Guida knew little of his character. She liked to think he was as noble as William, yet there was often something lurking in the depths of his eyes that made her uneasy.

Guida knew that they had been trained together and that they had been sparring ever since they could hold the batons. They both knew the other's fighting patterns and were both adept at blocking any advances. It was always interesting to see who would win each match, although some of their matches seemed to go on for ages.

Turning back to William, she wondered what it was about him that always drew her eyes. He had a sort of magnetism that she was helpless to resist. The fascination that had begun when he arrived with Isolde had not diminished. Now that she was getting to know him better, her interest continued to grow. She wondered when he would do something that would lower her opinion of him. She could feel her regard for him expanding in her chest, filling her with warmth and security, and yet it frightened her. Understanding the realities of their different situations, she needed to guard her heart to keep it from breaking.

"Pardon, my lady," Alys broke into Guida's thoughts. "You are being summoned by your aunt, Princess Gemma."

"Truly?" Guida did not attempt to hide her discomfort. "What can she want with me?"

"I cannot say, my lady."

"Very well. Thank you, Alys. I will come directly. It would do no good to keep the old hag waiting."

Upon entering her aunt's chamber, a chill crept over Guida as surely as if she were back outside. Her aunt's demeanor towards her had never been warm, but Guida was usually able to avoid much contact with her.

"I thought you would like to know that Isolde is to be married." Aunt Gemma actually looked pleased. "She is to marry Duke Alfred of Germany. He is one of the most prominent leaders in the empire and will provide a fine living for her."

"Oh." Guida did not know how to respond to such news. She hoped that Isolde would be happy, yet could not see how. Being betrothed to a man from Germany meant that it was unlikely the two had even met. It also meant that it must have been arranged for them and would likely not lead to an affectionate bond. Could that be the reason Giovan and his father had traveled there, to arrange this marriage? But why was Gemma telling her, and not Isolde herself? Isolde rarely spoke to Guida anymore, yet this seemed the type of thing she would have gloated about.

"Well?" Gemma's shrill voice sliced through Guida's reverie. "Are you not happy for her? I would like to remind you that this is the path you will follow. I know that your uncle is considering many suitable nobles and that he plans to have you married off soon. I am encouraging him to make the arrangements before too much more time passes. We would hate to see you wither away, becoming an old maid, simply because you aged too much before a suitable match could be found." Her aunt's eyes belied the intent to inflict pain behind her smooth tone and concerned manner. Guida knew all too well her aunt's opinion of her.

Guida's eyes narrowed in confusion. Did Aunt Gemma not know of her father's plan to arrange marriage with Giovan? Did her aunt and uncle really not speak to each other? "No, Aunt. I would not like that, either." If Guaimar did not wish to inform Gemma, Guida would not, either.

"No one cares what you would like." All pretense fled as her aunt's true nature rose to the surface. "I tell you this as a courtesy. I have seen the way that you moon over that *Norman*." Gemma's nose crinkled on the word. "You must know that your precious Guaimar at least has the sense not to allow you to marry a mere knight. Especially a foreign one." Gemma stepped closer and spoke so softly that Guida could barely hear. "You will never be happy as long as I have something to say about it."

Guida could hardly move. She knew the type of woman Gemma was, yet her vicious nature still took Guida by surprise at times. "As long as we are speaking plainly, Aunt, what is it that fills you with such hate?

For Guaimar as well as for me? I do not understand what makes you such a bitter, unhappy woman."

"Stupid, foolish girl! You are as ignorant as you are loathsome. My *husband*," she spoke as if spitting out rotten cabbage, "cares more for you than for me. Of course I hate you! How could I not? You have stolen the attention that *I* ought to have, the affection that I deserve. You ought to have been married off long ago. Guaimar is blinded by affection for you and does not wish to be parted from you. Because of this I must suffer your presence in my home.

"I suppose I ought to be grateful to you for one thing. Thanks to you and your careless idiocy, *my* son is now the heir of Salerno. I thank you for *that* kindness. Although, I confess that I rue the fact that you did not perish with John. How I would have rejoiced then. Unfortunately, I will have to content myself with you being placed in a miserable marriage and taken from my sight." Her aunt turned, and Guida took the opportunity to leave the room.

Guida was shocked. Her aunt was right; there was much to think on. Was she taking away some of her uncle's attention that should have been spent on his own children? Guida had never thought of that before. She had always loved her uncle and had never thought that there was anything wrong with it. Now, she was not so sure.

Chapter 22

Salerno – March 1038

William was at his wits' end trying to figure out different ways to approach Guida with all the problems Guaimar wished for him to fix. He could not say with certainty that they were all flaws. However, he knew how little his opinion mattered on the subject, so he kept his objections to himself. This time, however, Guaimar may have given William an impossible task.

"Well? What are we doing today?" Guida never did skirt around an issue.

"My lady," he began.

"Guida, please," she interjected. "We see one another every day. I believe that you have earned the right to dispense with formalities."

Nodding his agreement, he continued. "Guida, today's lesson is a bit more," he paused, "delicate than some of the others have been."

Her face lit up with mischief as she stepped closer to him. "You have my full attention, Sir." Oh, he loved it when she was playful with him. It happened so rarely that he considered himself lucky indeed when he was able to witness it. However, this time, he knew it would not last once she fully understood their situation.

He could not recall a time in his life when he had been more discomfited with a conversation. "Your uncle has noted that you do not respond well to," another pause, "well even the most innocent of touches from anybody." There. He had said it.

As he had predicted, her playfulness was instantly snuffed out. Fire flashed in Guida's eyes as she immediately took up her defense.

"You cannot mean that!" she snapped. "What right does Guaimar have to dictate every detail of my behavior?" She turned away and spoke under her breath. "Will there be no end of his pointing out my flaws? Am I really so unworthy?" Her voice cracked on the last word, and William tried to prepare himself to comfort the crying maiden. He could feel the frustration and hurt emanating from Guida, and wished more than anything that he knew what to do. Before he could think of a way, however, she spun back around to face him. Her face had paled and there was fear in her eyes, but no tears.

"What, exactly, did you have planned?"

So stunned was he by her reaction, he was left speechless for a moment. "My lady, Guida, when will you stop expecting the worst? We will, of course, start with something small." Extending a hand for her, he continued, "I want you to take my hand."

She squinted slightly as she returned his gaze. He smiled a little, hoping to put her at ease. Why was this so difficult for her? Then, just as his frustration was rising and his patience was fleeing, she extended her hand. As they touched, a jolt of warmth coursed from his hand up through to his shoulder. He had never had such a strong reaction to a woman. His grasp tightened as he searched her face to see if she felt it, too. How could she not?

"William?" Her voice was small, and questioning, but the fear was gone from her eyes.

How he wanted to pull her to him, to encompass her with his protection, his strength, his adoration. Did he dare? Did she want it as much as he did? For perhaps the first time since he had known her, he was unsure of her feelings. It made him doubt his own, so he let go of her hand. His felt more empty than ever before. Not knowing what to say, he merely bowed to her, then turned and walked away.

The dull reverberations from the clash of batons were welcome sensations after what William had just experienced. He still did not understand what had happened, or why he had reacted the way he had. Hoping for a diversion, he had immediately sought out Drogo to train. He did not want to think about feelings, or a blasted woman. The rigorous exertion of sword play would serve as ample distraction, and Drogo was a willing opponent.

Typically the brothers were so evenly matched that they each hoped for a way to distract the other. It often proved the only way to win the match. Unfortunately for William, he had several things distracting his mind today. It was not long before Drogo had him at the end of his sword, calling for him to yield.

"What has come over you, brother?" Drogo questioned. "I have rarely won a match so easily and it is not from my own skill that I have done so now." His voice held concern, which was not a sentiment that William wanted from his brother.

Angrily, he answered back. "Nothing. Let us go again." He returned to a starting position, challenging Drogo.

"No, I think not. You are no challenge for me today. Come find me when you are really ready to fight. But for now, you should go clear your head." Drogo began walking away, leaving William more out of sorts than before.

Deciding to go for a ride, he would give Valeur his head and hope that the freedom of the wind whipping his face would be more satisfying than his time with Drogo had been. Yet, when he reached the stables, he found that he was not the only one who thought a ride would be freeing. He found that Lady Guida's horse had just been saddled and was simply awaiting her rider, who would no doubt emerge from the castle momentarily.

Well, he would simply hope that Valeur could be saddled quickly. Then he could leave before she came out. He waited impatiently for the stable master to prepare Valeur, but was unable to depart before Guida's arrival. Hearing her footfalls on the loose gravel, he turned and saw her. Seeing her blush filled him with satisfaction. She appeared to not be entirely indifferent to his presence. The added color gave her a healthy glow that accentuated her dark eyes and the fullness of her perfect lips. No! He must think of other things.

"I see that I was not alone in thinking a ride would be enjoyable today." He tried to act as if her presence did not make every coherent thought leave his head.

Why was he so thrown off balance by her today? What had changed? He had been working with her for months and had never felt this unnerved before. He had even touched her before, although never with the same result as was had today. Perhaps it was due to his never touching her bare skin before. He had often taken her arm, but with the barrier of her sleeve between them. She had taken his arm in the past as well, but again there was the layer of fabric. Now that he had some perception of what actually touching her felt like, he was all too aware of the difference in their stations.

As a knight, he had no reason to even hope for an arrangement with her family to win her hand. She was so far above him that he may as well wish for a star for all the good it would do him. He looked back to her face and saw tales of amusement. Her mouth was turned up at the edges and her eyes squinted slightly, as if trying to puzzle out what he was thinking. He realized she must have responded to his earlier statement, and he had completely missed it.

"I am sorry, my lady. I was stuck in my thoughts." He felt like a bumbling idiot, but there was nothing to do about it now. Having already fled her company once this day, he was loath to do it again.

"I was merely inquiring where you had thought to ride. I did not wish to disturb you, so I thought to ride elsewhere." Her amused look fled, and she looked suddenly vulnerable. Was she worried about offending him by not wanting to ride out together? Was he offended? He had to admit that he was, a little.

"You are welcome to join me, my lady. I am going for the joy of riding, not in pursuit of any one particular location." Had he really just said that? She could join him? This ride was intended to put her out of his mind, not in the forefront of his focus. Yet, he could not allow her to venture out alone. That was his primary assignment after all.

The color rose in her cheeks yet again. If she kept doing that, he would be hard pressed not to stare at her for the whole of the afternoon.

"I would like that. Thank you, Sir William." By now, the stable master had William's horse readied. William moved to assist Guida onto Adrina's back before mounting Valeur. Grasping her waist, he lingered a moment before lifting her up. He would have rather held her in his arms, but he needed to banish such thoughts. Swinging her into the saddle, he forced himself to release her. Mounting Valeur, he led their horses through the gate and down the road away from Salerno.

William did not know where they were going, nor did he really care. He would attempt to make conversation with her, perhaps working on a few of her lessons. Just get through the ride and then retreat back to bed for the night. He knew that as things stood now, the fight for Guida's hand would be a slaughter, and he was not quite ready to give up his heart in that kind of combat.

Guida could not bring herself to focus on their direction. Neither of them seemed to have a preference, largely letting their horses pick their path. They had left the castle and turned north, away from the city.

William was the first to break the uneasy silence. "I am surprised that you were planning a ride today. I did not see a guard ready to accompany you. Did you plan on going alone?"

"You know that is not permitted. I would have found someone before leaving."

"You have not gotten any better with lying, my lady," he said, sounding slightly frustrated.

She groaned and her shoulders slumped. "What gave me away this time?" How could he see right through her every time? It was beyond aggravating.

"You glanced at me as if checking to see if I believed you."

She affected a haughty tone. "I find it rather poor conduct on your part to take notice each time."

Attempting to match her playfulness he responded, "Perhaps the lady ought not to make it so easy."

They both laughed, and the conversation continued in a much easier manner. Guida spoke of the forest and the love she had of it before, but it frightened her now. William shared stories of devilment that he and Drogo had gotten into as young boys. He spoke of the knight that he had trained under. She asked question after question of Normandy and his family there.

They raced their horses, laughing all the while. She attempted more falsehoods, but he caught them every time. It was perhaps the most enjoyable afternoon of her life, and Guida realized later that she had fallen a bit more for this handsome knight.

Chapter 23

Salerno – April 1038

S ir William, I wish for an update on my niece. How does she
fare?" William had been summoned by the prince several times
over the months since beginning his work with Lady Guida.
Each interview brought a little more of Guaimar's character into focus.
William's respect was growing for the man, affirming his natural
affinity. They shared a common purpose—helping Guida.

William released a breath of frustration. "Your Highness, in some
ways the lady appears to get better daily. Her confidence increases, yet it
is difficult to know if it is a lasting change, solely for my benefit, or
merely from increasing our familiarity with one other." William wanted
to be as honest as he could. He did not know how long the prince
would keep him at this assignment, but he wanted to do his best while
he could.

His opinion of Lady Guida continued to improve as he grew to know her, and he found that he truly wished to see her overcome her demons. She constantly showed a willingness to laugh at herself, or at him, and she was working hard. He respected her and her desire to not give up. She was determined to not be defined by one horrible experience, and William believed that they were making progress.

Prince Guaimar looked at him sharply. "Just how, uh, familiar are the two of you getting?"

Realizing exactly what worried the prince, William felt foolish for opening himself up to this line of questioning. "My lord, nothing has happened, or will happen between your niece and myself. We are merely becoming friends due to spending time together."

Guaimar released a heavy breath. "Good. You are a good man, William. I have no doubt of that. Yet you are a knight and not suitable for my niece. Do not let her beauty cloud your better judgment. You have a job to do. See that you do it. Is there anything else I ought to know?"

William chafed under the unnecessary reminder of his shortcomings. He was well aware of the distance between himself and the prince's niece. In fact, it was rare for that fact to be far from his conscious thoughts.

Bringing his mind back to the current situation, he added, "I am sure you have noticed, but Lady Guida appears to be losing weight. She has never been overly large since I have known her, yet I do not believe that she is eating enough now. Her clothes do not seem to fit as well as they used to, and her face is looking smaller than before."

Guaimar sighed. "I have noted this as well. I try to encourage her to eat, but she claims to have no appetite. I will send Berta to see her. Perhaps she can find some remedy that would help."

"There is one more thing." William hesitated, unsure how many concerns he should levy on this man. "I do not believe that Lady Guida is sleeping. She has not told me as much, but she does appear excessively tired. Her eyes often seem somehow out of focus when she is not actively engaged."

"Hmm. Your concern is noted. I will convey this to Berta and see what can be done. In everything else she is doing well?"

"Yes, my lord." William bowed his head slightly, out of habit.

"I am glad to hear it. I am grateful for your efforts with Guida. If Guy knew the full extent of what you were doing for his daughter, you would have his gratitude as well. I have not had much time of late to spend with her. I am consumed with reports of the raiding your fellow Normans are doing among my vassals near the borders of Pandulf's land. I have sent requests to Emperor Conrad and Emperor Michael for help. Emperor Conrad has responded. He is making his way here and will take matters into his own hands."

"Are you prepared to swear fealty to him, my lord?" William asked. "He will expect something in return when he arrives."

Guaimar slumped in his seat, something William had never witnessed before. Looking older than his years, Guaimar responded, "I suppose I am. I will not rise against Pandulf on my own. His forces rival my own in numbers, yet the Normans he employs are vicious fighters. I am not confident in our victory. It would be best to have the backing of the imperial forces. Pandulf would have no qualms going against me, but against the emperor? Let us hope not."

"When will Emperor Conrad arrive?"

"He is already on his way. I expect him by week's end."

This was news indeed. Would William be allowed to join in the effort to depose Pandulf? Or would he be tethered to the castle?

As if reading his thoughts, Guaimar answered, "I would like you to join the fight. Would you be able to draw away any of your countrymen? I am willing to offer a reward to those who wished to change sides."

"I do have friends who still work for Pandulf. It may be difficult for me to get through to them. Pandulf may not know me by name, but there were other knights who would know me, and know what I did to assist Lady Isolde. They will know that is the primary reason Pandulf has fallen out of favor with you. It would be dangerous."

"Dangerous, yes. Yet the lives that could be saved by limiting the actual fighting may be worth the risk. What say you?" Guaimar pressed for an answer.

After a slight pause, William said, "Yes, my lord."

Guaimar sighed in relief. "You are a good man, William. Now I can focus on easing the discontent near Sorrento, the area Guy now governs. And then there's the fighting in the south." Guaimar sighed again.

The prince ran his hand over his brow. Now that William was looking, he saw dark circles under the prince's eyes and a droopiness to his lids. The fighting must be worse than William had thought, to weigh on the prince this way.

"If I may ask, what are the reports from the south?"

"Civil war has broken out in Sicily. The Arab residents and the Roman rulers are not able to work together it seems, and they are fighting it out. I am not sure how long the Romans will be able to hold out, but it does not look promising for them."

"This is good news, is it not?" William asked. "If the Romans are busy fighting a rebellion in the south, then they are not causing problems on your lands."

"In that way, yes, it is good news. I am concerned that, once the Roman emperor realizes that they are on the losing side, he will approach me for reinforcements. The Romans are not known for backing down from a fight."

"I see." That meant William, Drogo and many of the Normans in Italy, would likely be shipped off to fight the Roman war. At least it would get William back to doing what he was trained to do. No more watching over Lady Guida. Was that not what he wanted?

If so, why did he feel as if a part of him would be missing?

He had never planned on staying in Salerno. But he realized that he no longer wished to leave. He wanted to remain close to Guida. Who would protect her with him gone? She had proven time and again incapable of taking care of herself. Realizing he cared for Lady Guida, he had to admit that he did not wish to leave her.

He shook his head to clear it. It was not certain that he would be leaving, after all. And he had his current mission to Capua to fill his mind.

Chapter 24

Guida nocked her bow, practicing just as William had instructed.

"Keep your eyes open," Guida reminded herself.

Taking another moment to settle her aim, she let the arrow fly. It struck the target in the left corner, near the edge.

Turning back, she grasped another arrow from the supply next to her. Nocking it, she attempted to focus.

Earlier, she had overheard Guaimar speaking to William, asking him to travel to Capua. She had initially been shocked that *her* knight would be asked to leave. Could not another man be given that responsibility? But she realized that it really must be William. No other man would have a chance of success in getting the Normans to switch sides. It was a wise tactic, but the thought made Guida incredibly angry. Her heart already ached for his absence. They had worked together so much over the past year that she had grown accustomed to his presence.

Was that really all it was? She was sad to have her teacher leave? No, she knew there was more to it than that. She would not miss any man more than she did William, not even her uncle. William was not merely her teacher. The friendship that had developed between them over the years meant the world to her, and she would understandably be upset to see him leave. He would be in danger, and she was afraid for him. What if something happened? What if he did not come back? Guida knew firsthand the danger that Pandulf posed to those she cared about.

Making a decision, she replaced the bow and arrow. Going to her chamber, she retrieved her bundle of knives. Guaimar had gifted her a set of her own well balanced knives for her last birthday. She had gotten quite good at it, and William had been right about it being a good emotional release. She could always take out her vexations on the trees.

Finding a knight willing to escort her to the clearing had been quite simple, and she was soon dismounting. Even before she began, thoughts of William crept back in. She tried to tell herself that he was a warrior. This is what he trained for. It was his primary purpose in life. She had seen him best the other knights many times. But what if he were captured? No. Surely he could handle Pandulf and his men, could he not? Alone? Absolutely not.

She raised her arm to throw, just as she had been taught, aimed at the tree and let the knife fly. It sank deep into the tree with a satisfying thunk, right where she had aimed it. Her next several throws flew just as true. She picked up her last knife. After this throw she would need to collect the knives from the tree. She was interrupted before aiming this last one.

"I believe you have finally mastered it." A deep voice sounded from behind her.

She slowly turned to face William. He was leaning against a tree watching her. "I thought you would be preparing to leave." She wanted to sound unaffected, but she failed miserably. She did not want him to go. What would she do without him? He was her protector, her security, and she was not ready to be on her own once more. Already she felt tossed about and lost.

"There will be plenty of time for that. I am seeing to a more important matter at the moment." He pushed off the tree and walked over to her.

She felt the blood rush to her face, and she felt a moment of satisfaction as she realized she must matter at least a little to him. If not, he would not have sought her out.

"What have you done with my guard? Disposed him most cruelly, no doubt." Keeping her tone light was her best option right now.

"He was usurping my position. He got only what was coming to him," William's smile was contagious.

"I would think you would be elated to have a break from me. After a year of hard labor you are due a small vacation." She smiled and tilted her head slightly to show that she was playing.

"My lady, do not imagine that what I have done with you was work," he said as he gazed intently into her eyes and took one of her hands in his. "I have enjoyed every moment of it." His voice had grown deeper and took on a slightly husky tone.

Her voice came out barely more than a whisper, and all hint of laughter was lost. "Really?" Her heart was pounding so hard she was sure he must be able to hear it. He stepped slightly closer, almost as if he couldn't help himself. Raising his other hand he cupped her cheek, rubbing her chin with his thumb. She couldn't breathe. What was he doing? They had never been this intimate before. She had not wanted to be this close to anyone in so long, but now she was afraid that he would realize what he was doing and step back.

"Tell me what you feel," his breath grazed her face as he spoke.

Having a coherent thought right now seemed impossible. She closed her eyes to try to clear her mind and come up with an honest answer. Her eyes popped back open as she realized what this feeling was. She looked directly into his eyes. "I feel safe." She saw the surprise on his face and then a slow smile, as he lowered his head to hers. His lips skimmed over her eyebrow, then down her cheek.

He pulled back to look in her eyes, seemingly asking permission without saying a word. She raised her head slightly and closed the gap between them. His kiss was gentle, as they both were hesitant. Her hands worked their way up his chest and then her fingers were curling in his hair. His hand slid from her cheek around the back of her neck as he slowly deepened the kiss. His tongue fluttered over her lips and then gently parted them as he tasted every inch of her mouth.

Her body shuddered with an unfamiliar emotion. This was so different from her previous experience that she could not believe they were even remotely related. How could a kiss from one man be heaven sent, when a kiss from another was hell? She brought her mind back to the present. Now that she knew how it felt to be close to William, she never wanted to be anywhere else.

William's head swam in unfamiliar waters. Perfection was not an idea he often held with, yet this moment was as near as he could imagine coming.

I must stop this. The thought came unbidden to his mind. This was not what he had in mind when he followed Guida to the clearing. He was simply going to bid her farewell in case he did not have another chance before the day was through. He knew her well enough to know that she would feel abandoned, and he wished to reassure her. That was all.

Breaking off the kiss, he could not bring himself to fully release her. He looked questioningly into her eyes, trying to see in them some form of encouragement. He knew he had no right to kiss her, yet he could not regret it. He would not leave her without her knowing how he felt about her. A line had been crossed, and there was no going back now.

"How did you do that?" She looked at him with bewilderment.

He could not help but laugh. He was so relieved that she was not terrified, and she had not pushed him away. She could have said almost anything and he would have laughed. "Which part? Shall I demonstrate again?" He tilted his head, ready to comply.

"No!" Tensing up, she pushed against his chest. He instinctively let go and she backed away several steps. The moment was lost, and he struggled to keep up with what was happening. There was no playful glint in her eyes. He honestly could not name what he saw in their depths. It was something that he had never seen in them before.

"How can you make me feel so safe and secure, all while knowing you are leaving? How foolish I must be. To let you kiss me like that and in nearly the same breath have to say goodbye! And what do you mean by kissing me in that way?" Now he recognized her anger, but it was still mixed with something new, something he desperately wished to understand.

"Did you think that because you are finally leaving you could do whatever you want? Do I mean so little to you that you are willing to take what you can and then never think of it again? I thought we were friends! I thought you might actually care about me. I thought…"

"Guida, look at me." It was a gentle command. "How can you say such things? Have I ever treated you with anything short of respect? Perhaps you are right, I am selfish. I selfishly wanted you to know how I felt about you. I wanted to make sure that you would think of me while I was gone, to know if you cared for me as much as I care for you.

"I ought to have done this ages ago, but I have been a coward, not wanting the time with you to end. I wanted to keep going the way we were for as long as possible. I knew that if your uncle ever heard of my doing anything like this with you, he would remove you from my presence. He might even have had me killed. He still might.

"But now I am leaving, not of my own choice, but by command. I want to be here to continue to protect you, but I have no control of this matter. I cannot refuse your uncle, and you know it! I am a warrior! It was never the plan to stay here taking care of you, but I would never trade this time with you, for I have treasured it!" His voice had risen in volume and intensity as he continued, but now he softened as he took another step toward her. "Guida, I love you. I have loved you for so long. Am I a fool? Do you not care for me?"

"You, you love me?" she whispered.

"More than anything!" he replied emphatically. Taking her face in both of his hands, he said, "Please, tell me you love me, too."

She took his wrists in her hands, and echoed his words. "More than anything."

Not able to stop himself, he kissed her again, this time less gently, putting everything he had into this kiss. He had never felt more at home or more at peace than at this moment. But it could not last.

When they finally broke apart, it was Guida who voiced his thoughts. "What are we to do now? You know that we cannot be together. My parents would never consent to my marrying a landless knight, and you cannot find your fortune tethered to me."

"I do not know," he sighed. "The Romans are always searching for soldiers. Perhaps I should go fight for them until I have earned enough to marry you."

"No!" she nearly shouted. "That is too dangerous! What if you were to be killed? I could not bear it."

"There is always danger, *ma cherie*. I have never shied away from it before. And you will no doubt marry. Your uncle cannot forestall the inevitable forever. I cannot stay here and watch as you are married off to someone else. I could not bear it. I think I must go."

"Wait, do not make a rash decision. Do as Guaimar asks. Go to Capua. Be careful. Think through our situation. Perhaps a solution will present itself while you are gone. But promise you will come back to me."

"For you, *mon tresor*, I will do anything."

Her heart fluttered at being called his treasure.

Chapter 25

Capua – May 1038

Gaining access to Pandulf's fortress had been easier than William had counted on. With a stroke of luck, he had found his old friend, Sir Aimery, guarding the front gate.

Grabbing William's arm, he forcibly moved him to the edge of the wall.

"What are you doing here?" Aimery hissed. "We are under orders to apprehend you on sight. They are old orders, but Pandulf has a long memory. The situation with Lady Isolde has caused Pandulf no end of troubles with Prince Guaimar."

"His troubles are far from over," William informed his friend. "I come with news. You have no doubt heard that Emperor Conrad is currently en route to deal with the duke himself."

"I have heard the rumors. But, why have you come back? You cannot be here simply to warn me," Aimery discerned.

"No," William confirmed. Pulling Aimery deeper into the shadows, he explained. "Prince Guaimar is concerned with the unnecessary deaths that this conflict will produce. He is offering to compensate any man who is willing to switch sides."

Aimery snorted, "Lucky for Guaimar, we have little loyalty to Pandulf. He is a formidable taskmaster, and does nothing to inspire his men. It will not be difficult to convince the others to join Guaimar. Leave it to me."

Later that night, Aimery smuggled William into the barracks that housed a majority of the Norman contingent in Capua, including William's friends Hugh and Peter, who had traveled with him across France into Italy. William was able to lay Prince Guaimar's offer before them and a discussion rose up on whether to accept. It was not a difficult campaign. Aimery had been correct in his assessment of the men.

"I must return to Salerno," William stated. "The details of your defection I leave to you and your men. I may not be able to send word when I will return with the emperor's forces, so you must be vigilant, do not let down your guard."

"We will be ready," Aimery assured him. They clasped arms, and William departed.

The castle was in a perpetual state of chaos. Everywhere one looked servants could be found scurrying from one end of the grounds to another, each looking more frantic than the last. Shouting was more frequent as everyone tried to accommodate their visitors. Emperor Conrad had arrived with his host of five hundred men. They had ridden hard, with no women to slow them down. Wenches travelled to the kitchens and back laden with trays of various vittles. Others carried clothing and bedding for the additional knights.

The emperor had made no secret of his wish to handle the needs of the area quickly and return to Germany. Over the past four years, both of the emperor's daughters had perished from illness, leaving him one lone son. He was understandably loathe to be parted from his wife and son, after experiencing such heartbreaking losses.

William met with Emperor Conrad and Prince Guaimar immediately upon his return to Salerno. Sir Enzo had been summoned as well.

"What news of the Normans, Sir William?" Prince Guaimar instantly jumped to the matter at hand.

"They have accepted your proposal, my lord. They stand at the ready, and will accept your command."

"Good. This ought to be a fairly simple matter, with Pandulf lacking his usual forces. Sir Enzo," the prince turned to the other knight. "I trust you have our men prepared as well?"

"Yes, my lord. Besides the emperor's five hundred, we have an additional two hundred at the ready. They will march to Capua on your orders."

The emperor chuckled. "This ought to be a great diversion. We shall leave at dawn."

William's heart sped up as they approached Capua the following afternoon. Other than his brief visit to persuade the Normans, he had not returned to Capua during the two years since he had joined up with Prince Guaimar. He knew that he would not be welcomed back. The company had made good time, considering how large it was. Marching seven hundred men through the wilds of Italy was no small feat.

No one knew what to expect in Capua. William was hopeful that Pandulf would not put up a fight, but there was no way of knowing until they arrived. He hoped that Aimery and his men had been able to keep their upcoming mutiny from the ears of the duke. If not, the fighting might be underway when the emperor arrived.

William was near the middle of the soldiers with Drogo and Sir Enzo nearby. They were followed by the emperor and the prince, who were surrounded by the rest of the men in an attempt to ensure the emperor's safety. William guided Valeur until he rode next to the prince.

A scout came riding to report to the emperor. "Over the next hill a small armed force awaits, your highness. Among them are a woman and small boy. They appear to merely be waiting for us."

Emperor Conrad scoffed, "The coward sends a woman to meet us? Guaimar, go, and see what is the meaning of this."

"Yes, my liege," Prince Guaimar acquiesced. "Enzo! William! With me."

As they crested a hill, they were confronted by the small armed force on horseback.

"Bloody bastard," Guaimar cursed. "The coward has sent his wife and son to meet us."

William experienced the heat of outrage flaming in his gut. How any man could utilize his own wife and child this way was beyond understanding. But it was another aspect of the opposing company that struck William. It consisted of his Norman brothers. As he watched, Sir Aimery and Sir Hugh left the safety of the group and approached the emperor's force.

"Your Highness." Sir Aimery addressed Prince Guaimar. "*My lord* Pandulf, Duke of Capua, knows of the crimes you have levied against him. He has offered up his wife and son as the emperor's prisoners. He hopes this measure will assuage the emperor, and insists that no further action be taken today."

Guaimar's face grew stormy. "Where is Lord Pandulf? Why is he not here pleading his own case before Emperor Conrad?"

To Aimery's credit, he did not cower before Guaimar. "He is not here, my lord."

Guaimar huffed with annoyance. "I can see that for myself," he said darkly. "I asked, where is he?"

William was grateful not to be on the other end of the prince's ire. This was a side of Guaimar unseen before today, and even William felt cowed by him.

Hugh answered, "I believe he is on his way to Constantinople, my lord. To the court of Emperor Michael. We, his Norman knights, have risen up against him, and he has been forced to flee."

"Enzo, William, bring me Lady Maria and her son," the prince demanded.

They answered in unison, "Yes, my lord."

William left Aimery and Hugh to negotiate with Guaimar, hoping that an arrangement would be reached and the Normans would swear fealty to the prince. Knowing Guaimar to be a fair and thoughtful man, it would allow his countrymen some security in this war driven country.

Chapter 26

Salerno – June 1038

There was a grand feast underway in the great hall. The servants in the kitchen had prepared the best of everything in order to impress Emperor Conrad and his host of men, a celebration for the peaceful resolution to the conflict with Capua. The great hall was more crowded than Guida had ever seen it. She knew the emperor never traveled in a small company, but actually seeing his party was an inspiring sight.

"My dear Lady Guida, what on earth do you do to keep yourself occupied here?" the emperor asked.

Guida felt nervous speaking with such a powerful man, but could not stay silent without giving offense.

"She runs quite wild, my liege," Aunt Gemma answered for her, and suddenly Guida wished she had been quicker to speak. She did not want her awful aunt to paint an unfavorable picture of her.

"I often ride out with Uncle Guaimar, your grace." Guida remembered to bow her head slightly as she addressed him. "I used to explore the woods quite often, but have not had much heart for that of late."

"That is a shame. I, myself, enjoy the woods. I do not have much opportunity to enjoy nature."

"I imagine you find yourself handling more important matters."

"Yes, the ruling of a kingdom does not allow one much leisure time," he agreed. "Now, tell me, why are you not married? I hope you will forgive me for speaking plainly. You are a lovely young woman. Your father ought to have arranged a marriage contract for you long before now."

As the ruler of the kingdom, he could speak to her in any way he saw fit, and she must answer. Choosing her words carefully, she responded, "My father has been quite preoccupied with the ruling of Sorrento, your grace. However, I believe he is working towards that very goal with a man who is currently out of the country."

"Now, Guida, you know that is not the reason," Aunt Gemma responded. Then speaking to Emperor Conrad, she added, as if letting him in on a secret, "She is not yet as refined as she ought to be, your highness. We are still working through some fundamental character flaws. It would not be right to inflict an innocent man with her quite yet." The words were spoken so sweetly, making it sound as if Gemma actually cared about the issue. The sweetness of her tone did not conceal the insults, however. Not wishing to argue with Gemma in front of the emperor, Guida clutched her hands together and looked down at them. She longed for the moment when she could politely excuse herself.

The emperor did not need to hide his feelings about what had been said. "Princess Gemma, are you questioning my assessment of this young lady?" he asked, his voice taking on a hardness Guida had not heard from him as yet. "I have stated that she is a lovely young woman. I will not tolerate another opinion on the subject." Conrad turned to the prince, and bellowed, "Guaimar!"

Guaimar, who had been conversing with Gaitelgrima and not following this conversation, turned to the emperor. "Yes, Your Highness?"

"You must see to getting Lady Guida married."

If Guida could have had the option, she would have gladly taken imprisonment over hearing herself discussed so openly among most of her closest acquaintances.

Taking the command in stride, Guaimar answered, "Yes, your highness."

"We do not want you to get so old that no one wants you, now do we?" Emperor Conrad said, turning back to Guida.

"No, your grace. Thank you," she answered, her mortification complete. She lost interest in the conversation and focused on the salt bowl in front of her.

Guida thought of the way she had seen some auctions held in Salerno and pictured herself as an item for sale. She lost her appetite—which was never very large—yet forced herself to keep eating just enough that no one would notice. She wished to avoid bringing additional attention to herself.

Searching the crowd, her eyes landed on William, as they often did. He was sitting with Sir Aimery, and she wondered briefly why he wasn't with his brother. For being family, she did not see the two of them together often. She found Drogo a few tables over from William, laughing raucously with some of the other knights. That group of men made Guida's skin crawl. She hated when she saw any of them around the castle. They were partly the reason Guida insisted on Alys accompanying her everywhere she went. The lusty look in their eyes mirrored her attacker's, and she hated that reminder.

Turning back to William, she found him looking back at her. Heat coursed through her as it did every time he had looked at her since his return. She could not read his expression, which added to her confusion. Having thought of him nonstop while he was away, she often relived those blissful moments they had shared just before he left for Capua. How she had longed for his return. He had been gone but two days, yet it had felt like an eternity.

And now he was back, and she could not bring herself to seek him out. What was the matter with her? She knew she loved him. So why was she petrified to speak with him again? What if he regretted kissing her? What if he forgot all about her once she was no longer the focus of his attentions? He was no longer tasked with her protection, after all. She could not bear the thought. So she avoided him. Stayed away.

Yet now they were in the same room. Thankfully they were seated at different tables, too far apart to even hear each other speak. But they could easily see each other. Guida's attention was never far from him. She saw him looking at her, and when she looked away, she could feel his eyes on her still.

She looked down at her trencher, still full of food. The sight brought the now familiar internal distress. Was it too early to excuse herself? She looked down her table and saw Guaimar was focused on her as well. Feeling all the blood leave her head, she was suddenly chilled to the bone. Had he seen her staring at William? Did he know what had happened between them? Would he guess? And if he did, what would he do about it? Would he send William away? So many questions, but none that she could answer. She needed to be alone. Quickly making her excuses to Emperor Conrad and her uncle, she fled the great hall.

Chapter 27

Salerno – June 1038

"W"alk with me, Sir William," Guaimar commanded amidst the dull thumps of batons. Since the arrival of Emperor Conrad, Guaimar rarely sat down to conduct his business. He seemed to always be on the move attending to one matter or another, deferring his seat in the great hall to the emperor.

"Yes, my lord," William answered. Giving command over the practicing soldiers to Drogo, William turned and followed his prince away from the practice fields.

Prince Guaimar had left most of his knights in Capua to ensure the peace with Sir Enzo in charge. Emperor Conrad had bestowed Capua and all of Pandulf's lands onto Guaimar, vastly increasing the prince's holdings. This also left Guaimar leading the largest contingent of Normans in Italy aside from those with Count Drengot in Aversa. Now, with Sir Enzo gone, the prince had raised William to head of the guard.

This took precedence over his duty to Lady Guida. Another knight had been temporarily assigned to ensure her protection. Her needs had decreased, and she no longer was a top worry to her uncle. For the time being, the emperor held the place of highest concern.

"I have met with the emperor many times over the past few days," Guaimar began. "Now that the business with Pandulf has been dealt with, there is another matter the emperor would like to handle while in this region. Count Rainulf Drengot. The emperor is assessing whether to view him as a threat or an ally. Now, I have my own opinion on this matter, but I would like to hear yours."

They were crossing the courtyard on a path back to the castle. The two men skirted around carts and animals, their owners within the castle walls for some business or other. William followed the prince's lead inside the castle.

"You know I have had naught to do with Drengot since I have been here with you. I have been in your service for a few years now and have not met with him during that time. However, I knew him some before he left Normandy. He is held in high esteem by his countrymen. He raised a force of 250 warriors before arriving in this area, and more flock to his side every day. I have paid close attention to any bit of news that I have come across concerning him. He is the undisputed leader of the Normans here, and that is not a position to be taken lightly.

"A rise to power like his, which he was not born to, comes with the loyalty of many other men. He is greatly respected and is considered one of the best of men, not just here, but back in Normandy as well. Many men have left their homes and families to join him. He is highly intelligent, well-educated, as well as willing to do whatever he sees as best for his countrymen. I am sure you know that he gained the title of

Count and the lands of Aversa from the Duke of Naples about six years ago; although, I believe it has yet to be ratified by the emperor.

"He has been a friend to the Lombards and has largely been fighting against the Roman Empire. He has had several run-ins with Pandulf and his men, though. It is hardly surprising given what manner of man Pandulf has proven to be."

Prince Guaimar was silent as he listened intently to every word William spoke. William now noticed they had made their way to the solar, where he knew Guida was likely to be. Would he see her there? They had not spoken much since his return, and he feared she might be avoiding him. He had behaved rashly before leaving for Capua. Perhaps she was regretting what had transpired between them. Though to know for sure would require actually speaking with her.

Stopping just outside the door, Guaimar turned and looked at William directly, bringing William's attention instantly back to their discussion.

"It is the matter of Drengot's title I wished to speak to you about. Emperor Conrad would like this dealt with while he is here and has asked my opinion on the matter. Whether he should ratify Drengot's title or strip it from him. Given what you know of him, what would your council be?"

"My lord, I believe that Drengot is a good and honorable man. I also believe that, given provocation, he would be a dangerous enemy. For the time being he is focusing his attention on the Romans and largely leaving the Lombards alone. The Romans are not your allies, so is it not good for them to be fighting someone else and not focusing on your people and lands? I would advise you to keep Drengot your friend by having the emperor ratify his title. Do not give Drengot reason to turn his attention from your enemy onto you. Let him fight your foe and secure those lands as an ally to you."

"Your argument mirrors what I have been pondering. I am pleased to hear that you have similar opinions to my own. I shall have the emperor confer Aversa on Drengot, on the condition that Drengot swears fealty to me. It shall raise his status while ensuring my own position. And it will take the care of that region off my hands. Thank you for your candor. You may go."

"My liege." William bowed and was about to depart as the prince opened the door to the solar. Standing just inside was Guida, looking very surprised to see William with her uncle. Her eyes grew large, and her cheeks quickly reddened.

Her reaction was not missed by Guaimar who looked curiously between the two. William smiled and bowed to Guida, wishing they were alone. He longed to take her in his arms once more. Instead, he said a quick, "My lady," turned, and left.

The next morning, William was summoned to the great hall to meet with Prince Guaimar and Emperor Conrad. His hands were sweating as he entered the room. The emperor sat in Guaimar's usual chair on the dais and another chair had been brought in for Guaimar.

William bowed low as the guard announced him.

"Ah, Sir William," the emperor addressed him. "I understand the prince has informed you about the matter with Drengot?"

"Yes, your highness."

"Very good. Now, I have taken into account the information you shared with Prince Guaimar and have decided my course of action. I will be leaving for Aversa on the morrow to meet with Drengot and to ratify his title as Count.

"There is another matter we would like to discuss with you." At this, the emperor glanced at Guaimar.

"I have received word from Emperor Michael of the Romans," Guaimar took over. "He is attempting to regain control of his portions of Sicily that have been taken over by the Arabs and has requested some men to aid him."

Guaimar shifted in his seat. "Pandulf has removed himself to the heart of the Roman Empire, Constantinople. It is my belief that if we heed this request for aid, we may be able to persuade the emperor to turn Pandulf over to us. We do not want him to gain enough influence in Constantinople to be able to return and regain his lands by force. I have decided to send a contingent of five hundred men. I would like you and the rest of the Normans now in my employ to be among them."

"Your highness," William bowed his head slightly, "I will gladly serve you by going. My one concern, if I may be so bold, is that I do not speak their language. It will be difficult to coordinate battle strategies."

The prince was quick to answer, "I am also sending a man named Ardouin, who will serve as an interpreter for you as needed. Bear in mind that he is a mercenary and, given the opportunity, he will likely betray you. Keep a close eye on him, and do not give him the chance. I am only sending him with you as he speaks Greek, as the Romans do, and that is not common in this part of the country."

"I know my men have been getting restless lately and will be happy to be of use." William, however, was not happy to be leaving. "When should I have them ready?" What would he tell Guida? She had been so unhappy when he suggested doing just this. And now he would have to make it a reality. He worried over her reaction.

Emperor Conrad looked hard at William. "We have heard tales of what your men do to stave off boredom. I confess, I do not condone their actions. It will please me to know that they are ably employed once again and the raiding of the villages will cease."

Prince Guaimar knew William did not participate in raiding villages. The knights in Capua were responsible for the raidings the emperor was referring to. He was quick to intercede on William's behalf.

"You have a few days to get everything readied. I would like the men to leave at the end of the week. Thank you for your assistance."

"Yes, my liege." William bowed and began backing out, but was halted by Guaimar who left the dais and approached him.

"I have one more favor to ask of you, William." Guaimar spoke quietly, and the emperor paid them no heed. He was already speaking with his other advisors. William and Guaimar walked together toward the door.

"Yes, my lord?" William asked.

"You know of Lady Maria and her son. I currently have them safely guarded in their guest chambers. I wish there were a way that they could be returned to their home." Guaimar looked side to side, then put his arm on William's shoulder and pulled him out the door into the corridor before continuing. "The emperor has forbidden their return, yet if they were to escape, we would be unlikely to pursue."

William tensed as he realized what the prince was suggesting. "Would it not be wise to wait until after the emperor departs?"

"My mind cannot rest knowing that I have imprisoned a woman and child. It is not right to make Lady Maria pay for the sins of her husband. My quarrel is with Pandulf, not his family."

"Are you wishing me to arrange this, or to personally see to their safety?" Having just been ordered to assist the Greeks, William's time was limited.

"I need you to go with your countrymen to fight for Emperor Michael. You know my men better than I. Find someone trustworthy and capable of protecting them. I do not trust all of the emperor's men, and do not wish anything to befall the lady while in my castle. Do it soon."

"Yes, my lord."

Relief flooded Guaimar's face at these words.

"You are a good man, William. I have truly been blessed with your allegiance."

William walked away as thoughts of how Guida would respond to this news swam through his mind. The ache in his heart threatened to consume him, the sense of loss palpable. *What else can I do?* he wondered. Duke Guy was determined to have Giovan marry Guida, and William could not stomach the thought. How could he stay here and watch? He could not.

He went to the guardhouse. He had another situation to sort out before leaving. He was determined to task Gregory with returning Lady Maria back to Capua. There were precious few men that William trusted with such a task. Gregory was technically still in training, but would not be for much longer. He had proven himself time and time again to be trustworthy, as well as capable. He would prove to be a fine knight indeed.

Chapter 28

L ooking down the shaft of her arrow, Guida aimed for the target at the end of the field. Archery had been William's second lesson. He felt she needed a hobby that would calm and settle her nerves. The focus necessary left no room for troubling thoughts. Well, she was certainly troubled now.

Learning William was leaving, Guida felt like her heart was being ripped out. She had always known there was no future for her with William. The daughter of a duke would never be allowed to marry a knight. Even so, she could not help herself. She had grown so comfortable with him, which was not normal for her as she was rarely at ease with other people. Seclusion brought her some peace, but not when she had to worry about unpredictable people nearby.

She let the arrow fly and it landed at the bottom of the middle ring.

"You have certainly improved since we began." William's deep voice shattered the silence.

Guida started, although she was not surprised that he had sought her out.

"It is no doubt due to our hours spent out here. A merciless tutor you were." She ought to have smiled, but could not force one.

"I take it you have heard." He took a step closer. She forced herself not to step back. Lesson three: do not retreat. That had been one of the harder lessons for her.

"Yes, I have heard. You are to leave, in search of the glory of battle. You will go and kill your fair share of men, and you will never return." She turned her back on him to hide the anger and sadness in her eyes. She picked up another arrow and nocked it on her bow.

"I am sorry to be at the end of your lessons. You have made so much progress, and I am proud of you." His voice was husky, and she wondered if he really was sorry to be leaving.

She aimed the arrow, trying to focus her mind. As if to prove him wrong, her thoughts ran wild, as did her shot. *What is he doing? Does he really care about my* progress? *He said he loved me, but does he truly? Why should I care? He will leave and never think on me again.*

William laid his hands on her shoulders from behind. "You are not clearing your mind," he whispered in her ear. "I can see the tension in you."

Lowering the weapon, she stepped out of his touch and turned to face him. "Why must you leave? I thought you cared for me. For us. I mean, for my uncle," she stammered. "For Salerno. Has not this become your home? Does that mean nothing to you? No, of course not. You left your home with your true family, and for what? Are you any better off here than you were there? Will you be any better off in Sicily than here?" *Do not cry. Do not cry.* She took a steadying breath.

"This is why I came here, Guida," he explained, taking a deep breath for patience. "I am a man for hire. I am not a man with a fortune who can choose his fate. For now, I must do this. I work for your uncle, and he is sending me. It does not matter what I want or who I care for. The result is the same. I must go."

"Then go. Do not let me keep you." The words were so full of sorrow.

"What would you have me do, Guida? I can do nothing more for you while I am merely a knight in your uncle's household. In order to have any sort of future at all I must go."

"What would I have you do? I would have you here with me! I would have you never leave. Let us spend our days together just as we have been. I thought we would have more time."

"You must know that we cannot stay this way. I cannot spend the rest of my life watching over you, playing the nursemaid. It is time for me to get back to my own life."

His words felt like a slap in the face. "I did not realize that was all it was to you. I would hate to take you away from your lofty ambitions of killing and stealing lands that belong to others." She could not keep the spite from her voice, nor did she try.

"You know that is not what I am doing! Those men do not deserve to be in power and they will continue to abuse that power for as long as they have it! I could never live with myself if I did not try to place that power into the hands of more worthy men."

"You mean into your own hands."

"Is it so wrong to want to have the power to help others? I can do nothing in my current position. I cannot even be with the woman I love. I will not remain this powerless! Why are you being so petty and selfish? I thought you would see the good that can come out of this."

"Petty and selfish?" She would not allow him to turn his back on her. "Is it selfish of me to want you here where you are safe? Where no one is trying to kill you? I suppose I am selfish, then."

"You expect me to sit by and watch as you get married? The emperor was quite explicit in that regard. Prince Guaimar and your father will not put him off forever. I can do nothing about that, but I will *not* sit by and watch. I have already altered my plans for you. I have stayed here for much too long, when I ought to have left long ago and searched for some way to advance my position. Instead, I stayed so I could be close to you. What a fool I have been!"

"I think it is past time for me to leave, *sir*," she bit out.

He caught her arm as she turned to leave. Taking a deep breath William took the bow from her and laid it down. He then took both her hands in his. "I do not wish to leave like this. I do not want my memories of you to be tainted by an argument."

She snatched her hands back. "It does not seem to matter what we want." She felt the tears threatening to fall, but she refused to let them. She turned and walked back to the castle. William did not follow. For the first time, she was able to lie and have him believe her.

Chapter 29

Salerno – April 1039

I s there nothing you can do?" Guida pleaded. "You are the only one father might listen to. Please, you must speak with him again."

"Guida, I have spoken with him." Guaimar glanced up at the priest, hoping he was not disturbing the sermon. "He will not be persuaded. Giovan will arrive today, as will your family. I am afraid it is too late to stop this."

Feeling the room closing in around her, Guida clenched her teeth to stop herself from screaming.

Guaimar looked at her and his eyes softened with pity. "I truly am sorry, my dear. I have done all I can."

The priest continued his discourse, but Guida did not hear a word. She knelt in silence, awaiting her doom. If her father had his way, she would be back here within the week, sealed for life to Giovan, a man she could hardly look at without cringing. William had not returned to rescue her from this fate. She was unable to grasp control of her own circumstances. The hopelessness closed in, threatening to consume her. Her prayers had gone unanswered. The God she had been taught to worship remained silent and unaiding.

The priest finished his sermon and the congregation filed out of the chapel. Guida remained, as she often did. She liked the solitude and solace that could be found in the empty chamber. She was blessed to have a chamber in her home that was dedicated to God. Not many people could claim that privilege. Yet she could, and she would not waste that blessing.

Why will you not help me? she prayed. *How can I find happiness married to such a man? He is not William.*

"*Patience.*" The word was spoken so clearly, Guida whipped her head around, searching for the source. The chamber was empty, save herself.

"Patience for what?" she asked aloud.

There was no further response.

With her thoughts running wild, she attempted to center herself once again in prayer.

Dear God, please keep him safe. Bring him back to me. Please, let him not be too late. She only allowed herself to voice those three thoughts, yet her heart could not be stopped from reaching for her God.

Making the sign of the cross, Guida left the chapel, making her way to the solar to join the rest of the family. As she neared the door, she recognized voices she would know anywhere. Her parents! Taking a fortifying breath, she entered the room to greet her family.

"Guida!" Maria rushed to throw her arms around her sister. "Oh, how I have missed you, dearest!"

"And I, you," Guida responded, stepping back to assess her sister. "You are growing into a lovely young woman."

Their mother, Lady Raingarda, took Maria's place, embracing Guida. "And you are still lovely yourself." Despite the words and their implications, Guida was happy to be reunited with her mother. It had been some time since they had visited with one another.

"Guida," her father's voice was harsh, and Guida was at a loss as to what offense she had already committed. "I would speak with you, immediately, alone."

"Y-yes, Father," Guida stammered.

She followed this man she used to adore down the corridor. They had lived apart for so many years; he was nearly a stranger to her now. He had become the man working to sell her off. He was a good man, she was still sure of that. Yet, she felt no closeness, regardless of affection, with him.

They entered a room Guida had seldom visited. Guaimar often used it when conferring with his advisors. There was a large table in the center with parchments strewn across it. A fire had been stoked and added a pleasant warmth to the spring day.

"Guida," her father began. "I am well aware of your feelings concerning the marriage contract with Giovan. I would like your assurance, however, that you will do nothing to impede the situation. As your father, it is my right to have you marry whom I please, and I will not tolerate any interference from you."

Taking a deep breath, Guida said, "Father. You know how much I love and respect you. I cannot, however, bow down to you on this matter. This decision of yours directly affects me and will for the rest of my life. I will not pretend to be at peace with it."

"Guida, if I have to lock you in the tower until the ceremony, I will. You do not understand the dangers awaiting an unwed woman. You need a husband. Giovan may not be perfect, but no man is. He will do just as well as any stranger."

Guida sank into one of the chairs. If she could, she would have sunk straight through the floor.

"My dear," her father's voice softened, "I do this for your own good. You must accept Giovan and appreciate the comfort and safety he will provide."'

Guida attempted to calm her racing heart. This would be her one chance to convince her father of the folly of this decision.

"Father," she said calmly. "You do not know Giovan as I do. He is a schemer, with no honor. He uses any woman he can to satisfy his own lusts. I could never be happy with such a match."

Her father's anger flared again. "You do not need to be happy. You need to be safe. I am confident that you will be happy again, in time. That is enough for me."

"But it is not enough for me, Father. Please, I beg you. Do not do this."

"That is enough! I will sign the contract, then leave the remaining arrangements to your mother. You will be Giovan's wife, and I will hear no more about it." He turned and left Guida alone.

Giovan's wife! Never! She could not allow that to happen. She knew with Giovan she could never be happy. But how could she stop her father? He had absolute control over her life now, and soon that control would be handed off to Giovan. She shuddered at the thought.

Chapter 30

Syracuse, Sicily – August 1039

U nable to sleep, William rose just before dawn. Making as little noise as possible, so as not to wake those around him, he lowered himself to his knees. It was a habit of his to pray before battle, and this morning would be no different. As was usual, his prayer included Guida, who constantly invaded his thoughts, as well as a plea for his own safety.

His prayer finished, he quickly dressed, then left the tent. Scanning across the predawn haze of the camp, he was unsurprised to find General Maniakes, the giant Mongol he served under. The General cast a dark shadow over the camp in the setting moonlight.

William recalled the first time he had laid eyes on the general. Rumor was that he was ten feet tall and as big as a bear. Upon seeing Maniakes himself, William could safely refute those tales as untrue. The reality was worse than the rumors. Maniakes was massive. By far the largest man William had ever seen.

The fate of these opposing armies would be decided today. The Emir had sent word to General Maniakes challenging him to single combat as a way to minimize deaths on both sides. Maniakes had agreed, informing William that he would be their champion.

"No rest for the hero, eh?" Drogo drawled from behind him.

"I am no hero," William scoffed.

"I was referring to myself," Drogo said with a laugh before he sobered. Grasping William by the shoulder, he added, "All will be well, William. Maniakes would not have chosen you as champion if he did not have confidence in your abilities."

William snorted. "Maniakes wins either way. Either I win, and he gets the glory of victory, or I lose, and he gets the satisfaction of being rid of me."

Maniakes had no love for the Normans under his command, and especially none for William, seeing him as a threat to his own power.

"Hmm." Drogo pretended to think it through. "That is a good strategy."

William swatted at him, but he ducked away.

"You better be fiercer than that when you ride out against the Emir."

"Do not worry, brother. I will not give Maniakes the satisfaction of my death." Focusing on the task ahead, he added, "I will be ready."

William sat upon Valeur, garbed in full battle armor, waiting for the signal for the duel to begin. Beneath his coned helmet sweat soaked his head, and rivulets ran down the length of his back. The sun was now full overhead and beat down upon the world, its intensity amplified by the metal armor.

Valeur nickered, eager to be set free. They were at one end of the no man's land between the two armies. At the other end, William could just make out his opponent, the Emir of the city. The military leader had oddly chosen himself to be the Arab's champion. Normally William would welcome the opportunity to be champion, but he had seen the Emir during the negotiations. Maniakes was a mountain of a man, but the Emir was not much less.

Pushing that aside, William chose instead to concentrate on the multitude of lives that would be spared as a result of this fight. Two lives risked with one that would ultimately be taken. Otherwise hundreds of men on both sides of the conflict would be slaughtered. That was not a risk worth taking if William had a chance to end it now. The image of Guida suddenly grabbed his attention, but he quickly pushed it aside, not willing to think on it.

Both armies took up a cry. The Romans and Normans chanting William's name and the Arab's chanting the Emir's. William let their cries soak into him, granting him the courage he needed. Saying a quick prayer, he set his eyes back on the Emir. A fly teased his face and he wished briefly for a free hand to swipe at it. Instead he clutched his kite shield in one hand, and a spear in the other.

He took a deep breath of the dusty air just as the flag lowered, signaling the start of the duel. Thundering hooves and clanging metal pushed the army's cries from his ears as he let Valeur go, barreling forward.

Lowering the spear, he aimed as best he could at the Emir's chest. The two warriors approached each other at an ungodly speed. At the last moment, the Emir lowered his spear below William's body. The crash of wooden spear shafts breaking mingled with the sound of a horse screaming its death cry.

Dropping his shield, William was thrown to the ground as Valeur crashed in a heap, the Emir's weapon lodged in the animal's breast. Blood spurted from the wound, clashing with the starkness of the landscape, distracting William for only a moment. Now, filled with rage, he turned to find the Emir had rounded his mount and was rushing back towards him.

William jumped away from the Emir's swinging sword just before it hit. Swinging his own sword back, it connected with the back of the animal's hind leg. Blood covered William's sword, and the horse stumbled. The Emir jumped off his mount, running back at William with his sword over his head.

Now on equal footing, and both with swords drawn, they circled each other. Realizing once more how much larger the Emir was than himself, William experienced a moment of doubt. Size was not the only thing that mattered in a fight, but it definitely gave his opponent the advantage.

The Emir swung for his head, but William ducked just in time, and made his own pass which also failed to land. Back and forth they went, clashing swords, until William took a false step during a swing. The Emir parried and kicked him in the chest. The blow sent William sprawling on his back, his sword leaving his grasp.

William's eyes grew wide as realization dawned that these could be his last moments. The image of Guida flashed in his mind, and he was filled with rage at the thought of never seeing her again.

As the Emir stood over him, William watched as the giant raised his sword in preparation of the death blow. As the sword descended, survival instincts took over and William crossed his arm over his body, hitting the flat side of the oncoming weapon with a backhanded swing, knocking the Emir off balance. Ignoring the new pain in his arm, William grabbed for his sword with his free hand and swung it across the Emir's midsection. The force of his blow nearly sliced the man in half. He was dead before he crumpled over William.

The combat over, he scrambled from underneath the fallen warrior. Covered in blood and entrails, William's stomach heaved. None of his previous experiences had prepared him for this specific horror. Taking off his helmet, hair soaked and dripping, he shakingly became aware of the cheers of his fellow warriors.

He had won, yet his heart continued to race with the thrill of the fight. Looking around, he saw his army celebrating for him, while the enemy stood in silent shock, much like his own feelings. After thinking he was going to lose, the reality of winning took a few moments to settle within him.

Turning back to his men, he raised his helmet in his hand and the cheers grew even louder.

He could see a small contingent of the enemy approaching Maniakes and his guards with a white flag raised. They had been beaten honorably, and now they surrendered. Drogo approached, wide-eyed and speechless.

The cheers of his men grew less chaotic as a single chant took form. Unable at first to make it out, the brothers gazed at the army and listened more carefully. The chant grew in volume and intensity until it rang out clear across the battlefield.

"Iron Arm! Iron Arm! Iron Arm!"

Chapter 31

H e cannot be as bad as that," Maria scoffed.

Maria's voice echoed through the empty corridor. The sisters approached the solar where they were to join the other women to begin the wedding planning.

"He can be, and he is. He is the worst sort of man. He takes what he wants with no care or thought for anyone else. I could never be happy with him!"

"Perhaps Father is right. You are thinking about this all wrong. It is not for you to be happy with him, but rather, for him to be happy with you."

"Maria!" Guida gasped, and stopped walking. "You do not truly believe that, do you? Do you not see that you, we, deserve happiness as much as any man?" *Do I believe that?* It had been some time since she had vocalized her opinions, and this one had escaped her almost without her thinking. Could it be that she was again beginning to feel her life held some value, regardless of what she had been through?

"Guida," Maria answered carefully, as if she were the older sister, "regardless of who I marry, I have every intention of being happy. I am responsible for my own contentedness, and I shall not forfeit that power in a marriage contract."

After a pause, Guida pulled Maria in for a tight embrace. "Oh, Maria! You have grown so wise." Letting go, she added, "Security and happiness are not the same thing. Giovan, I believe, would guide me beyond the bounds of self containment. His actions would forever haunt my footsteps through life. I fear we view marriage differently. I have no intention of selling my happiness for security, and I pray you never will either. I applaud your perspective, however. Perhaps you shall still find joy when your time comes."

Guida turned and resumed walking. Entering the solar she found her mother, Aunt Gemma, and Gaitelgrima. It was eerily silent, yet the air was thick with tension. Gemma wore her typical look of disapproval. Lady Raingarta and Gaitelgrima sported similar countenances of discomfort.

"Ah," Gemma began, "the lady of the hour. Thankfully, you did not allow our appointment to interfere with your daily schedule. I would be so put out to find we had inconvenienced you." She bowed her head with mock felicity, her words dripping with sarcasm.

"We are all quite aware of your disapproval, Gemma." Lady Raingarta snapped. "There is no need to be discourteous."

"Discourteous? Nay, *Sister*. I am merely attempting to convey the importance of arriving promptly when dealing with one's superiors."

"Superiority is better based on aspects of character than on rank alone."

"Mother," Maria interjected, cutting off any response from Gemma. "Let us focus on the tasks at hand."

Once again Guida was impressed with her sister's maturity and ability to handle those around her.

Lady Raingarta turned to Guida. "The men are signing the marriage contract as we speak, and Guaimar has ordered a feast for this evening to celebrate your betrothal."

"Oh, there is no need for that, surely," Guida attempted, not wishing to be the center of attention.

"The celebration is not simply for you, child," Gemma ground out. "As little as I think of you, my brother deserves the very best. Kindly keep your selfish opinions to yourself."

"My selfish opinions, Aunt Gemma?" Guida could no longer hold her tongue. "Your brother is the most conceited, sorry excuse for a human life I have ever encountered! Trust me when I say that I do not consider a betrothal to him worthy of a celebration. I would rather marry a leper than Giovan. This farce of a betrothal may be happening, but I give my word that I shall find a way to stop this marriage. Giovan's failings aside, I could never entertain the possibility of being tied any closer to you than I am already. Marrying any of your relations is a repugnant thought and something that I will never allow."

The faces of the other women registered their shock at Guida's outburst. This behavior was so far out of her usual sphere of conduct that not one of them knew how to respond. Even Gemma was rendered speechless. Guida herself was shaking with the rage that had been unleashed through her words. Feeling more in control of her future than ever, she turned and quit the room.

The feast that evening was a horrendous affair for Guida. Congratulations and well wishes seemed never ending, and the night could not conclude quickly enough. Lord Guy, having received word of Guida's earlier behavior, kept her continually under scrutiny. She felt his eyes boring into her as she attempted to eat.

"You look lovely this evening, my dear," Giovan said, leaning close.

"Your flattery is wasted on me, Giovan," Guida responded, with no warmth in her voice.

Smiling, he would not be deterred. "Flattery is never wasted. You will see. In time you will beg for a kind word from me." He placed his hand on her thigh and squeezed.

Swatting his hand away, she turned to him directly. "Let there be no mistake here, Giovan. I may have been unable to prevent this betrothal, but there shall be no wedding. Whatever it may cost me, I shall never marry you."

Giovan laughed. "You have such spirit! I shall thoroughly enjoy breaking it." He leaned back in and spoke with a voice of steel, "You have no power to stop this. Your fate is sealed."

"Why do you even want this? It is obvious you have no affection for me, nor I for you. What do you hope to gain?"

"Is that not obvious? You have sway with Guaimar. More than Gemma has, certainly. Once we are wed it shall not be difficult to convince you to do what you can to appease me, which will include asserting yourself with my plans for Guaimar."

"You think quite highly of your persuasive capabilities. Why would he listen to me?"

"Do not be coy, my dear. You know as well as I that he follows your guidance."

"Yes, now," she responded. "If my opinions were to change upon my marriage, which I will remind you will never be to you, he would no longer heed me."

"We shall see," Giovan said, as he returned his attention to the revelry.

Guida seethed inside, even as her resolve firmed into the toughest steel. She did not know how, but she would stop this wedding from taking place. She would rather die than subject herself to his mercy.

Rounding a corner that led to several bed chambers, Guida stopped and backed up to hide behind the wall. She had glimpsed Giovan entering the chamber that he had been occupying since arriving in Salerno. She had no interest in speaking with him, so she waited a moment, thinking that he would shut the door.

Once she thought it safe to continue, she began walking as silently as she could, not wishing to draw his attention from inside the room. As she passed his door, she realized that he had not shut it completely. She heard voices inside.

Curiosity overtook her. She leaned against the wall, this time keeping her head near the door opening, so as to hear better.

"She insists she will not marry me," Giovan stated. "She does not trust me, and she is not allowing opportunity for me to change her mind. I attempted again this morning, but she rushed the other direction as soon as she saw me." Giovan sounded like a petulant child whining to his nursemaid.

"You must try harder!" A woman's voice hissed. It was whispered and harsh, and Guida could not identify who the woman was.

Guida leaned closer, knowing herself to be the subject of their conversation. Placing her hand on the door to steady herself, she peeked inside the room, hoping to see who Giovan was speaking with. It was no use. The mystery woman was not within Guida's limited view.

"There must be an easier way to get to Guaimar," Giovan spoke thoughtfully.

"He does not trust me." The woman spoke more, but whispered too softly for Guida to make out all of her words. "...see him at meals...and there are far too many people around...do anything then."

"Why not enlist the help of one of the kitchen servants? There must be someone who can be *persuaded* to show their allegiance to you."

"No," the woman said disheartedly. "The servants are all loyal to him. I cannot think of a single one who would want to hurt him."

Hurt Guaimar? Guida's blood turned cold as she realized what the two were speaking of. She should not be here. If she were caught, there would be no one to warn her uncle of the danger he was in. And from his wife's own brother! No, she needed to find Guaimar immediately and relay what she had overheard.

She turned to leave and go in search of her uncle. As she removed her hand from the door, it shifted, and the hinges squealed in protest. Her breath hitched. She knew she would be caught in moments. Turning away from the door she raced down the corridor, not looking back.

Guaimar was not in his chambers, nor the solar. Neither was anyone else. *Where have they all gone?* Guida checked everywhere, finally asking the stable hand if Guaimar had taken his horse out. He had, so she needed to wait for his return. Thinking the chapel would be a safe place to pass the time, since Giovan had yet to set foot there since his arrival in Salerno, she went there. She had been praying for a few moments only before she heard the door open and close again. Looking up to see who had entered, she saw Giovan, leaning his back against the door.

"Do you think praying will help you now? I think God has better things to do than listen to the prayers of a spoiled, worthless woman." His cruel words were a warning; not that she needed one.

Searching the chapel for anything she could use as a weapon, she spotted several candelabras, but they would be too difficult for her to wield. She had a knife strapped to her calf, as well as one in her pocket. She never ventured from her chambers unarmed now. They would have to be enough should the need to defend herself arise.

"Giovan! Have you come to make your peace with God? I am certain He would love to hear your prayers." She spoke stiltedly, her entire body trembling. He must know that she had overheard him.

He advanced toward her as a sneer marred his face. "You know why I am here. A little mouse knows more than she should. And now she must be caught."

"I-I do not know what you mean." She knew playing the fool would not save her for long, but she hoped to stall him long enough for someone else to stumble upon them and rescue her. They were alone, certainly, but the setting was by no means private.

His eyebrows furrowed in fury. "Do not lie. It does not become you." He had nearly reached her, but she kept retreating, not sure what he would do once she was finally caught.

"Y-you cannot do anything to me. The castle is well guarded, and Guaimar will be back soon. You know he will not tolerate any unkindness toward me." At least she hoped he would not.

Bumping up against the wall, she realized that she had retreated right into a corner. He reached out and roughly grasped her wrist, and with his face inches away from hers, he whispered, "Guaimar will have enough to worry about once he returns. Trust me; he will not take time to think on you. Oh, my," now his voice dripped with sarcasm. "It would appear that there is no one here to protect you." His breath was hot and reeked from lack of care, while his grip tightened around her wrist.

Her free hand found its way into her pocket, and she quickly withdrew her knife. Touching it to his stomach, she applied enough pressure that Giovan stepped back in surprise. She opened her mouth to respond, but was interrupted.

"I would not say she was unprotected." A new voice joined in from the direction of the door. Guida turned to see her father standing on the threshold, rage emanating from his every feature. Guida took every unkind and uncharitable thought that she had recently had toward him and replaced them with gratitude.

Giovan, however, did not even turn around to look at Lord Guy. "This is none of your concern, just a small matter between me and my betrothed. Leave us!" The disdain evident in his voice did nothing to slacken her father's expression, which was growing more murderous by the moment.

Again, she opened her mouth, and this time said, "Giovan, as you see, I am hardly friendless. Now, you need to leave, before you are no longer able." Giovan paused for a moment, looking down at the knife that was still trained on his midsection. Realizing he could not win, he released Guida's arm and left the room.

Her father did not move right away. He stayed in the doorway, simply looking at Guida. He seemed to be waiting for her to explain the situation, but she just drew in steadying breaths and sat down in a nearby pew. He slowly walked over to her, and sat down next to her. They did not speak for several minutes.

Finally, he broke the silence. "Are you well, my dear?" His voice was all concern. At this moment, he was the dearest person in her heart.

She found her voice again. "Yes, I shall be well."

"I am proud of you, my dear," he said with a small smile. "You have shown great spirit, much more than I would have expected."

"To be honest, it was more than I would have expected as well," she laughed shakily. She had acted out of necessity, pushing aside her fear enough to protect herself, and she felt suddenly very powerful.

Bringing her thoughts back to the issue at hand, she asked, "Do you now see what sort of man Giovan is? Will you still insist on our union?"

Instead of answering, he asked, "What happened to cause Giovan to turn on you?"

Guida told her father the entire matter; after which he escorted her to her chambers. He then instructed her to bar the door and not let anyone enter until he or her uncle returned.

Sensing her discomfort, he tried to ease her mind. "Do not worry, Guida. There is no more to fear."

Looking him in the eye, she gave a small smile. "I am beginning to believe that, Father."

Then she shut the door and barred it as instructed.

Within the hour Guaimar showed up at Guida's door, informing her of Giovan's capture and imprisonment in the dungeon. Her father was currently interrogating him, attempting to ascertain the identity of the woman he had been plotting with. Both Guida and Guaimar suspected Gemma, but so far Giovan denied it.

"Your father told me what you did in the chapel. He is as proud of you as I am, I think. You showed such bravery and fortitude. You are truly an incredible woman, Guida."

Guida shifted uncomfortably under her uncle's praise. "I did not do it for praise. I did not have a choice."

Chapter 32

Salerno – October 1040

C heck." Guida smiled as she moved her queen into position. She had a dominant command of the board, and her uncle was not pleased about it. She saw his lips tighten and his nostrils flare just a touch, but she also knew the pride he took in her accomplishments would soften the loss for him.

"When did you become such a master of chess?" Guaimar stared at the board, weighing his options, which were limited. He finally chose to move his lone bishop to save his king.

"Checkmate." Guida stated, moving her castle to take his bishop, ending the game.

"My little niece has grown and can best me at my own game. Perhaps I should make you my chief advisor." Despite his defeat, he looked lovingly at Guida.

"I am just grateful you are not an ungracious loser. Also, keep in mind that I learned everything I know from you." Guida stood and bent down to kiss her uncle's cheek. She knew she was the better player, but she also knew the value of keeping powerful men happy. For this reason, she did not always allow herself the victory, winning just enough to make Guaimar feel they were on even ground.

"Another game, my dear?" He smiled, waiting expectantly for her response.

"Of course. I must allow you the opportunity to redeem yourself," she answered with a smile and sat back down. She absolutely loved these times spent with Guaimar. They were the highlight of her lonely existence, and she would not trade them for the world. Her relationship with her uncle had returned to what it had been before John's death. When William left, she had needed someone and Guaimar was the natural choice. She could not spend the rest of her life mourning the loss of William. Yet, she did still worry about him, and in her deepest secret fantasies he was always there.

"Uncle Guaimar, have you had word of the battles in Sicily?" Guida asked, wishing she had not sounded so tentative.

Guaimar sat back in his chair and watched intently as Guida set up the game pieces. "I have had news." His intense gaze belied the casual words.

She realized her uncle was watching for her reaction, but she was not sure why. *Does he have bad news? Is William dead?* Guida's hands paused in their work, and her breath hitched in her throat.

After a moment she was able to squeak out, "Oh?"

She had only heard William's name a handful of times since he had left the area. Now two years had passed, and hearing his name still made her heart speed up. Even now it felt like she would never be able to take a full breath again. Her grief over his leaving yet felt raw, but she had thought that she had kept her feelings secret. Yet, based on the way that Guaimar was staring her down, she was no longer certain of how sly she had been.

"Yes," her uncle supplied, "it will soon be finished."

"Is the fighting ceased, then?" Guida felt hope rising in her breast. "Have the Romans given up and relinquished Sicily to the Arabs?"

"Not entirely," the prince answered, "although, I think it will not be long now. The Romans have not fared well in this war. It seems the Normans abandoned them and have returned to Aversa. The court of Count Drengot has welcomed the warriors."

Will William come home? Guida's heart constricted as she digested this new information. Hope could be a dangerous thing when left unchecked. "Do you think any of the Normans will return here?" Dreading the answer, she still had to ask.

"Guida, why not ask what you really wish to know? Shall we not speak plainly with one another?" He leaned forward in his chair, piercing her with his gaze.

"Perhaps I should practice holding my tongue. Aunt Gemma certainly thinks I would do well to be more demure and silent." She grimaced as she thought of the many times she had heard those very words.

Guaimar smiled softly. "I rather like knowing what you are thinking. Please, do not allow Gemma to change who you are to fit her ideal. She is working that nonsense on our children." He visibly shuddered at the thought.

If speaking her mind was the way to get the answers she wanted, then she would comply. Then they could end this uncomfortable conversation. "I am wondering about Sir William."

"I suspected as much," he stated as he relaxed back into his seat. "Well, the last I heard he was well and whole, and in Aversa as well."

Guida released the breath she had been holding.

"I suspect he will come back, though he is under no obligation to do so. You know I have received many reports throughout this war. Although he appeared to be on the losing side of things, William's name kept coming up. He is a formidable warrior. He earned the nickname of William "Iron Arm" shortly after he left here, by killing the Arab ruler of Syracuse in single combat. But one man cannot win a war. The Normans are intelligent, and it is no wonder that they have now left the endeavor.

"Guida," Guaimar sighed, leaning forward once again. "I must ask. Do you have feelings for Sir William? Or is this mere curiosity?"

With her own sigh of resignation, she answered, "Would it make a difference either way? Do not worry, I know my duty." She could barely spit out the last word, and she knew that she had never been able to conceal much, even with William's lessons.

"You know I consider Sir William a friend. A good friend. He has done more for me, for us, than any other knight in my service. You know he would have been perfectly within his rights to ask for a reward for saving you from Pandulf's man, yet he never did. Nor did he ask for one when he first arrived with Isolde. Now why do you think that is?" He did not stop and await an answer, which was good, because Guida had no idea what to say. "And did you know that in his correspondence with me he always asks after you?"

Guida shifted in her seat, and her palms began to sweat. "Does he?" She sounded a little breathless, even to her own ears.

His voice softened even more, and he reached across the chess board to hold her hand between his. "You know how much I love you, Guida.

I only ever want to see you happy, but I must tell you this. I worry that you may have your heart set on Sir William. You know he does not own any land, and he does not possess a title. There is no possible way that my brother would approve such a union, so you must let William go."

"What does it matter?" Guida could not keep the hopelessness out of her voice. She knew all of this. After Giovan's treachery, her father had lessened his pressure to find her a husband, yet Guida could feel his unease growing once more through his correspondence with her. Her father was still searching for an acceptable husband for her, and he was narrowing the list. It was something she could not forget, no matter how hard she tried.

As frightening as that was, Guida knew her father would not marry her off to a complete stranger. He had promised as much when last they spoke. Guida had hoped that William would have returned by now with a plan that would allow them to be together. Knowing he was back from battle, yet still not here, filled her with fear that she had been forgotten.

"The world is not kind, Guida, especially to women. If we are fortunate, you will learn to love your husband more than any other man, but I know from experience that love in marriage is not likely. You must learn to think for yourself, or you will always be at the mercy of the men around you."

"I do not think I have the stomach for this, Uncle." She stood and took to pacing the room in her agitation. "I confess, this topic is not one that I enjoy. I fully know my duty, but I am worried about it. I have spent so much of my life here in your castle and have so rarely encountered anyone from anywhere else. I have no great skill with people and no assurance that whoever I end up with will care for me as you have."

Guaimar took a moment before answering. He stood and approached her. "That is a valid concern. I wish I could ease your mind. We both know how little influence I had in my own marriage, and my influence in yours may not lead to anything better." He squeezed her hand and looked back into her eyes. "I love you, Guida, and I pray to God that your future husband will as well. But you need to know that it will not be William, unless some miracle occurs to change his situation."

Guida squeezed his hands as well, and then took her hands away. "I know, Uncle. I love you, too. Now, are we going to play?"

"By all means."

Chapter 33

Aversa – January 1041

N o, no, no!" William's harsh yell stopped all the activity in the training yard. Not waiting for his former squire to return to his location near the quintain, he continued, "If you hold your lance loose like that, it will quickly be knocked away in a battle. You must remember to hold it this way, for better stability. Your strike will be more effective if you keep the lance steady."

He demonstrated the hold he wanted with his own lance by holding the handle between his elbow and the side of his body. They had been working on this all morning, and Gregory was struggling to let go of old habits.

"*Oui*, sir." His old response to his mentor always seemed to slip out whenever William was around.

"Again!" William shouted.

The two men separated to opposite ends of the field. William rode to the quintain, a training dummy suspended on a swinging pole, and prepared it for another pass. William noticed Drogo watching from off to the side.

Turning his attention back to Gregory, William gave the signal and Gregory spurred his horse. Man and beast barreled toward the quintain, gaining speed as they went. Gregory's aim proved true and his lance hit squarely on the dummy's shield. He used so much force that the quintain rotated too quickly and the sandbag counterweight hit him in the back as he passed. Not expecting the blow, Gregory was knocked off his horse completely.

"Yes! That's it!" William shouted. He dismounted and went back to help the younger man off the ground. As he spoke, he could not help but smile. "We'll make a proper knight out of you yet."

Gregory grimaced, "Now to do it while staying on my horse."

"Yes, well, there is always going to be something to improve upon." They reviewed different battle strategies as they made their way to where Drogo waited. From there, the brothers broke off and moved to the barracks for William to shed his armor.

"You should do it again until Gregory does it right, William," Drogo said disapprovingly.

Releasing a breath of frustration, William asked, "Must we really go over this again? Gregory is shaping up to be a fine knight. If he has an issue with the way he is being trained, he is free to seek help elsewhere." He looked over at his brother. "Is that really what you wished to speak with me about?"

At the reminder, Drogo's eyes lit with excitement. "No, in fact I came to inform you that Ardouin is here."

It took William only a moment to let that sink in. Ardouin was the interpreter that Prince Guaimar sent when William joined the fight for the Romans. "Here? Why?" William had not seen him since Ardouin had a disagreement with the Roman general over a horse. The general had confiscated the horse from Ardouin, who would not let the matter go. Things did not go well for Ardouin after that.

"He did not say. He wants to meet with a few of us tonight, including Drengot. We will meet in the great hall after the evening meal has been cleared."

William found it difficult to focus on anything throughout the meal. His thoughts were led to speculating the reason for Ardouin's presence. Gratefully, he did not have long to wait before the great hall began clearing out. William and Drogo made their way toward the dais where Ardouin was speaking with Count Drengot. Looking around, William recognized most of the men, some by face only, but some he counted among his friends. Among them were Hugh, Aimery, and Peter.

Ardouin looked around at the men before him. He had aged since William had seen him last. His face bore more wrinkles and his hair was whiter. His eyes were the same as William remembered: cunning and crafty, not to be fully trusted.

"I have come with a proposition for you all. I am sure you will understand when I say that I have no love for the Romans. Not after my run in with General Maniakes." William had heard of the incident and wondered briefly if Ardouin's wounds had fully healed. Ardouin had not appreciated that the Romans had cheated the Normans out of their fair share of the spoils of war. He had confronted Maniakes about it. Maniakes, instead of correcting the situation, had Ardouin publicly whipped.

Ardouin continued speaking, looking from one man to the next. "I am a Norman supporter and have proven that in the past. I have been recently in the town of Melfi, in Apulia, working in the Roman military. Melfi is still largely populated by Lombards from before the Romans invaded, and they are not pleased with the way they are being ruled. I have been laying the groundwork for some time to oust the Romans from the area, and believe that the time has come. The Romans have been so focused on Sicily that they have left the area of Apulia vulnerable.

"If you join me, we will take over all of Apulia, then we will split the spoils. Since I have laid the groundwork for this, I would take half of everything we gain. You would all split the remaining amongst yourselves."

Ardouin was obliged to stop as everyone started speaking at once. William turned to Drogo and was not surprised to see him smiling. "I can see what you think about this. It is written all over your face."

"It would be nice if I could tell what you were thinking as readily," Drogo responded. "What say you?"

William took a moment to consider. "This could be an amazing opportunity, depending on how the spoils are divided. We should settle on that before making any kind of commitment."

"Stop! Stop," Count Drengot shouted as he held up his hands to settle the chatter. "If we are to make an informed decision then we need to stop talking over each other. Iron Arm, what are you thinking?" William had risen in status amongst the Normans since the day he had earned that nickname and was not surprised to be singled out in such a way.

Instead of answering, William asked a question of his own. "Ardouin, do you actually plan on dividing everything? Riches, food, land?" It was the last of this list that William was particularly interested in. He had come to this country with the intention of gaining land and wealth, and this discussion could very well be the beginning of reaching that goal. It was also a necessary acquirement if he was to have any opportunity to be with Guida again.

Ardouin gave William an appraising look as he carefully replied, "Yes, half of everything. There are twelve of you, not counting myself, and we would make you each a chief leader and assign you the charge of a group of warriors. Apulia has more than enough for us all to share the spoils."

Once again voices rose as the men talked over each other. This time William raised his arms to calm the men. "And how many men do you expect us to provide?"

Drengot answered before Ardouin had a chance. "We are hoping to gather around three hundred men. I have pledged to provide one hundred warriors. William and Drogo, we were hoping that you would ride to Salerno to apprise Prince Guaimar of our plans and request additional knights. We ask the rest of you to gather at least ten men each. If Iron Arm can persuade the prince to send another one hundred, that would get us close to our goal."

William glanced at Drogo to assess whether he could answer for his brother. Drogo gave a slight nod of approval, so William answered, "That is a pitifully small number for such a campaign. We cannot accomplish all you suggest with a mere three hundred. We would need a way to increase that number."

"It is my belief that once this strike has begun, the Lombards will rise up and join us," Ardouin assured them. "I would not suggest such a design if I did not believe that to be the case."

After a pause, William finally answered. "My sword is yours. Now, how do we proceed once we have raised our forces?"

Ardouin's eyes gleamed with excitement. "I will return immediately to Melfi and prepare my allies for your arrival. As soon as you have gathered together, you will travel across the mountains and meet me in Melfi. Send a message before you arrive, and I will ride out to meet you and guide you into the city. If all goes as planned, you will be able to immediately occupy Melfi and set up a center of command.

"From there, we will be able to reach out to other nearby cities such as Venosa and Lavello. These inland cities are only lightly fortified by the Romans, but mostly populated by Lombards. There will not be much of a fight if we are able to raise the forces we have talked about. This all needs to be done quickly."

"Once we have taken over the inland cities," William interjected, "we will need to meet again and assess the state of our forces. By that time, the Romans will know that we are taking control. They may reroute their army to meet us. We need to attack hard and as quickly as we can. Surprise will be our best weapon. The coastal cities will be much better fortified with defenses, as well as with manpower. I think it would be impossible to successfully take over any of them before the Roman army is mustered and sent to meet us in open combat."

"I agree," Hugh jumped in. He gave William a thoughtful glance and then addressed the group at large. "We must be willing to face the inevitability of actual combat. The Roman forces will outnumber our own, but I believe with the new cavalry techniques Iron Arm has been teaching, we would still be able to defeat them."

Ardouin, not to be cut out of the conversation, said, "We should also have the support of most of the population. Once they see that we are rising up against the Romans, I believe that we will have more Amalfitans rally to our side."

William had a worry tickling his mind. "How large do you imagine the Roman army will be once they come against us?"

The room that had been buzzing with whispers and plotting, instantly silenced. It seemed that every man wanted the answer.

Ardouin suddenly paled, and William saw doubt in his eyes. "It is difficult to say. There are many factors that make it impossible to estimate with any degree of certainty."

"We do not need an exact number," Peter spoke for the first time, "but we deserve a straight answer. You are asking us to put our lives, and the lives of those men we muster, in jeopardy."

Ardouin took a large breath. "Two of the biggest factors will be how soon they find out what we are doing, and how soon they try to come up against us. If they try to fight us right away, then they will not have time to muster much of a force, perhaps three to five hundred men. If they wait until they have gathered more men, they could come with upwards of a thousand. But, by then I expect our numbers to have increased as well."

The room was stone silent. The men glanced at each other, attempting to gauge what each of them were thinking, but none wanting to be the first to speak.

Finally William broke the silence. "Do you really believe that the populace will join with us?"

Ardouin's color came back and he nodded. "I do. They are discontent with being governed by people so disconnected from them. I believe they will readily join with us, if we prove that we are able to win. We will prove that when we take control of the inland cities."

The discussion continued, with William lost in his own thoughts. If they were successful, and William did not perish along the way, this could be his path to becoming a land owner. It was not a title, but it was the first step. This could be the answer that would allow him to be with Guida, assuming she was not married already. It had been nearly three years since he had last been with her. Certainly that was enough time for her situation to have changed. And if she was still unwed, could she still care for him at all? She had told him she did not care, but could he change that? Would he be able to gain her affection once more?

William's attention was drawn back to the issues on hand when Count Drengot, who had remained mostly silent thus far, spoke up. "Are there any other questions or reservations? Or are we all in agreement with this plan?" The men all nodded or voiced their assent. "Good. I would ask all of you to set out at first light to see to your assignments."

The men turned once again to Ardouin, as he continued the instructions. "In order to prevent the Romans from getting wind of our designs, do not speak of this to anyone you do not trust to be discreet. Speed will be our greatest ally. Pray, return here as soon as you are able with the required men. Thank you all."

The men all moved to leave. Drogo turned to William with a smirk. "Life just got a lot more interesting."

"Indeed it did."

Chapter 34

Salerno – February 1041

William was happy to be back in Salerno, although it would not last long. It had been a cold journey. As he entered the great hall, he did not stop inside the door. Instead, he went directly to the giant fireplace to begin warming himself before finding a seat. As he began to regain feeling in his extremities, he looked around the familiar room and saw the prince entering through a side door. The men both smiled and approached one another.

"William, my friend! Welcome back." Prince Guaimar grasped William's arm in greeting. William returned the gesture heartily.

"Prince Guaimar, you are a welcome sight."

"Come, join me on the dais. The servants are beginning their preparations for the evening meal, but we mustn't let that stop us from catching up."

William followed where the prince had indicated, sitting in the chair next to the prince's usual one. He waited until the prince sat down and then occupied his own seat.

"Now, tell me what you have been about," the prince demanded. "I have not heard from you since you arrived in Aversa." Prince Guaimar showed real interest, as he leaned forward slightly in his chair and fixed his eyes on his friend.

The two spent the time telling tales until the meal was ready to be served. William spoke mostly of one battle or another, regaling the prince with stories of the men he had fought beside. Guaimar spoke of the affairs of the kingdom since William had left to fight in Sicily. William was nowhere near being this man's equal, but that did not stop Guaimar from treating him as one. William was struck once more with how much respect he had for the man.

"How is your family?" William's genuine interest was evident in his voice.

All mirth dissipated as the prince responded. "They are well, mostly. We have moved on as best we can, but John is still constantly in my thoughts. Now Gisulf will be my heir. He is four years old and quite unruly. Truth be told, he favors his mother's disposition. I fear for him already."

William laughed heartily. "I imagine all of your offspring will be unruly. How many are you up to these days?"

Guaimar's eyes grew soft. "Besides Gaitelgrima, I have got two boys and a darling little girl. You will not see them tonight, though, as they eat with their nursemaids."

"There is plenty of time to teach Gisulf what type of man he ought to be. Do not give up on him yet. And Princess Gemma, how does she fare?" William knew theirs had not been a loving marriage before but was hoping, for his friend's sake, that something had changed in the past few years.

Guaimar let out a tired breath. "Oh, she will be here shortly. She can never turn down an opportunity to goad me, especially in front of others. Gemma has never made life easy for anyone, and it seems to be worsening as time goes by. It is nothing I cannot handle for my own sake, but she is not always kind to Gaitelgrima, and she torments Guida to no end. I do not understand her ire." William certainly did not envy the prince's marriage. "Enough of this," Guaimar sighed. "Tonight we will speak of happy things. How long will you stay with us?"

As they continued conversing, the great hall began to fill. The tables and benches had been moved into place and trenchers were being set out. William had not paid much attention to the activity around him, being so involved in the conversation. However, as the meal was about to begin, he felt his eyes drawn to the side door that the prince had entered from earlier. He did not know what reception to expect from Guida, given how they parted. His heart raced at the thought of seeing her again.

Finally, she entered. She had changed little in the few years he had been gone. She was still a rare beauty, the most alluring creature he had ever seen. She had an over gown of the deepest green with wide sleeves the color of fresh cream. The color of her gown complimented her raven tresses that were intricately braided in a crown around her head. Ribbons that perfectly matched the green and white of her gown were twined throughout the braids.

"Guida." The word was barely a whisper. Before William even thought, he was up and striding toward her. Finding himself quite suddenly standing in front of her, he fought the urge to take her in his arms.

William took Guida's hand, bowed low over it, murmured a soft, "My Lady" and laid a gentle kiss on her hand. Her fingers twitched slightly. As he straightened, he looked into her flushed face. Her teeth were clenched tight, and her eyes flashed. She evidently had not forgiven him for leaving. He shouldn't have been surprised, but he had hoped. Hoped for some understanding, hoped for forgiveness, hoped that time would have soothed them both without diminishing their love for one another. How foolish he had been.

"Shall we sit?" He led her to her chair next to Gaitelgrima. The prince had by now been joined by his wife. William had not had much interaction with Princess Gemma, but he knew enough not to engage her in conversation. He was instructed to take the seat next to Guida, as had been his place the previous times he had dined with the royal family. It was the perfect location to speak with her, but would she allow it?

"Guida," he began. "I just want to say…"

Her chair legs scraped loudly against the stone floor as she stood up, interrupting him.

"I apologize, Uncle Guaimar, but I have suddenly lost my appetite. Pray excuse me." She turned and moved straight out the door she had entered only minutes before.

He's back. Guida could not seem to think of anything else as she marched down the corridor to the tower. After not seeing him for so long she would have thought that her anxiety over being in his presence would have lessened. That did not seem to be the case, however. She had been hoping that once she saw him again she would finally be able to see him for what he really was— just a man. This idea had fortified her enough to enter the great hall. And he was just a man, but a potentially dangerous man, at least dangerous for her. How could she guard her heart from him? She had not been able to in the past, and she felt every bit as vulnerable now.

He had risen higher in status since he had last been in Salerno, although he still lacked any land of his own or any title. His name had always come up whenever anyone spoke of the unrest and recent battles in Sicily. She shook her head, wishing she could shake her love of him so easily.

Climbing the stairs to the top of the wall, she thought of her love for William. Was this to be her life? Always wanting, always missing a man she could not have? She now understood his reasons for leaving, but that did not lessen the pain it caused.

She forcefully chanted an internal mantra. *He is just a man. He is no different than any other knight. He is just a man.* She said these words over and over as she paced the top of the outer castle wall. Her words formed clouds of vapor as she spoke. She should not have walked out, but she could not just sit there next to him as if nothing had happened. As if she had not professed her love for him, and he had quickly abandoned her. She just was not that strong. He had worked so hard teaching her how to defend herself, but that was only the defense of her body. How could she defend her mind? Her heart? Those lessons had been missing from her education. And why did William's opinion of her matter to her so? Even after not seeing him for so long?

She had meant to eat, but could not force herself to sit next to him. Knowing he would be in attendance, likely seated near her usual place, she had prepared herself as best she could. Alys had taken extra time with her hair and dress. It was foolish, she knew, yet she had desperately wished to impress him when she saw him again. And now she was out in the freezing night without any furs, yet her blood was pumping like fire. She hoped the weather would cool her down.

His warm lips on her hand had been nearly more than she could bear. How she had wanted him to take her in his arms, and assure her of his love. The thought of his kiss sent new heat coursing through her.

Yet, without saying a single word to him, she had walked out. There was much she wished to say to him, but nothing she could utter with such a vast audience. How was she to be expected to sit in normal conversation with him, when all she wished was to be in his arms? She desperately wanted him to tell her that he never should have left, that he loved her still, and he would never leave her again. But it was no use. He was a warrior, and why would he wish to be shackled with her?

She stopped her pacing and looked out the crenel closest to her. It was too dark by now to see anything beyond the castle, but that did not stop her from looking. How she used to love sitting in these when she was smaller. And how Brunhild had hated it! She was too big to sit there now, but she was not too big to stand on it. She glanced around to make sure the guards were looking in different directions, then hiked her skirt up enough to step up on the stone.

Resting her hands on either side of the battlement, she closed her eyes. Her thoughts focused solely on the wind, as if the wind and the darkness could take away her dark thoughts. She lost track of how long she stood that way, focusing on her breathing and trying to banish any thoughts of William, or Brunhild and John, as their memories were always linked now. Thinking of one always brought the others to mind. The memories were too painful, and the reality of the present held no balm.

Guida suddenly found herself yanked backward from her waist and dropped unceremoniously to the stone floor. A scream ripped from her throat, and she heard the guards at either end of the wall come running. In her mind, she was immediately transported back to the mercy of a man she did not know. Her hand flew to the knife she always kept strapped to her calf and within half a second she had it aimed at the figure lurking over her.

"Put that away before you hurt someone!" William's face was contorted with unconcealed anger.

Guida took in a staggering breath and lowered her weapon. She quickly stood up off the cold stone floor, brushing off her skirts. Not even trying to temper the anger in her voice, she asked, "What do you think you are doing? I could have killed you!"

Ignoring her response, he continued. "I suppose it should be comforting to know that nothing has changed since I left. You still do not think before you act and every action leads to more pain for those around you." William waved the guards off, and Guida watched as they went back to their posts.

"What are you talking about?" Confusion contorted her features.

"Do you honestly not see how jumping off the castle wall would hurt your uncle? He has already lost one child; he does not deserve to lose you, too." He turned away and ran a hand through his hair.

"I was not jumping off the wall! And how dare you act as though you know me! For three years you have been gone. Did you really think I would be the same now as when you left? Well, one thing has changed. I am no longer your responsibility." She could hardly breathe through her anger. "You know nothing of my life now. Nothing of importance. Do not presume to know me."

Her words were cut off as William stormed over to her and grabbed her fiercely, with one hand grabbing her arm and the other hand behind her head forcing her lips to his. The harshness of it took her breath away, and she fought against it. She pushed against his chest, but he was immovable. After her initial panic, she realized the fire that had erupted in the pit of her soul was different than what had burned there only moments before.

Her body responded like the traitor it was. She melted into him, and her arms slid from his chest up to his shoulders. One got tangled in his hair and the other wound around his neck pulling him closer. Her lips parted as a groan of pleasure escaped. That sound seemed to shake her out of the madness she had plunged into. Ripping her head away from his, she attempted to step back. William slowly loosened his grip on her as he stood breathing heavily.

Wordlessly, she turned back to look through the crenel once again. She could not think of a single thing to say to him. Oh, how she wanted to hate him. She had spent so long trying to convince herself to let him go, and yet he had her completely undone and unsure of herself in a matter of moments.

"Guida." For the first time tonight he sounded a little unsteady. "Will you please look at me?"

"Why? What more do you need? What more will you take from me?" Her voice hitched, and she realized she was crying. She could not remember the last time she had cried. The strength she had been finding in herself seemed to have deserted her. Her fury dissolved, and all that was left was immeasurable sadness. Sadness for what she had lost, and for what could never really be hers.

"What have I ever taken from you?" His words sounded a little stronger as he became defensive.

"I cannot do this anymore. I have tried everything I can think of to get you out of my head, out of my heart. I fear I will never be free of you. And yet, I can never have you. How can you leave me for so long, then unexpectedly return, and kiss me like that? Like you had never been away, had never stopped loving me."

She whirled around to face him, and even took a step closer. "You accuse me of being selfish, thinking only of myself. You are no better than what you accuse me of. You are selfish, taking whatever you please with no regard for who gets in your way. What about *my* choices? What if I did not want to kiss you? What if I never want to kiss anyone?" *It matters not. I am just a woman, here to please any man who wants me.* "I will never be free." The last was said as an afterthought as she turned away again.

"Free from what? What in your life here could you possibly want to be free of?" He sounded truly curious.

"YOU! Why can I not be free from you? Why do you come back and torture me? Your words, your soul, your lips! How can I ever be free when you come back to tease me, to torment me? I hate you! I hate what you do to me whenever you are near. I hate that I want to be close to you at the same time I want to stab you in the eye! I hate that you leave like I do not matter and yet kiss me like you love me. I hate that I have no idea what you really think about me, if you even think about me. I hate that I do not know when you are going to leave again, and when, or if, you will ever come back." Her voice that had started out so strong had quieted to nearly a whisper. "And I hate that I love you still."

William stood there just staring at her for the longest moment of Guida's life. She waited for another moment, then started to turn away to flee back inside the castle. William's arm shot out and grabbed her hand. His grasp quickly softened, and he brought his other hand up to caress her cheek. His thumb stroked her lower lip, and her entire body trembled.

"Do you mean it? Do you really still love me?" he asked, unsure.

"What difference would it make? I can never have you."

"Oh, Guida." He rested his forehead on hers. "I realized I loved you from the moment you were thrown from your horse, and I did not know if you would yet live. I have never been more frightened. The fear of losing you is always in my thoughts. Every move I make is strategically thought out so as to move me closer to you, regardless of it seeming otherwise. I currently have no land, no wealth to speak of, and no way to provide for you. But that is about to change." His voice held hope. Hope that had been so lacking in Guida's heart. He lifted her chin to look in her eyes. "I want nothing more than to have you with me, always."

He bent his head and kissed her again. There was no fierceness in this kiss. No anger or frustration. This kiss was all tenderness and gentle longing. This kiss left her with no doubt as to his affection. His lips skimmed over hers and his hands slowly encircled her waist. There was no pressure for what would come next. There was only this moment and the hope that it would never end. But it must.

"But you left me." All of Guida's pain was released in a flood as her tears returned. "And you will leave again. I am left to wait, with no way to know when, or if, you will return. I barely escaped my father's last plan to have me marry. I may not be as fortunate again."

William pulled her close, encircling her within his arms. "I left because there was no other way. But now, a path has opened itself up and there is finally hope. If we can wait just a little longer, we can marry and be together always. Then I promise to love you forever and to protect you from all I can. Please, stop fighting me." He wiped her tears away as he spoke.

Guida stepped back out of his reach. "Have you gone completely mad? You know that with my father a Duke I could no sooner marry for love than I can control the weather. I am at the mercy of some of the most powerful men in the empire. You know this! Why would you do this to me?"

"Because I want to know what *you* want. If I am to pursue this, I must be assured of your affection. I will not chase you if you do not wish it."

She could think of no logical response, so she gave into her instincts. "I-I should go. It's colder out here than I thought." She turned and fled back into the castle and to her bedchamber, feeling like the coward she was.

Chapter 35

Salerno – February 1041

G uida?" She jumped in her chair at the sound of her name.
Both Guaimar and William were watching her intently. She
could not have said which one had spoken to her, as her
attention had been elsewhere. Part way through breaking her fast she
had lost focus, having not slept most of the night as her thoughts
tumbled over everything William had said.

"What could possibly have taken your attention so entirely?" There
was a laugh in his voice as Guaimar winked at her.

Did he know what happened last night? Had one of the guards
talked to him? Why would he be happy about it? No, he must not know
anything. He would definitely not be happy if he knew. What could she
possibly say? *My apologies, Uncle, but I have fallen in love with a knight.
And not just any knight, but a Norman besides, as well as a friend of yours. I
cannot seem to think of anyone or anything else.* She knew she could not

say any of that to either man, let alone to both. Guaimar already had his suspicions about her affection for William, but as yet did not know how deep it ran. Best to shift the focus onto someone else.

"Sir William, how does our home compare with the court at Aversa?" she asked. "I have never been to a Norman court, and I am curious about the differences with here."

"Was that really what you were thinking of?" His gaze told her he knew it was not, but he would let it pass if she really wished it.

She gave a slight nod, not liking to lie, but also not willing to answer honestly.

"Very well." He proceeded to compare the two castles, as well as the surrounding areas. Guida paid very little attention, since she really was not interested in the information, but it successfully took the focus off of her.

When a break in the conversation came, Princess Gemma spoke up. Her voice was dripping with disdain and sarcasm. "So, Sir William, what are you doing back here? Do not tell me that you just missed us all terribly and decided to pay us a visit."

William suddenly looked a bit uncomfortable. "There is some business that I would like to speak about with Prince Guaimar."

Gemma looked like she had finally found something to interest her. "Oh, really?" she drawled out. "And what would that be?" She leaned forward as she spoke, as if she could not wait to hear the answer. Guida thought she had a bit too much intensity in her gaze and wondered why she would be so interested in William. Gemma never showed much interest in anything, aside from vexing Guaimar, which she did with great skill, or being cruel to Guida and Gaitelgrima.

"It is a bit sensitive, my lady, and hardly appropriate at this time. Much too serious to dampen such a pleasant meal. Prince Guaimar, would there be a time today that you would be able to meet with me?"

"Of course! Guida and I often ride after we break our fast. Why don't you join us? Guida never stays near me, preferring to let her horse run wild. There will be ample time for discussion."

Princess Gemma snorted in disgust, a sound much below her dignity. Guida glanced at her and shivered from the ice crystals shining from Gemma's eyes.

William arrived at the stables before the prince and Guida. The stable servants were working on saddling the horses, and there was nothing for him to do but wait. He should be thinking of what to say to Guaimar, but all he could think of was the man's captivating niece.

He had spent most of the previous night thinking of her, as well. What had come over him? She was exquisite, but William was hardly the type of man to let that distract him. Many beautiful women had crossed his path over the years, yet none of them compared with Guida. He had tried to put her from his mind since leaving Salerno, but the moment he saw her last night it became achingly apparent how unsuccessful he had been.

The sound of a door opening and closing interrupted his thoughts. His gaze flew to the castle where he saw Guida walking toward him. She moved with such grace that all he could do was stare. She wore large furs over her simple riding habit with a very large skirt, which would keep her perfectly modest while riding. Her habit was a deep blue that looked black in the early morning light. Flowing free and unfettered, the natural waves of her hair cascaded down, covering her upper arms.

How he longed to run his fingers through that river of tresses and feel the softness of it.

She looked up and locked eyes with him. There was a feeling of electricity in the air and he did not realize he was moving until he stopped in front of her. Why did that keep happening? It was like something was drawing them together independent of conscious thought.

They stood silent for just a moment before Guida cleared her throat. "I wish to apologize for my behavior yesterday. When I saw you, I forgot all of my manners and reacted on impulse. That is not how a lady behaves. Pray forgive me." Her well rehearsed speech sounded as such, and he smiled in spite of himself.

"For which part? Surely you do not regret all of it." Why was he goading her? *I should be down on my knees trying to convince her of my love.* He decided to switch tactics. "You look lovely, my lady. And about last night..." He stopped as Guida put up her hand.

"I do not wish to speak more of last night."

He turned to walk beside her back to the stables, taking her hand and placing it on his. "Very well, tell me about your horse. How has she fared since last I was here?" He remembered how much she had loved her horse and hoped to be able to draw her out with simple conversation.

He was right. Her face broke into a smile, and all signs of her frown were wiped away. She began speaking quite animatedly and only stopped when Guaimar joined them. The stable hand assisted Guida into her saddle, and they were off. As soon as they cleared the castle gate, Guida spurred her horse into a full gallop. The prince and William did not speed up, however.

Guaimar laughed as he watched her leave. "She does this every time. Says she wants to ride with me, but quickly forgets I am even here. She will be back when her horse tires."

"How does the lady fare, my lord? Truly?"

Guaimar eyed him with furrowed brows, and William felt his measurement being taken. "I would not know. She refuses to speak about it, but now and then I sense it still troubles her. I know that she worries about being in another situation where she would need to defend herself. Alys has told me she still dreams of it. Wakes up screaming one night and sobbing another, yet she will not speak of it.

"She has taken your lessons to heart. If taken by surprise, she is likely to fight, and never leaves her chamber without a knife. We have all learned how to avoid being on the receiving end of her ire. But, I do not know how much she consciously thinks on it. I wish she would confide in me as she used to. Those days are long past, I am afraid. Perhaps she would speak with you, since you were her savior after all. Would you try? I know it is a lot to ask, but I would rest easier if I knew a little of what was going on in her head."

"Of course I can try, but I cannot see that she would share with me when you have been unsuccessful."

"It may be a fool's hope, but it is hope nonetheless. If only there were a better way to protect those who cannot protect themselves." Guaimar mused.

"My lord, I have been giving this very thing a lot of thought. Have I ever told you about my father's second wife?"

Guaimar looked confused at the change in subject, but answered. "I did not even know you had one."

"One day, shortly after marrying my father, Fressenda caught me chasing my sister Beatrix through the orchard with the intent to harm her. Beatrix was much smaller than I, but she had the temper of the devil. She took offense at something that I had said and in retaliation broke my favorite wooden sword. I was so angry!

"Fressenda, thankfully, arrived before I laid hands on Beatrix. She was outraged by my behavior, and I expected a lashing. Instead, that dear woman sat me down, and talked to me. I attempted to defend myself and explain what Beatrix had done, but was given no opportunity. Fressenda took that time to teach me that no matter what offense Beatrix was guilty of, it could never be cause enough for me to lay hands on someone smaller and weaker than myself. I would always have the physical advantage over my sister, and it would never be appropriate to press that advantage."

"Not everyone is as fortunate with their childhood teachings." Guaimar said thoughtfully.

"No, they are not. It is unfortunate. I have vowed with myself, and with God, to follow this principle, and I will pass it on to those with whom I have influence."

"I believe that I would like to imitate your example in this. I have some influence over the men who work for me. We will see if we can make even a small difference. Thank you, Sir William. I have surely missed your council. Now, what is it that you wished to discuss with me?"

"That is quite the intrigue." Guaimar had listened to William's explanation without much comment. True to his character, he wanted all possible information before making any decisions. "If this plot goes your way, it would mean a great deal to you Norman chiefs. Not just the spoils of war, but land to go with it. That is a prize indeed. I can easily see the temptation. This is basically what you and your countrymen came here for. I would like to know what you would do if this goes your way?"

"That is a valid question, my lord. You know that I consider you a friend. That would not change. If I were to possess any land I would continue to be loyal to you. I would consider you the lord of my lands for you to do with as you see fit, as long as I am able to retain them. We both know the value of having neighboring allies."

"Yes, that would be beneficial. When are you needing an answer?"

"I would like to leave in two days to return to Aversa. I will need your answer by then."

"Very well. I shall think on it. You must speak of this to Guida. She is upset already, but I know it will be worse if she believes you are staying. She does not handle change well."

"If that is your wish, my lord," William conceded.

Guaimar looked William full in the face. "I am certain you know how Guida feels about you, William. I would ask you to be kind. Do not fill her head with hope that may come to naught."

William could not hide the shock he felt hearing these words. He had not realized that Guaimar suspected anything of them. "My lord, you must know that Lady Guida and I have never…"

Guaimar raised his hand to silence his friend. "There is no need for denials or justifications. I know you, and I know Guida. If I had been concerned for her welfare where you are concerned I would have addressed it well before now. Any fool can see how in love with each other you are. In my heart I truly wish I could sanction your marriage.

"Unfortunately, Guida is not my daughter to give as I see fit. She must have Guy's blessing. If you are successful in this plot of yours, I believe you may be able to convince him to accept you, assuming he has not found another husband for her by then. For my part, I will try to prevent any matches that may present themselves, as I have done thus far. I have known for years of your attraction to each other and your shared affection. I believe with you she would be happy as you would strive to please her and bring her joy. I do not know how much longer I will be able to put Guy off, however. I suggest speed in the upcoming months."

William could only stare at the prince, dumbfounded. Had he really just heard Guaimar correctly? Was he giving William his blessing?

"Prince Guaimar," he finally replied, "this is more than I could have ever hoped for. Does Guida know that you would bless our union?"

Guaimar threw his head back and laughed. "If she did, do you think she would have slighted you at supper last evening? No, my dear boy, I believe I shall leave you to carry those sentiments to her. But remember, nothing is for certain. You still must conquer Melfi. Start with that. Then return and see what awaits you."

Her ride this morning had been invigorating, but still Guida felt restless. How could she be expected to sit demurely in the castle when she had so much on her mind? A walk through the forest was precisely what she needed. She made sure to have her knife strapped to her leg, as she had done every day for the past two years. She also put an extra blade in the pocket of her skirt, and snatched up her blade pouch.

Walking through the forest had been one of the harder things for her to deal with since her attack. She longed for the peace that she had always found in the stillness of the trees. That peace had fled, along with her sense of safety and security. She had learned from William that to get over a fear, one must face that fear, so she had begun returning to the woods last year. It had taken her many times before she began to release the fear she had been living with.

Now she was able to again feel a semblance of peace here. Of course, she never ventured out of the castle without a guard. Life had taught her that lesson quite well. So she walked through the trees, knowing her guard was there, but paying him no heed as he trailed behind her.

Pausing for a moment, she listened to the sounds of the forest. The breeze rustled the leaves of the trees. Birds called out to one another. Various insects went about their daily hunt for food. The occasional susurration of some small creature foraging along the forest floor. Oh, how she relished these sounds! She closed her eyes, and taking a deep breath, enjoyed the cacophony.

A twig snapped and she had to fight the urge to turn to it and draw her knife. *It is merely the guard. There is no reason to fear.* Even so, anxiety rose up in her chest, like a great blackness that sought to destroy everything in its path. Her breaths became shallow, and her heart threatened to burst from her chest.

She could not open her eyes. The entire world was darkness and fear, and Guida was alone. So alone. There was no sound but the pounding of her heart in her ears. No sight but the darkness. Her nails cut open the skin on her palms, and the pain drew her out of her fear. She slipped her hand into her pocket and drew out her knife as she whirled around to face her attacker.

"Honestly, Guida? Will you forever greet me with a knife drawn?" William stood just feet away from her. He reached out and took the knife from her hand, his eyes taking stock of the cuts in her palm. "What have you done?"

She began to breathe again. Great gasping breaths that still did not seem to give her the air she needed. William pulled her to him, encircling her within his walls of safety. She clung to him as her breathing slowly returned to normal. He murmured reassurances into her ear as he rubbed circles along her back. As her senses returned, so did her defensiveness.

"Will you ever stop sneaking up on me?" she asked, stepping out of his embrace. "What are you doing out here?" It was better to be on the offensive. No sense in giving him more information than she needed to.

"Your uncle asked me to check up on you. He is concerned." He gave her a scrutinizing look.

She scoffed and shook her head. "Still acting as nursemaid."

"It is evident his concern is warranted. What other person do you know who draws a weapon whenever approached?"

"It is only you that I draw my weapon on. No one else continually sneaks up on me."

"Perhaps I should confiscate your weapons, then." He gave a slight grin.

"What are you doing here, William?" she sighed, in no mood to play. "Why did you come back? I am not conceited enough to believe you came back for me."

He furrowed his brow and thought for a moment before answering. "I have come to request soldiers from your uncle. There is a plan afoot that could change everything. It is just a beginning, but I can feel it, Guida. Everything rests on these coming events. If everything goes as I hope, I will soon be a landowner." His face shone with ambition. Guida had never seen him look so hopeful.

"What sort of plan? Is it something that will hurt my uncle in any way?" She could not believe that William would plot against Guaimar, but she had to be sure.

"Do you not know me better than that?" Anger flashed across his features before he relaxed. "Why must we always fight?"

"It eases the pain. Anger is an easier emotion than longing or fear." She had never vocalized this idea before, but the truth of it seeped into her soul.

He did not immediately respond, but drew closer to her while gazing into her eyes. "What frightens you, *mia tesoro?*" He took her hands in his and pulled her closer still.

"What frightens me?" she laughed. "Thankfully, not as much now as in the past. But right now, I am afraid of giving myself over to hope. I am afraid of further disappointment. Afraid of being left behind. Afraid that you will never truly come back for me. We have been apart for so long, how can you still love me?"

"The same way that you still love me. I can see it in your eyes and have felt it in your kiss. You have ever been present in my thoughts. I will not let you down, Guida. For both our sakes, I will make this campaign successful, and then your father will consent to our marriage." The earnestness in his words resonated within her as he pressed his lips to hers, and she rested in the strength he offered.

Chapter 36

The Banks of the Olivento River (Apulia) – March 1041

A rdouin was true to his word. The gates of Melfi had quickly opened for the Normans. Later, William learned that Ardouin had sung their praises to the Lombard populace, saying they had been sent by God to deliver them from the hands of the Romans. Whether the Lombards believed that was still to be seen, but it had been enough to get them through the gates, which meant the city was theirs.

That had been several weeks ago. The Norman force had spent the time since sending out raiding parties to different areas throughout Apulia, working to gain more control over the land. They now possessed the nearby towns of Venosa and Ascoli, with more sure to follow. The Lombards saw that William's people were helping them fight off the Romans and were beginning to join their efforts, making the Normans a force to be reckoned with.

"My Lord Iron Arm," Gregory began. Several of the men had begun calling William this, saying that he soon would be a lord, in truth. "The Romans have mustered their forces and are now several thousand strong. They are marching towards us as we speak."

"So it is here, on the banks of the Olivento River that we shall meet them." William had known that the time for this battle was drawing nigh and had been able to muster most of the chiefs, Hugh and Peter among them. Some were still out raiding, so the force against them vastly outnumbered the Norman-Lombard contingent. God would surely have to be with them if they were to win the day. The fact that the Romans were no match for the Norman knights under normal circumstances might not be enough to swing this battle their way.

"How many men have we been able to gather?" Count Drengot asked. The chiefs had gathered for a quick planning meeting in the predawn hours before the battle was to take place.

Peter was the first to respond. "Our last count was three hundred knights and six hundred foot soldiers." Every man in their circle knew that with those numbers victory was anything but sure.

Drengot turned his eyes to William. "We must pray the new fighting tactics Iron Arm has been teaching the men will be enough to turn this battle. If not, this may be the end of our campaign."

"We all know that we are the superior fighters here. It will be enough." Drogo chimed in, confident as ever.

A commotion stopped the men's conversation, and they turned to see what had stirred the company around them. Two soldiers marched toward the chiefs escorting a man dressed in Roman battle armor.

One of the soldiers spoke up. "We found this man approaching our camp. He says he has a message for Count Drengot."

Drengot stepped forward. "Let him speak, by all means. I am most anxious to hear what the Romans have to say to me."

The Roman stepped forward, still holding the reins of his horse. "I have a message for you, sir, from *Katepano* Michael Dokeianos, military leader of the Roman army. He knows that, by now, you can see how outnumbered you are. He offers you the chance to leave. Return to Lombard territory, and spare yourself the outcome of a bloody battle. You cannot win this. Better to stop now than needlessly waste the lives of your men."

Hugh marched over to the messenger, and looked him in the eye. He then turned to the Roman's warhorse. Raising his gauntleted fist high in the air, he brought it down on the back of the horse's head. The mighty warhorse immediately dropped. Dead.

The entire assembly was silenced. Not one man wanted to draw attention away from the message that Hugh was sending to their rivals.

It was only fitting that Hugh be the one to break the silence. Turning back to the messenger, he said, "You have our answer. Return to your *katepano*. Tell him we will meet him on the battlefield at dawn."

The messenger, who looked to be moments away from being ill, was escorted back out of the camp. Drengot turned his attention to Hugh, clapping him on the back and laughing aloud. "I could not have said that any better. You truly have a way, Touboeuf."

"Yes, I felt that they needed to be reminded who they are dealing with." He looked back at the lifeless body of the horse. "It may have been excessive, but it ought to be effective."

William had to ask, "Did you know you could do that?"

"It is not something I practice, Iron Arm," Hugh laughed out. "I never even thought about doing something like that before, and it is not likely to be something I will ever do again."

"How unfortunate that you killed such a fine animal," Drogo mourned. "You really ought to have hit the messenger and left us with the horse." Drogo looked as if he had just witnessed his own mother's funeral.

"Trust Drogo to feel more sympathy for an animal than for a man. I am sorry for your pain." Peter said with thinly veiled hostility, causing William to wonder what was amiss between the two men.

Drengot put an end to the banter. "Come on, men. We have a battle to prepare for."

Chapter 37

Guida and Guaimar rode out at their usual time. Instead of immediately giving her horse her head, Guida stayed near her uncle. Shifting uneasily in her saddle, she stole a few glances at her uncle as they continued down the road.

"What is troubling you, my dear?" Guaimar asked with a chuckle. "You may as well speak, for you are not currently at peace."

"There are many rumors coming from Apulia. What news have you received of the fighting? I cannot believe everything that I have been hearing, and I would like to know the truth."

"I have received word from some of my men, William among them. The Norman forces met with a much larger Roman army several weeks ago in a pitched battle."

"That's not a common occurrence in war, is it? I had just imagined men sieging castles and attempting to defend strongholds. The thought of the generals agreeing on a time and place for battle had not occurred to me. I suppose I do not have a clear picture of what actually takes place."

"No, not common, but not unheard of. I am uncertain what led to both sides choosing to agree to it, but it has happened. Count Drengot had been leading the Normans..."

"I had heard that William was leading them," Guida interrupted.

"Listen, my dear," Guaimar instructed. "Count Drengot had been leading the Normans with Ardouin leading the Lombards. Not long into the campaign, the Normans began looking to Sir William to lead them. They began the battle by charging with their cavalry in the center and their foot soldiers flanking the edges. They were victorious despite the odds and won the day.

"They have since had their numbers increased by more Lombards in the area that are now willing to fight against their Roman overlords. It is proving to be a hopeful situation, as the Lombards would rather be friends with the Normans than under the rule of the Romans. They are also being joined by more Normans who arrive in the country every day. My men report that Sir William is an easy man to follow. He inspires those he fights beside, and they would all follow him unquestioningly."

"Is not that a good thing? I would think that it would be good to have a man who has proven loyal to you rising up among the Normans. Will William truly gain much from this endeavor?"

"Of course. He was appointed one of the chiefs who will split their spoils evenly. He will need to send some of that here, to compensate for the men I supplied. But beyond that he will keep all that he can. That includes land. He is bound to be in a much better position when he returns from this venture."

"Assuming he returns," she said quietly.

"He still has a long road ahead of him in order to gain full control of all of Apulia."

"But will it stop there? What will they do after they gain Apulia?"

"Is that not enough?" he laughed. "I believe they will be satisfied once they gain more of a foothold in the area. Besides, they may be able to rout the Romans out of Apulia, but that does not mean they won't come back. The Romans are not known for easily letting go of their territories. They will not take kindly to these usurpers. We need not worry about the Normans gaining too much control. William is my friend and ally. I am more certain of his character than I am of nearly any other man. I would much prefer having him ruling as my neighbor than any of those foolish thieves to the East."

"Yes, only William is a lone Norman. The Normans as a whole have not pledged allegiance to one side or the other. Up until now they have been simple mercenaries fighting for the biggest purse. How do you know that they will stay on our side?"

"My dear, these are uncertain times. We are, none of us, loyal to one side our entire lives. Men must choose every day who to flatter and who to contend with. The only person you can truly trust is yourself. You are smarter than half the men I employ and keep in my house. I love you dearly, yet I cannot predict who you would follow next year, or in ten years. So much around us will have changed by then. You will likely be married and may adopt many of your husband's views on who to form alliances with and who to be wary of. Some of those views will doubtless be different than my own. This is why you have to only trust yourself."

"Are you saying that we may be on opposing sides someday? How can you say that? I love you, Uncle, and I respect your opinions. How could I ever see things differently?"

"Well, we are not on opposing sides now. Let us speak of happier things and enjoy the rest of our morning."

Chapter 38

William's head was swimming. He could hardly see straight, let alone stand erect. He was freezing one moment and in the fires of hell the next. Months of war and strategy meetings and sleeping out in the elements had finally taken their toll. Now his body fought against itself with fever.

That dreaded word. Fever. How many mighty men had been dragged down to death by fever? Yet, William was too headstrong to allow it to best him. Besides, they were scheduled to meet the enemy army on the morrow for their second pitched battle. There was still more planning to do with the other chiefs. He did not have time to rest while his body struggled through this internal fight.

"You look dead already." Drogo was never the voice of comfort, but William would have struck him if he had the energy to do so.

The chiefs were meeting inside William's tent, and William was grateful to be out of the sun.

"Why not lay down in the corner there. That way you can rest while still listening and advising us." Peter suggested.

"I think I will. Thank you." He fairly flopped onto his pallet, causing his head to throb all the more. How could he fight tomorrow when his head was being ripped apart from the inside today? He prayed that the fog in his head would lift before he was required to.

"Perhaps we could simply lure the Romans into the river and have them all drown," Drogo suggested. "It would certainly simplify matters."

It was not really a possibility, but in his weakened state, William hoped for an easy battle. Having the river close during their first battle had certainly aided the Normans. They had found that few of their enemies were able to swim and were soon drowned. This next battle, although in a different location, would also take place near a river.

The men ignored Drogo and kept discussing their plans. William paid no heed to who was speaking as he closed his eyes in a vain attempt to block out his pain.

"We are outnumbered again."

"Yes, but as we saw last time, numbers are not the only factor leading to victory."

"Not the only factor, but not one to be dismissed, either."

"Our cavalry is much better trained. We have the techniques that Lord Iron Arm has taught."

Unable to remain focused on the discussion, William's mind drifted. With his eyes closed, he could see the hundreds of bodies left in the wake of this campaign. The images of men cut down before their time would likely never leave him. Men on both sides had perished, but the

Normans had fought strategically and, so far, had won the day. *Is it worth it?* Faces floated through his memory. Faces belonging to the men he had killed. Some belonged to older men who had already lived a full life, at least William hoped that they had. Others were still in their youth, many younger than even Gregory. These faces would stalk William's dreams for as long as he lived.

"William," Hugh interrupted William's thoughts, "you have studied war theories. What must we take into account while devising our strategy?"

Please, God. Let my mind be clear, and help me lead these men regardless of my health. Do not let this be how I die. Not now, before I make it back to Guida.

William was one of the few men in the company who could read, let alone who had been able to read any military and war strategy writings. William suspected that was one of the deciding factors which led to him leading this group of fighters.

"There are five pertinent factors to account for when laying plans for war," William answered from his pallet. "Of those five there are three that ought to be our primary concerns. These are the weather, terrain, and order of deployment.

"We have our cavalry, and they are vital to this fight. But we must not discount the role that our foot soldiers must play. We need a plan that will utilize both of our forces."

William's focus drifted as Drengot took command of the planning. Drifting in and out of sleep, he only responded when he was directly spoken to. He would have Drogo share any vital decisions with him after he had a chance to rest some more.

William woke to find Guida standing over him. Kneeling next to him, she placed her hand on his cheek. "William, my love." He grasped her hand and pressed it to his lips. He pulled her down to lay with him. Resting her head on his chest, he never wanted her to move. Wrapping his arms around her, he felt content, complete.

"I am almost there, Guida. I am so close, but I cannot see the end."

"You must! You have to finish this, or we can never be together." She turned to gaze into his eyes.

"I am worried. I need you with me." He tightened his hold on her, afraid that she might slip away from him.

"I am always with you, mio vita, cuore mio. *My life. My heart. But, you must get up and fight for us. Fight, and then return to me."*

William stirred from his delirium long enough to feel the loss of Guida's absence, yet comforted with the thought of her, he fell into a restful slumber.

Chapter 39

Salerno – July 1041

R acing down the corridor, Guida's skirts flew, threatening to tangle and cast her to the ground. Her footfalls smacked against the solid stone floor, announcing her presence well before her arrival at Guaimar's chamber. Having just learned that a missive had come for him from Apulia, she could not rest until she knew what news it held. She desperately needed to know if William was still alive. Nothing mattered beyond that.

Her dreams had changed over the past weeks. Gone were the faces of those who had haunted her for so long. They had been replaced fully by William. She dreamed of him needing her. She was his strength, and it filled the darkness of her soul with purpose. Feeling needed was new for her. Although it came in the night and was likely not real, it changed the way she saw herself.

Reaching Guaimar's chamber, she found the door ajar and heard Guaimar and Gemma fighting inside. She started to back away until she heard her name, and she leaned in closer again to hear.

"Guida should not even be here! She needs to go home. Let her own parents care for her. I am sick of having her here!" Gemma yelled. These outbursts were becoming commonplace, and no longer surprised Guida. The sting of such comments had not lessened, however.

"She does not wish to leave, nor do I wish her to. This is her home! I will not cast her aside!"

"Guy asks too much of you, of us," Gemma continued, as if not hearing her husband. "He must find her a husband and then we can be rid of her! I want her gone!" Her voice lowered, and Guida leaned in closer to the door to hear. "Your own son died because she was too weak to protect him. How can you still care for her?"

"Woman, stop!" Guaimar's tone deepened with warning. "You will not bring my son into this, as if you cared for him. I have never raised my hand to a woman, but that may easily change if you persist. It was not her fault, and I will not have you accusing her of it! Guida was a victim, the same as John." His voice softened as he asked, "Where does this hatred come from? What has Guida done to deserve your disdain?"

"Do not touch me!" Guida heard the swish of skirts and loud steps moving to the door, and she jumped back. There was nowhere to hide in the open corridor, and she knew Gemma would know right away that she had been eavesdropping, but there was nothing to be done now.

Gemma exited the chamber and faced Guida.

"Aunt Gemma, I..." Guida began, but not knowing how to continue.

Gemma stared coldly at Guida and then turned and walked away. Guida turned back to the now fully opened door and found Guaimar watching her.

"Uncle Guaimar, I did not mean to overhear. It was wrong of me." Her head hung in shame as she confessed.

"Do not worry yourself about it, my dear. This is just Gemma being Gemma. Let us not think on it."

"Uncle, why have you kept me here? I love you, but maybe there is some truth to what she says. For whatever reason, I am a source of misery for her. She is your wife. I would understand if you wished to be rid of me."

"I fear nothing will remove the hatred in her heart." Guaimar looked older than Guida remembered, as if he had aged a few years in the few short hours since she had seen him last.

"Thank you for what you said to her."

"Of course. Now, what do you need?"

"Oh! I nearly forgot. I heard that you had news of the fighting." All thoughts of her aunt disappeared as she returned her focus to William.

"Yes. Come in and you may read the missive. It is there on the table." He turned to sit in a chair near the fireplace. It was too warm to have a fire, but Guaimar stared into the blackness as Guida read.

...Iron Arm down...fever...roused to lead...Normans refuse to back down...fight with fierceness...force three times their size...cavalry charged the center...foot soldiers flanked edges...

Guida skimmed over the account of the battle hoping for more information about William.

...took down many men despite fever...sizable war bounty for Normans...respite from fighting...hopes of gaining support...next target...stronghold at Montepeloso... south of Melfi...workable strategy.

Your servant ___

But is he alive? She turned back to her uncle. "Is this all of it? This cannot be everything."

"Guida, just ask what you want to know." He said with a sigh.

"Does William yet live?" Her voice sounded small in the large chamber.

"I believe he does. He is one of the leaders, and I would think his death would warrant a mention." His eyes narrowed, and he leaned forward in his chair. "Guida, that was a great victory, but it does not guarantee William for you."

"I know, but it gives me hope. Thank you." Kissing her uncle on the cheek, she turned and left.

Chapter 40

Near Montepeloso – September 1041

One more battle, one William was determined to win. He was more than ready to be done with this entire adventure. With what he would gain from this battle, he would be able to return and seek Guida's hand. He would be a landowner at last. Combined with the riches he had been stocking up, he had finally made a future with Guida possible. He would build her a home and give her anything she could ever want.

"We should just assault the castle," Hugh suggested.

With the planning meeting continuing, William forced his mind back to it. Hugh had no patience and was always pushing them to rush right into battle. He did not have a head for strategy, and William had to make sure that he did not sway the other chiefs to follow his rash words.

"If we assault the castle," William pointed out, "they have the benefit of the castle defenses. We will lose more and more men before we can finally breach the wall, assuming we are able to breach the wall before we are weakened beyond being able to finish the campaign. No, we need to find a way to have them meet us on equal ground."

Drogo answered, "They have already refused to meet us in another pitched battle. They have realized they cannot beat us that way."

"We need to think of a way to make them...reconsider," Drengot said with a slight tilt of his head.

"Suppose we starve them out?" William mused. "A siege would take time, but the cold weather hasn't set in yet. We are not in a rush, are we? We just surround them and assure that no food goes in. Eventually they will run out and be forced to meet us."

Drogo jumped on the idea. "We could speed up the process by getting rid of their animals."

"We cannot just slaughter all of them," Peter said, vehemently disagreeing with Drogo.

"Is there a way for us to take them and keep them for ourselves?" Count Drengot asked. "I do not want everything destroyed before we take control of the area and render it useless."

"We must send a scout to see when the animals are let out to pasture," William instructed. "He can assess if there is a way for us to get them. Hugh and Drogo, I want you two in charge of this. Make certain you are not found out."

"We know how to be discreet, William," Drogo said derisively, as he led Hugh out of the tent.

"That man does not know the meaning of discretion," Peter muttered.

Ignoring him, William huffed, "Now we wait. Get some rest, all of you. We all must be at our best for this battle, however it comes about." The men all filed out of the tent, leaving William alone with his thoughts.

Chapter 41

Salerno – October 1041

A few days later Guaimar found Guida at the top of the castle wall. "Will you never tire of this view?"

She turned loving eyes on her uncle. "Never! I will love it until the day I die."

Guaimar grunted and rolled his eyes, "Always so dramatic."

Guida laughed and wrapping her arm through his, resting her head on his shoulder. They both gazed over the forest, lost for a time in their own thoughts.

"I do not wish to interrupt your solitude, but something has come up. Something that I believe will delight you. Will you take a walk with me?"

"Of course," she said, allowing him to guide her from the wall.

"A situation has arisen in regard to Sir William."

Guida stopped walking and faced him. She felt blood drain from her face. "Is he...?" She could not even say the word.

"No, no, my dear girl," he answered as he patted her cheek. "He is alive and well. I am sorry to make you worry." They began walking again. "No. He has been appointed by the other Normans as the Count of Apulia, which drastically changes his situation."

Stopping yet again, Guida could only stare straight ahead. "What does that mean? How can the Normans appoint anyone with a title?" This could not be true, could it? After these years of waiting, would William truly come back for her?

"Well, technically, Count Drengot can bestow titles, as long as they are beneath his own. This puts William on equal footing with Drengot, which is not exactly proper. In order for this title to mean anything, it would need to be ratified by someone of a higher rank, such as myself or the emperor."

"Was not the agreement for the chiefs to split everything evenly? Are the other chiefs given titles as well?"

"The others are made barons under William. They elevated William, as a show of respect for the leadership role he played."

"Will you ratify William's title then?" Guida could not believe this news of good fortune. When William left Salerno, he had possessed next to nothing. Now he was titled with land, wealth, and power.

"This is the heart of what I wished to speak to you about." They had arrived at Guaimar's business chamber. Leading her to a chair near the fireplace, Guaimar continued. "It seems the Normans suddenly have a solid foothold in this country. This will affect the politics of the other nobles, myself included. I am concerned about the Normans continuing to increase their influence and power and would like to ensure their continued alliance with me."

A feeling of dread settled over Guida. "How do you propose to do that?" She asked hesitantly.

"I would like you to marry him."

Guida slumped in her chair, an enormous weight forcing her down. How could she respond to that? It was everything she had wanted for years, but the reality did not bring the joy she had longed for.

"I expected a much different reaction, Guida." Her uncle's gaze was intense. "I thought you would be pleased. Have I misjudged your feelings for the man?"

Guida shook her head in confusion. "I hardly know, Uncle. I need to think on this. Could we speak more of this later? I would like to get some fresh air."

"Of course. I'll expect you back for the evening meal." He kissed her cheek. "I would sooner see you with William than with some other noble whose character is less deserving. Take that into consideration, my dear."

"Yes, Uncle." She turned and walked away.

Guida's need to escape was overwhelming. Leaving the castle through her and John's secret way, she began to run. No guard could help her now; the need to escape consumed her. She ran for as long as her legs could carry her. As her legs began to give out, she reached out to grasp a tree trunk, successfully bringing her to a full stop. Turning, she sat down in one swift movement. As she leaned back against the tree, her mind revisited the dark thoughts she had been trying to run away from.

She needed air. Her chest rose and fell in the usual manner, although quicker than normal, yet she felt no benefits of the action. Her head felt too light and there were black spots encroaching on her vision.

Getting married. She was getting married. And to the man she loved! So, why was she so unhappy? Why did tears come to her eyes at the thought? Was it simply the fact that she was a pawn in the political game? Guaimar needed a way to link this rising Norman with the empire to ensure his loyalty, and she was in an ideal position to be that link.

No. Guaimar could have married her off at any point to any number of men, and he had stayed his hand. Her father, too, could have forced his will. Thankfully, for her sake, he had not pushed her.

Then why did she feel the need to scream? In fact, that was just what she did. She screamed, and screamed, and then screamed some more. She was in the middle of a forest with no one else around, and she was determined to find some emotional release.

When her throat was on fire and she could no longer produce the energy needed for such an exercise, she finally stopped. She thought of William. For all she knew he might not yet know of her uncle's plan. *What if he does not wish to marry me?* After all, he had been gone so long. He may have decided that he did not love her like he had thought. *What will I do then?* Nothing. There was nothing she could do about it.

Having no real experience with marriage, she thought of those she had seen. They were anything but happy alliances. Guaimar had been married for many years, and Guida had never witnessed any affection between them. Her own parents' match had been anything but blissful. Her father dominated his wife and had never left her in doubt as to who was in charge. Her mother enjoyed precious little freedom because of him. For how much Guida just wanted to be loved, she did not see marriage as the means to achieve that goal.

The growing shadows indicated the lateness of the hour. Guida needed to return to the castle soon if she was to join the family for supper as Guaimar had requested. Wiping her tear-stained cheeks, she stood up on wobbly legs, and turned back.

After only a few steps, she saw a couple of men, still a good distance away, but moving in her direction. She continued on her way, surprised at her lack of panic. She surreptitiously removed her concealed daggers, one from her pocket and the other from inside her stocking, hiding her hands in the folds of her skirt. She was not at ease, yet her faculties seemed to still be functioning, and she was not dissolving in anxiety.

The closer the men grew, the quicker Guida's heart pounded. Hoping that she would be allowed to pass by unhindered, she moved to the side of the path.

"Look what we have here," the shorter of the two men said.

"She is a pretty little morsel, I do say," the other answered.

Guida continued as if to pass by, but the tall one stepped in front, blocking her path.

"You would not leave me here with only this sorry sot for company, now would you?" the tall man asked.

"Please, excuse me," Guida said, attempting to sound braver than she truly was. "I must be going."

"Yes, she said you would not come willingly," the short man said.

"She? Who?" Guida asked. "You must have me mistaken for someone else."

"I do not think so, my lady," the tall one said with a twist of her arm. "We know exactly who you are."

"Then you must know that I cannot come with you. My uncle is expecting me back."

"Yes, well, your aunt is not as keen for your return, unfortunately." The short man took a step toward her, and she pulled out a knife and held it in front of her.

"Not another step," she informed them, "or I will slit your throats."

The short man laughed at her threat and continued forward.

Guida took a quick breath, then let fly her first knife, catching the man in the middle of his left thigh.

Anger flashed on the other's face, and he made to grab her. Spinning out of his reach, she slashed unsuccessfully at him. When she came back around to face him once more, she stabbed him using her momentum to force the blade into the soft part of his abdomen. The sickening sound of punctured skin met her ears and blood gushed out, covering her hand. The man cursed as he slumped at her feet.

Turning back to her other opponent, she found him limping away yet keeping his eye on her. She took a threatening step toward him, bloodied hand and knife outstretched. The trembling limb disconcerted her, but her mind was clear.

She watched him struggle out of sight, only then allowing herself to move. Half running, half stumbling, she made it back to the castle wall, meeting Sir Enzo.

"My lady, we were coming out to search for you," he said, taking in her bloody and disheveled state. "What has happened?" he asked with more urgency.

"Two men attacked," she said, pointing behind her. "One stumbled off, but the other will still be on the road."

Sir Enzo issued commands to the few men with him, who quickly left to seek her attackers.

"Go get cleaned up, my lady. My men and I will handle the rest."
Guida nodded and turned to the castle.

The steaming water of her bath soothed her muscles, yet her mind
could not erase the events of the day. Over and over again she relived
those brief moments on the road.

Suddenly she sat upright, splashing water onto the floor. Gripping
the edge of the wooden tub, her fingertips grew white as another
memory took hold.

What had they said? *"...your aunt is not as keen for your return."*

Her aunt had sent them. Was it Gemma that the men had been
referring to? Nodding to herself she realized it could only have been
Aunt Gemma. No one else hated Guida enough for an ambush such as
this.

If so, did that mean it was also Gemma that Giovan was with when
he plotted to kill Guaimar? Guida recalled hearing a woman's voice at
the time. It must be Gemma, but she did not wish to believe it. Yet, the
truth of it settled in her heart. She had no other aunt who wished her
any ill will.

"Are you well, my lady?" Alys asked as she reentered the room,
carrying clean clothes for Guida.

"Help me out," she demanded. "I must speak with my uncle."

Chapter 42

The two men's horses trotted through the newly fallen leaves in unison. Gregory had insisted on accompanying William back to Salerno. He had been given the option many times over the years to join with any of the other chiefs, but he had remained loyal to William and refused to leave his service. Gregory had long since finished his training, and William considered the younger man one of his closest friends. So why had William not told him the reason for this journey?

"You are white as a sheet, sir. You look more frightened than I have ever seen you."

William grunted. He did not wish to be drawn into conversation right now. His thoughts were a jumble, wondering what his reception would be. Did Guida really want this match? Given the way she had received him the last time, he could not imagine her welcoming him with open arms. A knife to the throat, perhaps, but not joy. In fact, it might be wise to scout out the castle ramparts before approaching to be certain she was not lying in wait with her bow to kill him before having to be wed to him. At this point, he honestly did not know what to expect.

She had loved him at one point, but that had been years ago. Their interactions since that time had been so volatile. He had loved her as well. He still did, if he was honest with himself. She was the primary reason he was yet alive. Without the strength that thoughts of her brought him, he would have succumbed to the fever he had suffered months ago. But that hardly mattered right now.

Many things could have changed while he was gone. Could she have met someone new? Someone else who had won her heart? Was she being forced into this arrangement against her wishes? What was he thinking accepting Guaimar's offer? How could he have accepted before he saw her again? He ought to have returned before sending his answer. As much as he desperately wanted to marry Guida, he would not take an unwilling bride. If she did not want him, he hoped that Guaimar would be forgiving on the matter.

In battle, he had the courage of ten men, yet at the threshold of matrimony he was nothing short of a coward. He must focus on his forward momentum. He would be there soon and see Guida. She would not hide her feelings from him. She never had.

"Do not look so solemn. You look like you are attending your own funeral." Guaimar teased with a smile. The family had gathered in the great hall to welcome William back. Guards had seen him approaching on the road and informed the prince. William would be ushered in any moment now.

Most of the gathering were happy to be seeing William again. Thankfully, Aunt Gemma was not here to dampen the excitement. After relaying what she knew to her uncle, Guida had learned that Gemma had been confined to her chambers, where she could be guarded at all times. Both of Guida's attackers had been apprehended, and during their interrogation they corroborated Guida's assumptions.

Guida, however, seemed to be the only one not overjoyed about being there. She did not wish to greet William in front of her relations. How she longed for a private reunion.

The outer doors opened and William entered, along with Sir Gregory. William walked directly to the family and bowed, first to Uncle Guaimar, then to Gaitelgrima, and finally to Guida. Uncle Guaimar wasted no time in taking up all of William's attention, asking him seemingly endless questions about his recent adventures giving Guida time to study him.

He was certainly still quite handsome, although there was something different about his eyes. They looked worn somehow, and not simply from the weariness that his journey would have caused. When she had first met this man, he had laughter in his eyes. Throughout the next few years she had seen friendship in them, and later, love. Now, it was as if he were purposefully avoiding her gaze. What could be hidden there that he would not wish for her to see?

"Shall we retire to the solar, where we will all be more comfortable?" Uncle Guaimar began moving before anyone could respond, but stopped when William spoke up.

"My liege, if you will permit it, I would like to speak with Lady Guida. We can speak more this afternoon."

"Of course! I ought to have realized that you would wish to discuss your upcoming wedding first. By all means, there will be plenty of time for our discussion later."

Then turning to Guida, but still avoiding her eyes, William asked, "Would you care to take a ride with me, my lady?"

Guida had not spoken a single word since William had entered the room. She did not want to go for a ride with him, or speak with him, or even see him. What if he saw through her thin façade and saw the quaking woman she was? She was so frightened that he would be unhappy with this arrangement. Perhaps that was what was lingering just out of sight. Regret.

She slowly nodded. "Let me change my dress, and I shall meet you at the stables."

"What are you doing, William?" Guida would avoid the issue no longer. They might as well get this unpleasantness over with.

"I am riding my horse, my lady." he replied in an attempt at humor.

"I am not amused, *sir*. You know what I mean. Are you not pleased that we are to be wed? Are you taking me off alone to cancel our wedding and to save me some embarrassment, rather than say it in front of my relations?"

William did not answer. Stopping his horse, he dismounted and approached Guida. He reached up to assist her off of her horse. She allowed him to assist her down.

Grabbing the reins of both horses he tied them to a nearby tree. He then began walking into the forest.

"Where are you going? I assumed we were going to talk about this, so why are you leaving?" His silence was not helping her nerves.

"Come along!" he called back to her.

They only walked a short ways into the woods, just enough to not be seen from the road, should anyone pass by, but close enough to still see the horses.

"Now," William began, "I am not changing my mind. I would, however, like you to know my views on marriage. I have had the benefit of seeing both happy and cheerless marriages. My father and my mother did not care for one another. Their marriage was similar to your aunt and uncle's. My home was a miserable place, and I often dreamt of being anywhere else. Then my mother died. Not one tear was ever shed by my father, and I was torn between being heartbroken at losing my mother and relieved that the fighting was over." He turned and sat on an old tree stump.

"Soon after my mother passed, my father met Fressenda. She was everything that my own mother was not. She instantly loved us all, and she showed it in her every action. She took the time to teach us what we needed to learn, as well as taking care of our basic needs. She was kind and loving and never once yelled unnecessarily at any of us."

He paused, sighing and running his hand through his hair. "My father married her soon after, and our home was happy for the first time I could recall. My father dotes on Fressenda, and she adores him. That is not to say that they have never fought, but it was different. They were not out simply to hurt one another. They fought over differing opinions but never out of enmity. They never let the other one feel that they were unloved in any way. That is the kind of marriage that I want. I believe, I hope, that you and I could have such a marriage. You loved me once. Do you love me still?"

He looked at the ground, but Guida could feel his vulnerability. The conflicting sight of the fierce warrior admitting his deepest desires was almost more than Guida could manage. Her previous feelings of being powerless and thrown about by the events of life seemed insignificant to William's wide open heart.

What am I supposed to say to that? She really had no words. So instead of answering, she walked to him and took one of his hands in hers. His focus shifted to their hands, as did hers, and she felt her fears melt away. She loved this man. No matter what happened, even after all of these years, she still loved him. Giving him a tentative smile, which he did not see, she raised her other hand to caress his cheek.

"Look at me, William." It was barely a whisper.

He lifted his head, and she had a glimpse of the little boy he must have been. Serious and unsure. His eyes held hers and she found herself leaning in. She rested her forehead on his.

"You have been honest with me, and I shall be honest with you." She closed her eyes, and leaned away again. "When you first knew me I was a weak, naive maid. I allowed good people to die because I did not understand the dangers of the world. But I am no longer that woman. I have learned to protect myself, as well as those around me. I have become strong and capable of fighting my own battles. However, that strength is not everything. I have found that I still lack the most important thing of all. You. All I need, all I will ever need, is you."

"Oh, Guida." He stood up and took her face in his hands. Lowering his head, he kissed her. It was not a kiss of passion, but one filled with hope for the future.

Chapter 43

Salerno – November 1041

You look well, Daughter," Lord Guy stated as Guida greeted
them on the steps of the castle. Her family had just arrived.
Lady Raingarta and Maria would help with the final planning
of the wedding which would take place in three days time.

"It is good to see you, Father. Mother." She curtsied to each in turn.
Then, turning her attention to the young woman who stood a little
behind them, she exclaimed, "Maria! I am so pleased to see you." Guida
walked over and kissed her sister's cheek. Then, taking Maria by the
arm, she turned back to her parents. "Come, I will show you to your
chambers. You must be weary after your journey."

She escorted her parents to their chambers, leaving them with a
promise to see them at supper. Then turning back to Maria, she asked,
"How does this castle compare with Father's? Having never seen it, I
must confess, I am curious."

Maria squeezed Guida's arm as they walked. "It is nothing like here. This castle is well established and finished. Father's construction has been slow. He has little time to spend overseeing the construction. He is far too busy attempting to appease the people. They were sorely abused by Isolde's parents, and it takes time to build up trust with a new lord."

Guida could not help but smile. "You certainly have grown. I see that father has not spared your education. I am glad of it."

Brushing Guida's comments aside, Maria continued. "We are working still on the outer buildings and a solar in the top of the east tower. It is smaller than this, but Father has allowed for enough room to have more built on later as he expands his holdings. It will be lovely, I am sure, when all is completed. For now, the furnishings are bare, and we lack all of the fine tapestries and ornaments that are present here. To be perfectly honest, this seems a bit opulent after so long in Father's keep."

"Even so, I wish that I could see it. With me getting married now, I have no idea when I will be able to visit." Guida sighed wistfully.

"When do I get to see Sir William? Is he still handsome? Or is he terribly scarred from his years at war? I want to hear everything!" Maria now sounded the very epitome of an excitable young woman, and it did Guida's heart good to hear it. There was no heaviness weighing her sister down from the cruelties of the world. Her sister had been well protected.

Guida smiled at her. "You will be able to judge for yourself this evening. For now, would you like to see my wedding dress?"

Maria squealed and grabbed Guida's arm again. "Oh yes, please."

The dress was laid out on Guida's bed when they arrived in her chamber. Alys had been adding extra embroidery and beads to it as she had the time. It was a lovely overdress with tree branches and leaves embroidered through the bodice.

Maria's brows lowered. "But, it's green."

The simple statement held much of meaning. Green symbolized young love, which was a common enough color for a bride to wear. Few people who were witnesses of the wedding procession to the church in town would comment on Guida's choice of gown. However, her mother had worn blue for her wedding, the symbol of purity. Her grandmother, and her great grandmother, and so on, had all worn blue. Guida would be the first in a long chain of ancestors to not follow tradition.

"Yes, it is green," she conceded.

"Are you not afraid of what Mother will say?" Maria eyes were wide with wonder.

"I must confess, I am slightly concerned." Guida sat down on the bed and her shoulders slumped.

"Then, why? I am sure you have a lovely blue gown. Let's look through your clothes and see what our options are."

"No!" Taking a deep breath, she calmed her voice. "No. I have made my decision. Green it shall be."

Maria's brow wrinkled once more. "But why?"

"Did no one ever tell you?" She did not know why, but she had simply assumed her father would have shared the account of her youthful experience with her mother and sister. And then she remembered. She had asked Uncle Guaimar to not spread the details of her attack with her parents. It would seem he had honored that request. Even after all these years they had not received word of it.

"Oh, Maria! The world is a terrible place." Guida told her everything. She would not deny her sister a view into her private thoughts and memories. Maria was in need of someone to prepare her for the world that she lived in, since their mother had never prepared either of them for anything.

"But William saved you before any loss of virtue. And now for him to marry you. That is so romantic!" Maria's eyes held a far off look.

Guida grabbed Maria's arm and shook it a little. "Trust me, there was nothing romantic about it. It was the single most horrific day of my entire life! Do not simply dismiss it. You do not know what it is like to have the deaths of innocents on your head! You do not know what it is like to be exposed like that. To be touched, bruised, defiled by some unscrupulous devil of a man. To feel so dirty, even after years have gone by. To know that no man would want you if they knew. To feel so small and helpless and alone." Wiping the tears from her cheeks, she continued. "Being always afraid. Never knowing who to trust. Feeling your whole life has just been defined by an experience that lasted mere moments. Those moments have made me who I am today, for good or ill."

Maria had moved Guida's dress at some point in the retelling and sat next to Guida on the bed. Now she slid closer to her older sister and wrapped her arms around her. Guida continued to cry, letting out more than just remnant tears of that day long ago. Her tears carried her frustrations with the world and her anxieties over the coming days.

"Do you still feel that way? Afraid?" Maria asked.

Wiping her face, Guida answered, "No. It took me years to overcome it, but I no longer live in fear." She thought of the men she had injured on the road. She had not mentioned that to anyone, and she would not burden her lovely sister with the knowledge now. "I realize now that I have power within me. I am not defined by my experiences, but rather by my responses to them. Besides, I do love William. I love him more than I ever thought possible, and I will show him that love every day of our lives, beginning on the day of our wedding with the color of my dress."

"That is so romantic," Maria gushed. "You have every right to wear green, if you wish it. And I will support you. I cannot speak for mother, though. I fear that you still have a bit of a fight on your hands."

Chapter 44

Salerno – December 1041

Guida had spent no time alone with William since the first day he had returned. He had been shut in with her father and uncle working on first the marriage contract, then on their plans for the future. Evidently, William and Guida would not be remaining in Salerno for long after they were married. Uncle Guaimar had his sights set on Calabria in the south and wanted William to lead the campaign. Guida had strong feelings about these plans, but had not been allowed into the strategy meetings. She was being given no say over her future, which was typical, yet galling.

Now the day for her wedding had come, and Guida had awoken early. Indeed she had hardly slept at all. She could not remain still, either. She would only sit for moments at a time before jumping up and pacing the floor. She was nervous about what this day would bring. Her entire life was about to change and she had conflicting feelings about it.

She decided to go to her favorite spot on the battlements of the castle. After today she did not know when she would have another opportunity, if ever. Leaving her room in her current state was a risk as she still wore her dressing gown with her hair cascaded down her back in an unruly tangle, but she did not care. It was too early for most people to be awake, let alone be out and moving about. Sliding her feet into her slippers, she pulled a fur on over her night dress and left her bedchamber.

The castle was darker than she was used to. She did not often venture from the safety of her room after saying goodnight to the family, so she never saw the corridors with so few torches lit. Thankfully, she knew the way so she did not bother with bringing a candle; yet, she was keenly aware of the dismal hues around her. She passed a few guards on her way up, but none of them paid her any heed, for which she was grateful.

The moon was high in the sky when she exited into the night. Soon the sun would rise and she would watch as God revealed the beauty of the earth by shining His orb of light onto all living things. She walked distractedly along the wall, dragging her hand along the parapet. About halfway to her favorite spot, she noticed a dark shadow ahead of her. Suddenly she felt foolish. She should have known he would also be awake. Her heart skipped a beat as she continued her approach.

"You are up awfully early, sir."

"I could say the same for you. I wondered if you would make your way up here." William turned toward her and leaned his back against the wall.

She moved so she had a clear view out of the crenel, not wishing to miss the first rays of the sun. "Well, here I am." Suddenly feeling shy, she did not know what else to say. She was grateful for the darkness that cloaked them so he could not see her uncertainty.

Moving, he stood directly behind her. She was trapped between him and the wall, yet she did not panic. Her heart sped up again, in a way that was not at all unpleasant. She could feel his warmth encasing her, and she relished this new feeling of safety. As she identified it, she turned to look him in the face.

"What is it?" He looked genuinely concerned and took a step backward. She was not ready to be parted from him, so she reached out and grabbed hold of his tunic. He did not need any more encouragement. He bent his head and claimed her mouth with his own. It was as if all of the tension and anger of the past was being erased. The closer their bodies got together the farther away the rest of the world felt. His hands grabbed her around the waist and hoisted her up to sit in the crenel. Her legs were wrapped around his torso as she held on for dear life. She loved this man more than anything. This perfect moment stretched on and on until Guida finally pulled away.

"I need to breathe!" She kept her arms around his neck as his hands rubbed circles on her back. They both tried to catch their breaths.

William brought one hand up to caress her cheek. "What are you thinking?"

She eyed him, wondering if she should tell him the truth. "I was thinking how perfectly happy I am right now, in this moment."

He pressed his forehead to hers, as he had done in the past. "Me, too. Guida, I love you."

"Really?" she whispered.

"Guida, how could you ever doubt it?"

"The day you returned long ago, I confessed my love for you, but you did not respond in kind. You kissed me, which left no doubt in my mind that you wanted me, yet you did not say the words."

William chuckled. "You silly woman. Everything I have done since first setting eyes on you has been to get to this point, where I could finally make you mine." He kissed her again, without all the passion, but with all the tenderness she could ever hope for.

"You have seen me at my absolute worst, and you probably know me better than any other living soul. You know my strengths and weaknesses, my virtues and vices."

"Yes, I do," he answered with a sly grin. "You are the most determined, faithful, honest person that I have ever met. You have more courage than most of the men who follow me. You are full of faith in God and reflect His love for his people. You are more beautiful than any woman should be allowed to be, and I cannot wait to have you all to myself."

Thinking on other marriages, she asked, "What if I am no good at being a wife?"

William turned her gently around, wrapping his arms around her waist from behind. They both watched for the sun to appear over the horizon. The beginning of a new day, the day they would begin their lives together. She rested her hands on his arms as she basked in his presence.

"I know what that man did years ago left its marks on you," he continued, "but those have only added to the incredible woman that you have become. That experience has led you to develop new skills and has strengthened your mind by teaching you more about the world. I do not want some naive maiden who might wither under the harsh realities of life. You have already been tested, and I know what you do in the face of adversity. I have not always shown you the respect that you are due. But I will spend the rest of my life, however long that may be, attempting to show you how deep my love for you is."

Guida was silent as his words seeped deep into her soul.

William continued, "You are like the sun. See how it rises slowly, almost tentatively? It takes time to grow into the blinding mass it is meant to be. The heavenly body that gives us light and heat and upon which we depend. You are like the sun in many ways. You are tentative with strangers, and with new experiences, yet given time, all may see how brightly you shine. I consider myself blessed indeed to be witness to any of your light."

She turned in his arms and snuggled close to him. He just held her, and she knew that as long as he was there she would be safe and loved. Just as the sun banished the darkness of the world, so their love would banish any fears that came her way. The future was bright indeed with William at her side.

ACKNOWLEDGMENTS

I will be forever grateful for the multitude of people who have helped me along my journey in writing this book. My husband, Stephen, brainstormed with me and was especially helpful choreographing fights scenes as well as some of the more tender scenes which was so fun and meant the world to me. I am grateful for his patience as well as his encouragement. I am grateful to all those who saw the potential here, especially my eldest son's announcement to our local librarian that his mom was going to be a famous author.

I have been fortunate to have found such caring and wonderful beta readers and am grateful for their input. I also must mention my critique group, the Nebo Novelists, who have helped make this work fun and enlightening. My editor (janasbrownwrites.com) was fantastic to work with and I credit her with making this book what it is. I am so grateful to my arc readers and Dawn Loper for proofreading the near final manuscript.

I have been thoroughly fascinated by the story of the Hautevilles and am pleased to share some of this history with you, my dear readers. The majority of the historical events I have used for this work came from the book written by Gordon S. Brown titled *The Norman Conquest of Southern Italy and Sicily*. I also used war tactics from Sun Tzu's *The Art of War*, although I realize that it was unlikely for the men in my narrative to have any knowledge of that work.

Many of the characters and events in this work of fiction are factual; however, I have taken literary license and changed a few things in order to create a story that made sense to me. If you are interested in learning more about the Hautevilles or Prince Guaimar or any of the other historical figures mentioned in these pages I encourage you to read Gordon S. Brown's book.

www.ingramcontent.com/pod-product-compliance
Lightning Source LLC
Chambersburg PA
CBHW020259200626
46816CB00001BA/368